The Candy Cane Cupcake Killer

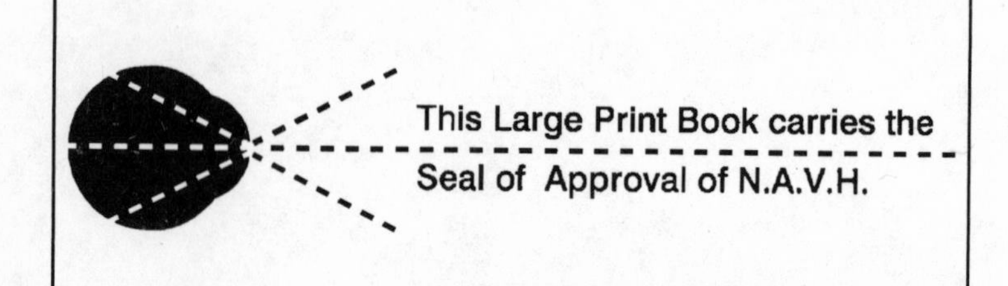
This Large Print Book carries the
Seal of Approval of N.A.V.H.

A FRESH-BAKED MYSTERY

THE CANDY CANE CUPCAKE KILLER

LIVIA J. WASHBURN

WHEELER PUBLISHING
A part of Gale, Cengage Learning

GALE
CENGAGE Learning

Farmington Hills, Mich • San Francisco • New York • Waterville, Maine
Meriden, Conn • Mason, Ohio • Chicago

Wheeler Publishing, a part of Gale, Cengage Learning.

Wheeler Publishing Large Print Cozy Mystery.
The text of this Large Print edition is unabridged.
Other aspects of the book may vary from the original edition.
Set in 16 pt. Plantin.

LIBRARY OF CONGRESS CATALOGING-IN-PUBLICATION DATA

Names: Washburn, L. J., author.
Title: The candy cane cupcake killer : a fresh-baked mystery / by Livia J. Washburn.
Description: Large print edition. | Waterville, Maine : Wheeler Publishing, 2016. | © 2015 | Series: Wheeler Publishing large print cozy mystery
Identifiers: LCCN 2016012735 | ISBN 9781410488633 (softcover) | ISBN 1410488632 (softcover)
Subjects: LCSH: Newsom, Phyllis (Fictitious character)—Fiction. | Baking—Fiction. | Murder—Investigation—Fiction. | Weatherford (Tex.)—Fiction. | Large type books. | GSAFD: Mystery fiction.
Classification: LCC PS3573.A787 C36 2016 | DDC 813/.54—dc23
LC record available at http://lccn.loc.gov/2016012735

Published in 2016 by arrangement with New American Library, an imprint of Penguin Publishing Group, a division of Penguin Random House LLC

Printed in the United States of America
1 2 3 4 5 6 7 20 19 18 17 16

Dedicated to my husband, James;
my daughters, Joanna and Shayna;
and my friends Shilo Harrington
and Shelly Toler Franz

CHAPTER 1

Sam Fletcher sang, "Ohhhh, jingle bells, shotgun shells —"

Phyllis Newsom shook her head and said, "Not that version, Sam. Have you no respect for the classics?"

"Maybe I've just got a different definition of *classics,*" Sam said with a grin. Then he leaned forward to peer through the pickup's windshield and went on. "There's Barney McCrory, an old friend of mine from when I was coachin'. Mind if I stop and talk to him for a minute?"

"That's fine," Phyllis told him. "There's still a little time before the Christmas parade is supposed to start." She raised the plastic container in her lap. "As long as I get these cupcakes to the square before the tree lighting."

Sam pulled over into the parking lot of an auto-parts store that was already closed for the evening. Less than a block ahead, Weatherford's South Main Street was blocked off by orange plastic cones. Beyond them, the city's annual Christmas parade was forming.

Businesses, civic groups, and school organizations had floats or decorated flatbed trucks loaded with hay bales, where people would sit and wave at the spectators gathered along both sides of the street. They would be followed by the high school marching band, which would play "Here Comes Santa Claus" to herald the arrival of the jolly old man himself.

Except Santa wouldn't be riding in a sleigh this year but rather in a fancy horse-drawn carriage decorated with garlands and lights. He was already in place in the carriage, Phyllis noted, surrounded by "elves" who were actually cheerleaders from the high school. She thought the girls' elf outfits were a little too skimpy and suggestive, but that was nothing unusual.

She wondered idly who was in the Santa suit and white beard this year. Usually it was some local politician or celebrity. Appearing in the Christmas parade was good publicity. And, not to be too cynical, she reminded herself that it accomplished some good as well, because the big bags of toys in the carriage with Santa were the result of a citywide collection drive and would wind up in the hands of needy children on Christmas morning.

Up at the end of the parade route was the courthouse square, with the majestic old courthouse outlined by festive lights. After the parade, the towering Christmas tree on the courthouse lawn would be lit; then everyone would enjoy snacks provided by the local churches. Phyllis had agreed to bake something for her church's effort, and in the plastic container she held was the result: a new treat she had dubbed candy cane cupcakes.

They were vanilla cupcakes with peppermint buttercream frosting, and had been garnished with crushed pieces of candy canes. Sam had sampled them and declared them delicious, and so had Phyllis's friends Carolyn Wilbarger and Eve Turner, the other two retired teachers with whom Phyllis shared a big old house on a tree-lined street a few blocks away from where they were now.

It was a chilly evening, appropriate for early December, and Phyllis was glad for her coat as she got out of the car, holding the container for the cupcakes, and followed Sam toward the carriage. There was plenty of hubbub as the parade participants got ready. The man in the driver's seat in the front of the carriage didn't notice them until they drew alongside the vehicle. Then Sam called, "Hey, Barney."

The man turned his head to look down at them, and a grin split his weathered face. He wore jeans, a sheepskin coat, and a broad-brimmed cowboy hat. A white handlebar mustache stood out in sharp contrast to his deeply tanned face.

"Sam!" he said in a booming voice. "You old dog! Haven't seen you in ages!" He was wearing gloves as he held the reins attached to the six-horse team, but he took the one off his right hand and leaned over on the seat to extend his hand toward Sam, who took it in a hearty grip. "How you doin' these days?"

"Fine," Sam replied. "Barney, this is my friend Phyllis Newsom. Phyllis, Barney McCrory."

With exaggerated politeness, McCrory reached up and took off his hat. He held it in front of him and told Phyllis, "Ma'am, it's an honor."

"I'm pleased to meet you, Mr. McCrory," Phyllis said.

"Oh, shoot, call me Barney. Mr. McCrory was my father, and he's been gone a mighty long time, Lord rest his soul."

"Is this your carriage and team?"

"Yes, ma'am. The folks organizin' the parade asked me to give 'em a hand this year, and I'm glad to. It's for a good cause, after all." McCrory clapped the hat back on his head and gave Sam a solemn look. "I was sure sorry to hear about Vicky, Sam. She was a mighty fine woman."

"Yes, she was," Sam agreed. His late wife had been gone for several years, having succumbed to cancer, like so many others. Phyllis knew how difficult the loss had been for Sam, and she was glad that their friendship had been able to help him get over his grief, at least to a certain extent.

Sam continued. "How are Allyson and Nate?"

Phyllis thought a shadow passed briefly over McCrory's face, but the man sounded genial as he said, "They're fine. They haven't gotten around to makin' me a grandpa yet, but I figure it's only a matter of time."

Sam turned to Phyllis and said, "Barney's daughter and her husband both played ball for me up at Poolville when they were kids. Really nice couple. They were high school sweethearts."

"That's how Sam and me got to be friends, from when my little gal was on the girls' team." McCrory added, "I've got a little ranch up in that part of the county."

Sam chuckled and said, "Don't let him fool you. That ranch isn't what you'd call little."

McCrory waved a knobby-knuckled hand. "That's enough talk about me," he said. "I recall now why your name's familiar to me, Miz Newsom. I've read about you in the paper."

"Well, you can't always believe everything you read," Phyllis said, thinking that he was talking about the stories involving the various crimes she had solved over the past few years. She had saved some innocent people from being convicted of murder and she was glad of that, but she didn't like dwelling on the sordid nature of the cases.

People who committed murder usually had a pretty ugly reason for it.

As it turned out, though, that reputation wasn't what McCrory meant. He said, "You're supposed to be just about the best baker around here, especially when it comes to pies and cakes and cookies and suchlike."

Phyllis had to laugh. She said, "I wouldn't let my friend Carolyn hear you say that. She might take exception to it."

"Well, you're the one who's grabbed first place in most of the contests, like that one over at the state fair." McCrory grinned and wiggled his bushy white eyebrows as he pointed at the plastic container in Phyllis's hands. "What you got in there? Somethin' good to eat, I'll bet."

"It's the snacks my church group is providing for after the tree lighting —"

"How about a taste?" McCrory asked.

"Oh, I'm not sure I can do that —"

"You see, by the time the parade's over and we all circle back around here to let folks off, then head up to the square, all the best stuff's liable to be gone already. And I know if you made those cupcakes, they'll all get snatched up right away."

"He's right about that," Sam chimed in. "Folks know by now that if you made it, it'll be the best thing there."

"You two are just a couple of old flatterers," Phyllis said sternly, but, truthfully, she was pleased by the comments. Even so, she wasn't sure she should allow Barney McCrory to wheedle one of the cupcakes out of her.

"If you give me a cupcake, I might be able to persuade Santa to let you ride on this here sleigh with him," the rancher said, still grinning.

"First of all, this isn't actually a sleigh," Phyllis said, "and I don't want to ride on it. I'm not fond of the idea of hundreds of people looking at me."

"You're not a county commissioner." McCrory inclined his head toward the backseat of the carriage, where Santa was sitting with the cheerleader elves. "That's Clay Loomis wearin' the suit this year."

Phyllis knew the name. She had seen it on enough campaign signs during the past election. Clay Loomis was the longtime Parker County road commissioner. In addition to being charged with the upkeep of the roads in their area, the commissioner also dealt with the sheriff's office and other county business.

Loomis must have heard his name, because he leaned forward and, through the white fake beard he wore, asked, "What's going on up there, Barney? Not any trouble with those horses of yours, is there? They look pretty nervous to me."

"Nope, just visitin' with a couple of friends before the parade starts," McCrory replied. "Which should be just about anytime now." He turned his attention back to Phyllis. "So, if you want me to try one of those cupcakes, ma'am, you'd better go ahead and give it to me now."

Phyllis didn't know whether to be flabbergasted or amused. *He* was the one who'd practically been begging *her* for a cupcake.

She decided it was better to be amused, and laughed.

"Oh, all right," she said, and loosened the lid on the plastic container. She reached into it, brought out one of the cupcakes, and started to hand it to McCrory. Seeing that she was a little on the short side for the job, she gave the cupcake to Sam, who passed it along to McCrory.

"I am much obliged, ma'am," he told her. He lifted the cupcake to his mouth and took a big bite of it, leaving buttercream frosting and little bits of crushed candy cane in his thick mustache. After he swallowed, he said, "Lord have mercy, that's mighty good! Are they havin' a contest? 'Cause if they are, this little darlin' ought to win!"

"No, the goodies are just for people to enjoy," Phyllis said.

"They'll sure enjoy these." McCrory took another bite, then said around it, "Looks like the parade's gettin' started. I'll see you folks later. Sam, next time don't let it be so long 'fore we get together again."

"I'll make sure of it, Barney," Sam promised. He lifted a hand in farewell, then started along the street with Phyllis. The two of them headed for the courthouse square. The marching band had begun playing Christmas songs. People who had gathered along both sides of the street to watch the parade clapped and sang along with the music.

Phyllis and Sam moved as far away from the street as they could get so that the crowd wasn't so dense around them. They were able to walk fairly quickly toward the square. Sam rested a hand on Phyllis's arm just above her elbow, and she was glad to have it there. She wasn't that fond of crowds.

They had gone only a couple of steps when Sam's hand suddenly tightened on Phyllis's arm, as if something were wrong. She glanced over at him and saw alarm on his rugged face.

"What is it?" she asked as her hands gripped tighter on the plastic container. She wasn't sure why she did that. Instinct, she supposed. It wasn't like somebody was going to come along and try to rip the cupcakes out of her hands.

"Something's wrong with Barney," Sam said.

Phyllis looked at the carriage and saw that Barney McCrory was doubled over in the driver's seat. He crouched there, bending forward for a couple of seconds, and then let go of the reins and crumpled into a heap, half on the seat and half on the floorboard of the driver's box.

Without Barney's firm hand to control them, the already skittish horses lunged toward the marching band.

People in the crowd began to scream, which just spooked the team that much more.

The tubas were bringing up the rear in the band, as usual, and the high school boys playing them must have realized something had gone wrong behind them. Several of the instruments let out strident blats as boys scrambled to get out of the way. More screams filled the air as the music stopped and the band members began to scatter.

With his hand still clasped around her arm, Sam swung Phyllis around and said, "Come on!"

She had no choice but to go with him as he ran toward the parking lot where they had left the pickup.

"What are you doing?" she asked breathlessly.

Sam had fished his keys out of his bluejeans pocket with his other hand and pushed the button on the attached fob to unlock the pickup's doors. As he threw the driver's-side door open, he told Phyllis, "Get behind the wheel and go after that carriage!" He pressed the keys into her hand.

"What?!"

"We've got to stop it before somebody gets hurt!" Sam said as he ran to the back of the truck. He climbed into the bed and added, "Come on, Phyllis!"

Though it seemed crazy to her, she knew he was right about one thing: Somebody was going to get hurt if that runaway carriage wasn't stopped. She slid the container of cupcakes across the seat and pulled herself behind the wheel.

She wasn't sure what Sam had in mind, but she cranked the pickup's engine to life, threw it in gear, and wheeled out of the parking lot. The carriage was a block away, and the horses were picking up speed now that the marching band had cleared the street. The team weaved around one of the floats, causing the carriage to sway back and forth dangerously.

"Run over those cones!" Sam shouted through the pickup's back window.

Phyllis stopped thinking about it and acted. She pushed the gas pedal down and the pickup leaped forward, crushing the plastic traffic cones under its wheels.

CHAPTER 2

A few of the uniformed band members had started to come out into the middle of the street again to stare wide-eyed after the carriage that had nearly run over them. But they scurried out of the way again as Phyllis drove toward them.

Actually, she wasn't going very fast yet, but the pace already seemed breakneck to her. *I'm not some . . . some Hollywood stunt driver,* she thought. What sort of lunacy was going through Sam's mind right now?

She honked the horn to warn the drivers of the floats to pull over to the side of the street as much as they could. The pickup flew past them.

Phyllis's pulse pounded. She hoped she wouldn't have a heart attack right here and now.

A sharp rapping on the window beside her made her jump a little. Sam was trying to get her attention. She rolled the window down and called, “What?”

He leaned down and said through the open window, “Pull up beside those horses and get as close as you can!”

“What are you —,” she started to ask, but it was too late. He had straightened up already and couldn’t hear her over all the commotion.

They were right behind the carriage now. She saw Clay Loomis and all the cheerleaders huddled together. She couldn’t hear them, but in the glare of the headlights she could see that their mouths were open, and she figured they were screaming as they hung on for dear life.

Up ahead, hundreds of people had gathered on the courthouse lawn. The horses and the carriage were headed straight toward them. And though people had started to realize they were in danger and were trying to get out of the way, it didn’t look like all of them would make it.

Sam was right. Somebody was going to get hurt if they couldn’t stop the runaways.

Somebody was *already* hurt. Phyllis remembered the way Barney McCrory had collapsed. He must have had a heart attack, she thought.

She pressed harder on the gas and turned

the wheel. The pickup swung out to the side and began to draw even with the carriage. Phyllis got a good look at the terrified face of Clay Loomis, who had torn off the fake beard and white wig.

Then she was past the carriage and alongside the frightened horses. Their eyes rolled wildly as they ran.

"Get closer!" Sam shouted through the window.

Phyllis didn't know who was more scared: her, the horses, the people on the square, or Loomis and the cheerleaders.

But there is a time to be timid and a time to be bold, she told herself, and like it or not, this is a time to be bold.

She moved the pickup closer to the horses.

She gasped as she saw Sam's image appear in the big side mirror. He was leaning far over the edge of the pickup's bed, clinging to the cab with one hand. A scene from an old Western movie that was one of Sam's favorites flashed through her mind. She had watched it several times with him, and now she was afraid he remembered it, too.

Sam clung to the cab with his right hand and reached out his left arm as far as it would go. Phyllis saw that she wasn't close enough and edged the pickup over a little more. Sam stretched out his lanky form over what seemed like an impossible distance, and his hand closed around the harness of the lead horse on his side of the team. He hauled back on it.

"Ease off the gas!" he called to Phyllis. "Don't brake!"

She understood what he meant. If she stopped too short, it might jerk him out of the truck bed. She took her foot off the gas and let the pickup's momentum slow some on its own.

"Now give it some brake!" Sam told her. "Easy!"

Phyllis's hands gripped the steering wheel so tightly, it felt like it was going to snap off. She rested her foot lightly on the brake, felt the pickup respond, and then pushed down a little harder.

She had to stop smoothly. That was the key.

They were less than a block from the square when the pickup finally came to a halt. So did the team.

Sam called to the crowd, "Somebody come grab hold of these horses! Be careful not to spook 'em again, though."

Several men hurried out and grasped the harness so the horses couldn't bolt again. Sam let go of it and sat down with his back against the cab, his chest rising and falling rapidly. As Phyllis got out of the pickup, she saw how hard he was breathing and was afraid that he was having a spell of some sort.

"Sam!" she cried. "Are you all right?"

"Yeah, just a mite winded," he told her. He summoned up a smile. "That was a little nerve-rackin'."

"Nerve-racking! I thought you were about to jump out of the pickup and go sailing out over that team like John Wayne in that *Stagecoach* movie!"

"Yakima Canutt," Sam said.

"What?"

Sam didn't answer. Instead he pushed himself to his feet as a worried frown replaced his smile.

"We got to find out what happened to Barney," he said.

For a brief moment, Phyllis had forgotten all about McCrory's mysterious collapse. She had been so relieved that Sam was all right, she hadn't been able to think about anything else.

As he climbed down from the pickup bed, she turned toward the front of the carriage. Sam moved past her and pulled himself up on the metal step the driver used to climb up and down from the box. He reached over and took hold of McCrory's shoulder.

"Barney! Barney, can you hear me?"

But when Phyllis saw the way McCrory's head lolled limply as Sam shook his shoulder, her hopes sank. She had seen enough dead men to recognize the signs.

A couple of seconds later, she realized just how bizarre it was for a retired schoolteacher to have such a thing go through her mind.

That just went to show the kinds of unexpected turns her life had taken over the past few years.

In the back of the carriage, the cheerleaders huddling around Clay Loomis were still crying and whimpering. They were safe now, but that knowledge hadn't caught up with their terror. Loomis had stopped yelling, but he was still wide-eyed with shock.

"Step back!" a man's voice ordered. "Clear this area now!"

Phyllis turned to see Chief of Police Ralph Whitmire, along with several of his officers, hurrying toward the carriage. Whitmire, a stocky, graying man and a good cop, stopped short as he recognized Phyllis and Sam.

"Oh, no," he said. "What are you two doing here?"

Although Whitmire had never demonstrated the level of hostility toward Phyllis that the local district attorney had, she knew he wasn't happy about the way she seemed to turn up at so many crime scenes.

Of course, this wasn't really a crime scene — just a tragedy that could have been much worse. She was convinced that Barney McCrory had suffered a heart attack and died.

"Chief!" Clay Loomis piped up. Lingering fear gave his voice a high-pitched squeak. "Chief, we were almost killed!"

"You're all right now, Mr. Loomis," Whitmire assured him.

Sam stepped down from the driver's box and said, "Looks like Barney didn't make it, Chief."

"We'll let the EMTs deal with that," Whitmire said. He nodded toward an ambulance that was maneuvering through the crowd at little more than a crawl. The vehicle's lights were flashing, which washed out the more festive lights on the courthouse and the other buildings around the square.

Phyllis knew the two young men, Calvin Holloway and Ted Brady, who got out of the ambulance when it came to a stop. They were friends of her son, Mike, who was a Parker County sheriff's deputy.

Tonight they wore dark blue Windbreakers with big letters on the back that read emt. Phyllis couldn't keep her mind from flashing back to a hot summer day several years earlier when Calvin and Ted had been summoned here to the courthouse square because of another death. She wasn't likely to forget that time, since it was part of the first murder case with which she'd been involved.

As the two of them hurried up, carrying handheld cases full of medical equipment and apparatus, Chief Whitmire told them, "Looks like a heart attack."

"Anybody else hurt that we need to check on first?" Ted asked.

"Not that I'm aware of." Whitmire put a hand on the edge of the carriage and asked Loomis and the cheerleaders, "Anybody hurt in there?"

Several of the girls shook their heads, and two answered in shaky voices that they were all right. Loomis scrubbed a trembling hand over his face and said, "I'm not hurt, Chief, at least as far as I know right now."

Calvin and Ted climbed to the driver's seat, one on each side of Barney McCrory, and began checking his vitals. Phyllis was pretty sure they would find that he didn't have any.

A voice behind her boomed out, "Good Lord, Phyllis. What happened? Eve and I saw you driving like a bat out of — Well, you know where bats fly out of."

Phyllis turned to see her friends and housemates, Carolyn Wilbarger and Eve Turner. Carolyn was her oldest friend and also her longtime rival in baking contests. She went on. "You and Sam looked like you were in one of those stupid action movies he likes so much."

"I felt like it, too," Phyllis admitted. "I'd just as soon never do that again."

Eve, who was shorter than the other three members of their little circle of friends, rose on her tiptoes and craned her neck as she peered through the crowd of police, paramedics, and bystanders at the carriage.

"Is that poor man dead?" she asked.

"I'm afraid so," Sam said. "He'd just started drivin' the carriage in the parade when something happened to him."

Carolyn looked at Phyllis and asked with a frown, "Where are those cupcakes you made? That man didn't eat one of them, did he?"

Phyllis had a hollow feeling in the pit of her stomach as she said, "Well, as a matter of fact . . ."

"I knew it," Carolyn said. "He ate one of your cupcakes, and then he died."

"Oh, don't make it sound like that," Eve scolded. "I'm sure the two things don't have anything to do with each other."

Sam snorted and said, "Of course they don't. Shoot, we all had cupcakes from the same batch, didn't we?"

Chief Whitmire turned his head to look at them, as if he had just become aware of the conversation, and asked, "What's this about cupcakes?"

Phyllis gestured vaguely toward the pickup and said, "I brought some candy cane cupcakes with me for after the Christmas-tree lighting. Mr. McCrory talked me into giving him one."

Calvin leaned over from the driver's seat, where he had been examining McCrory, and said, "That explains what's stuck in his mustache, then. I couldn't figure it out. It's frosting, isn't it?"

"I'm afraid so," said Phyllis.

"The ME will do a tox screen," Whitmire said. "But surely your baking didn't have anything to do with what happened this time, Mrs. Newsom."

Phyllis didn't care for the way the chief said *this time,* but there was nothing she could do about that. Her reputation was what it was.

She was distracted from those gloomy thoughts by the arrival of a number of people who had rushed up to the carriage.

Some of them were uniformed members of the high school marching band, while others were adults. All of them were intent on the same thing, though: getting to the cheerleaders in elf costumes, who were still on the carriage.

The newcomers were boyfriends and parents of the girls, Phyllis decided, as a lot of hugging and crying and asking "Are you all right?" went on. Chief Whitmire looked annoyed, which made Phyllis think that he wished he could keep the girls away from everybody until he'd had a chance to question them. In this crowd, though, that was going to be impossible.

Another couple arrived on the scene, looking upset, but they appeared to be too young to have a daughter in high school. The woman, who had auburn hair and was quite pretty, was trying to push through the crowd to reach the carriage as she cried, "Dad! Daddy!"

The fair-haired young man with her took hold of her shoulders and said, "You need to stay back, Allyson. You don't want to get in the way of the paramedics. Let them do their work."

Sobbing, she tried to pull away from him, "That's my father up there!"

"I know, but there's nothing we can do to

help him. That's somebody else's job."

Phyllis could tell that the young man was trying to keep his voice calm and steady, but it shook anyway.

Sam stepped over to them, put a hand on the young man's shoulder, and said, "It'll be all right, kids."

That was a lie, of course. Barney McCrory was dead. But Phyllis knew Sam was just trying to comfort them the best way he could.

The young woman turned to Sam and exclaimed, "Coach Fletcher!" And then she pulled him into a hug as she broke down. Awkwardly, he patted her on the back as she said between sobs, "You . . . you don't understand. When I saw my father earlier today, we . . . we had a big fight. Those angry words can't be the last thing I ever say to him. They just can't!"

That told Phyllis she'd been right when she thought she saw an unhappy look cross McCrory's face earlier when Sam had brought up the man's daughter and son-in-law. McCrory had been upset about the argument, too, it seemed. Such an assumption was a bit of a leap, but Phyllis's instincts told her it was correct.

One of the EMTs, Ted, hopped down from the carriage and approached Whitmire.

He and the chief talked quietly for more than a minute. An angry expression appeared on Whitmire's face as they spoke. Phyllis couldn't make out anything the EMT said, but she heard Whitmire's response as he demanded, "Are you sure?"

With a grim look on his face, Ted nodded. He said something else, then turned back to the carriage to assist his partner as he started lowering Barney McCrory's body from the seat.

Knowing that he probably wouldn't answer her, Phyllis asked Whitmire, "What was that about, Chief? Mr. McCrory died of a heart attack, didn't he? I know you'll need an autopsy to be sure —"

"We'll need an autopsy, all right," Whitmire interrupted heavily. "It appears that the deceased was shot. This is murder."

There was still a lot of commotion going on up and down the street, but next to the carriage, a stunned silence fell for a moment until Carolyn said, "Well, at least he wasn't poisoned. Now no one can blame those cupcakes of yours, Phyllis!"

Chapter 3

After everything that had happened, the parade couldn't go on, of course. And the police couldn't keep the bystanders — and possible suspects — from leaving, either. There were too many people and not enough cops for that. Phyllis saw the frustration on Whitmire's face, but there was nothing the chief could do.

Nothing he could do about that part of the investigation, anyway. He turned to her and Sam and said, "The two of you talked to McCrory just before the parade started, right?"

"That's right," Phyllis said.

"That's when this cupcake business came up."

"Yes. But now that you know —"

"No offense, but I don't know anything yet except that McCrory was shot. And I shouldn't have mentioned that." Whitmire sighed and shook his head glumly. He muttered, "I guess I should have expected it by now." He became more businesslike as he went on. "Were the two of you the last ones to speak to the victim?"

"Maybe," Sam said. "I don't remember seein' anybody else say anything to him before the parade started." He nodded toward the carriage, where Clay Loomis was sitting alone now. All the cheerleaders had gotten out of the vehicle. "I reckon one of the folks back there could have said something to Barney, but I don't recall seein' him turned around, talkin' to them."

"Well, I'll ask Mr. Loomis about that later," Whitmire said.

Phyllis said, "There was a little bit of time right after the parade started when Sam and I were walking in this direction. I wasn't watching the carriage then."

"How long was that?"

"I don't know. Twenty seconds, maybe."

Whitmire asked Sam, "How about you? Were you watching the carriage the whole time?"

"I was lookin' in this general direction," Sam said, "but I wasn't really payin' that much attention to Barney. I was lookin' at the crowd and the parade and all the lights . . ." Sam frowned in thought. "But I saw him kind of rock back on the seat a little, and then he started to stand up. I knew he wouldn't be doin' that while he was drivin' the team unless something was wrong."

Whitmire nodded and said, "You two will have to come down to the station and give statements. Too many witnesses have wandered off already. I'm not letting the two of you get away."

Carolyn was standing close enough to hear the chief's words. She said, "That sounds rather ominous. Should Phyllis and Sam bring a lawyer with them?"

Wearily, Whitmire shook his head and waved off the question.

"No, no, they're not being charged with anything —"

"You're not supposed to even question them without letting them know their rights," Carolyn went on. Both she and Phyllis had fallen under suspicion of murder in the past, and that had caused Carolyn to look at the local law enforcement in an adversarial light most of the time.

Chief Whitmire was starting to look annoyed, and Phyllis didn't want Carolyn to get arrested for interfering with an officer or obstructing justice. She turned to her friend and said, "It's all right, Carolyn. I'm not worried about it. I waive the right to counsel."

"So do I," Sam said. "I don't have anything to hide."

Carolyn said, "Hmph. We've seen before that innocence doesn't always mean much in this town."

Whitmire looked like he was about to say something angry, but before he could, McCrory's daughter, Allyson, stepped up to him and asked, "Where are they taking my father, Chief?"

Calvin and Ted had loaded McCrory's body onto a gurney and were wheeling it toward the waiting ambulance. Whitmire said, "They'll take him to the funeral home. My office will keep you informed about the situation, ma'am."

"The situation," Allyson repeated. "What does that mean?"

"There'll have to be an autopsy. You're the deceased's daughter?"

"That's right. I'm Allyson Hollingsworth." Her face was red and puffy from crying, and tear streaks on her cheeks reflected the myriad lights all around. But she was more composed now than she had been a few minutes earlier. She nodded toward the fair-haired man beside her and added, "This is my husband, Nate."

"I'm sorry for your loss. I'll need to talk

more to both of you, so why don't I have one of my men take you down to the police station, and I'll meet you there shortly?"

Allyson stared at him in disbelief.

"You're *arresting* us?" she demanded.

"No, not at all," Whitmire said. "I just need to get statements from both of you. I realize this is a terrible time to be bothering you —"

"Yes, it is," Nate Hollingsworth said coldly.

"But we're just following procedure," Whitmire forged ahead. He signaled to one of his men. "This officer will take you to the station."

"We can't go in our own car?"

"It'll be simpler this way. He can show you exactly where to go. And then he'll bring you back to your car when we're done. I hope it won't take very long."

Nate looked like he wanted to argue, but Allyson said, "All right, if we've got to, let's get it over with. But I'll have to get to the funeral home and talk to them about the . . . the arrangements . . ."

Her face started to crumple into sobs again. Nate put his arms around her shoulders and drew her against him.

"You can talk to the funeral-home people in the morning," Whitmire told them.

"There'll be plenty of time."

He is right about that, Phyllis thought. It would probably be at least several days before McCrory's body was released, since it would take that long for the autopsy and the other parts of the forensics investigation to be carried out.

The police officer ushered them away from the carriage. Whitmire turned back to the vehicle and said to its visibly shaken passenger, "I'll need to get a statement from you, too, Mr. Loomis."

Even under these circumstances, the politician's natural arrogance asserted itself. Loomis said, "You know who I am, don't you, Chief?"

"Yes, sir, I do. I still need a statement from you."

"This has been very upsetting —"

"We won't keep you any longer than we have to." Whitmire motioned another officer over to them and spoke briefly to him, telling him to escort Loomis to the station.

"But . . . but I'm dressed like Santa Claus!" Loomis objected. "This is humiliating."

That protest didn't do any good. He went off with the second officer.

Phyllis asked Whitmire, "Are you going to

put us in the back of a patrol car, too, Chief?"

"No, I don't think that's necessary." He pointed with his thumb at Sam's pickup. "This is your vehicle, Mr. Fletcher?"

"Yep."

"You can take it down to the station as soon as my officers get the street cleared enough to turn it around. Just let whoever's working the reception counter know when you get there, and they'll pass the word to me."

Carolyn said, "It sounds to me like a gathering of the suspects."

"Hardly," Whitmire said. "Oh, and one more thing."

"And now he sounds like Columbo," Carolyn muttered.

Whitmire pretended not to hear her. He said, "Where are those cupcakes you were talking about?"

"They're in the pickup," Phyllis said. "I suppose you want me to bring them in so they can be analyzed."

"No, actually. I was thinking that maybe you might not mind if we ate some of them," Whitmire said. "I don't think I've heard of candy cane cupcakes before, but they sound really good."

■ ■ ■ ■

The police department was on Santa Fe Drive, which ran parallel to and several blocks east of South Main Street, where the Christmas parade had been scheduled to take place. Once Sam was able to move his pickup, it wouldn't take long for him and Phyllis to get there.

As Sam drove, Phyllis said, "I'm sorry about your friend. Mr. McCrory seemed like a nice man."

"He was. Barney McCrory was a real charmer . . . when he wanted to be."

That comment made Phyllis cock an eyebrow. She said, "I take that to mean there were times when he wasn't that way."

"You should've heard some of the cussin'-outs I got when Barney didn't agree with the way I was playin' his little girl on the basketball team. After some games, it felt like he spent an hour in my face, tellin' me what a lousy coach I was." Sam shrugged. "Maybe he was right."

"I highly doubt that," Phyllis said.

"I never really held it against him, though," Sam went on. "Shoot, if you're a good parent, you can't help but get involved with your kid's life at school, whether it's academics or athletics."

"Yes, but some of them get a little *too* involved," Phyllis pointed out.

"Yeah, no doubt about that. Barney never crossed the line about Allyson and the team, though. Not *too* much, anyway. And that was just his way. He was like that about plenty of other things. Hard chargin' all the time, straight ahead. He held himself to a high standard, and he felt like everybody else ought to be the same way." Sam shook his head. "It's hard to talk about him in the past tense. Somebody as vital and bigger than life as Barney was, it seems like he'll be around forever."

"And yet that can change in an instant," Phyllis said. "To be honest, I've come to feel that way about you, Sam. Like you'll always be around." Her voice caught a little as she went on. "And then I see you doing something like leaning over so far that you're practically falling out of the pickup while you tried to stop those horses . . ."

She couldn't talk anymore. At the time, she had been too caught up in what she was doing to think too much about how dangerous Sam's heroic actions were, but now, when she realized just how easy it would have been at that moment for her to lose him, it was like a cold hand clutching at her heart.

Her left hand rested on the seat beside her. Sam reached over with his right and laid it on top of hers. She turned her hand and laced her fingers together with his.

"I'm not goin' anywhere," he said quietly. "I plan to be around for a good while yet."

"I hope so." She tried to lighten the mood a little by saying, "What in the world did you mean when you said . . . Oh, I don't even remember what it was now. It didn't really sound like English, though."

"When are you talkin' about?" he asked.

"When I said something about John Wayne and *Stagecoach.*"

"Oh." Sam laughed. "You mean Yakima Canutt."

"I know I've heard you talk about that before, but I can't recall what it is."

"He," Sam said. "That's the name of a famous Hollywood stuntman. He's the one who jumped on the stagecoach team in the movie, not John Wayne. In fact, he did it twice: once when he was doublin' one of the Apaches, and once when he was doublin' the Duke. Remember the fella who falls under the stagecoach and the wheels go on either side of him?"

"I suppose. Yes, I think so."

"That's Yak, too. Best stuntman there ever was."

"How do you remember all these things?" Phyllis asked.

"Trick brain," Sam replied with a grin. "Just don't ask me what I had for lunch yesterday, because odds are I can't tell you." He turned off the street into the parking lot of a sprawling redbrick building. "Anyway, we're here."

He was right. They had arrived at the police department. Sam parked, and they went inside, shivering a little because the chilly December wind had gotten stronger during the evening. A cold front had blown through, and according to the forecast, the temperature was supposed to drop close to freezing by the next morning.

It was warm inside the police department lobby, though. As she and Sam approached the counter, Phyllis wondered if Allyson and Nate Hollingsworth and Clay Loomis were already here. They probably were, and there was a good chance Chief Whitmire was already questioning one of them.

She wondered also if the chief would handle the investigation into Barney McCrory's murder himself, since he'd been the first officer on the scene, or if he would turn the case over to one of his detectives. She knew several of those detectives from previous cases.

Sam told the officer at the counter who they were, and that Chief Whitmire had asked them to come in and give statements. She thanked them and told them to have seats in the waiting area, adding, "The chief will be with you shortly."

Phyllis supposed that answered her question about who would be heading up the investigation, at least for the time being.

They waited for about thirty minutes before a door opened and Whitmire came out. He looked even more tired and harassed than he had at the murder scene. He said, "I'm sorry to have kept you folks waiting. Mrs. Newsom, we'll start with you."

"You don't want to talk to the two of us together?" Sam asked.

"No, it's standard procedure to interview witnesses separately."

Phyllis knew that and wasn't surprised. She stood up, gave Sam a smile, and followed the chief along a corridor to an open door. They went into an interrogation room, which looked like the ones on TV and in the movies, Phyllis thought, only a little nicer. The walls were painted a neutral cream color rather than the common institutional green. The table in the center of the room wasn't scarred, and showed signs of having been polished at some point. The two straight-backed chairs weren't exactly comfortable, but the one Phyllis sat in didn't make her squirm in discomfort, either.

Whitmire sat down on the other side of the table, placed a small digital recorder between them, and began, "Interview with Mrs. Phyllis Newsom —"

He didn't get any further than that before the door burst open. A chunky, dark-haired man carrying a briefcase hurried into the room and exclaimed, "Don't say another word, Phyllis!"

CHAPTER 4

"D'Angelo!" Chief Whitmire said as he stood up. "What the devil are you doing here?"

"Saving my client from illegally incriminating herself," the newcomer replied.

"Mrs. Newsom waived the right to counsel."

D'Angelo looked at Phyllis as if he were badly disappointed in her. He said, "You did? Never waive any of your rights. Never. They're what this country was built on."

"She's not being accused of anything," Whitmire said, visibly holding in the irritation he felt. "I'm just taking a witness statement from her."

D'Angelo waved that off and said, "Doesn't matter. She still needs legal representation."

"No, I don't, Mr. D'Angelo," Phyllis said. "I didn't do anything wrong."

"Everyone who deals with the police

should have an attorney with them, looking out for their interests."

A realization came to Phyllis. She said, "Carolyn called you, didn't she?"

D'Angelo hesitated, cocking his squarish head to the side, before replying, "I'm not at liberty to say."

Phyllis sighed and shook her head. D'Angelo didn't have to admit it. It was just like Carolyn to let her distrust of the authorities get the better of her common sense.

Actually, though, she wasn't upset to see Jimmy D'Angelo. She and Sam had known the bombastic defense attorney for a while, ever since he had represented the primary suspect in another case they had been mixed up in. In fact, D'Angelo had hired them to act as investigators in that case, giving them some legal standing for a change, and had said that he might call on their services again.

According to Sam, that made them private eyes. Phyllis didn't think it was quite that simple, but she didn't see any point in arguing the matter.

D'Angelo set his briefcase on the table and went on. "I was told there was some question about a suspicious death and some cupcakes you baked."

"The cupcakes had nothing to do with it," Phyllis said. "Poor Mr. McCrory was shot, not poisoned."

Whitmire leaned forward and said, "Speaking of those cupcakes, where are they, Mrs. Newsom?"

D'Angelo pounced on that.

"If you don't suspect Mrs. Newsom, why do you want her to turn over the cupcakes as evidence?"

"I don't! I want to eat one of them, blast it! I haven't had any supper."

Clearly, that wasn't the answer D'Angelo had been expecting. He blinked, frowned, and said, "Oh." Then, more businesslike, he asked Phyllis, "Did you agree to this?"

"I did," she told him. "Somebody should get to enjoy them."

"What kind are they?"

"Candy cane cupcakes," Phyllis said.

D'Angelo licked his lips and nodded.

"That does sound good," he admitted. "Where are they?"

"I forgot and left them in Sam's pickup. It's parked right outside, though. You could go back out to the lobby and tell him to get them."

D'Angelo looked at Whitmire and said, "Chief?"

Whitmire waved a hand.

"Go. And when you come back, bring Mr. Fletcher with you. To heck with procedure."

That was something Phyllis had never expected to hear Ralph Whitmire say. But, obviously, this had been an unusual evening all the way around.

D'Angelo left his briefcase on the table. He told Phyllis, "Don't answer any questions while I'm gone," and hurried out of the interrogation room.

Once D'Angelo was gone, Phyllis said to Whitmire, "I'm sorry about that, Chief. I don't know what Carolyn was thinking."

Whitmire grunted and said, "I do. She was thinking you can't trust the cops. A lot of people feel like that these days. A few of them — very few — have some justification for that. But that's not the case here. You're not in any trouble." He paused. "Although from what I saw, that was some pretty reckless driving you were doing. Not that you had a choice about it. Somebody else would've gotten hurt for sure if you and Sam hadn't stopped that carriage."

"I thought Sam had lost his mind, but he knew what he was doing."

"Good thing, too," Whitmire said. He leaned back in his chair and frowned. "You know, it occurs to me, we've been assuming that just because McCrory was shot, there can't be anything wrong with those cupcakes."

"There can't be," Phyllis said. "I baked them this afternoon. I made three dozen of them. The batter and the frosting were the same for all of them. Each of us ate one of them when they were done. Sam ate *two,* as a matter of fact. None of us have shown any ill effects from them."

"They were never where anybody else could have gotten at them?" Whitmire held up a hand before she could say anything. "Wait a minute, you don't have to answer that. I don't want D'Angelo thinking that I'm trying to trick you or anything like that."

"Of course not. And I don't mind telling you, the cupcakes I took to the parade tonight never left my kitchen until I put them in that container. No one else was around and had access to them, just the four of us. And none of us had any reason to want to hurt Mr. McCrory. None of us even knew who he was except —"

Phyllis stopped short. Sam knew Barney McCrory. But from what Phyllis had seen, she knew he considered the old rancher a friend. And anyway, Sam would never hurt anyone, of course.

She knew how a detective might think, though. Sam knew McCrory, so it wasn't beyond the realm of possibility that Sam could have known that McCrory would be driving Santa Claus's sleigh in the parade, too. And Sam could have guessed, based on his familiarity with McCrory's personality, that the man would beg one of the cupcakes from Phyllis . . .

"What are you thinking, Mrs. Newsom?" Whitmire asked.

"I'm thinking maybe you're more suspicious than you're letting on, Chief," she said. "Not of me, but of Sam."

"Why would I be suspicious of Mr. Fletcher?" Whitmire asked blandly.

Instead of answering that question directly, Phyllis said, "It doesn't work. *I* took the cupcake out of the container and handed it to Mr. McCrory. Even if Sam wanted to hurt him — and it's absolutely insane to even think that — he couldn't have known which cupcake I'd give him. He'd have had to tamper with all of them, which means that innocent people would have been hurt, maybe even killed. That's just not possible, Chief. It's not."

Whitmire surprised her by laughing.

"I agree with you a hundred percent," he said. "I've been telling you the truth all along, Mrs. Newsom. I don't suspect you or Mr. Fletcher of anything. I'm grateful to you for what you did. I just want to know what you saw before the incident took place."

"Oh."

"I have to admit, though," Whitmire went on, "that's pretty impressive — the way you put together that chain of evidence and reasoning on the fly. I can see why you've been able to figure out some of those other crimes." He chuckled again. "You've got a diabolical mind."

"I . . . I . . ." Phyllis didn't know what to say to that. And before she could figure out an appropriate reply, the door of the interrogation room opened and Jimmy D'Angelo came in again, followed this time by Sam, who carried the plastic container filled with cupcakes.

"You didn't try anything underhanded with my client while I was out of the room, did you?" D'Angelo asked.

"Not at all," Whitmire said. Phyllis didn't contradict him. The chief stood up. "Mr. Fletcher, sit down here. Mr. D'Angelo and I can stand."

"I'm fine," Sam said. "I'll just perch a hip here on the table, if it's all right with you, Chief."

"Sure. Are those the famous cupcakes?"

Sam grinned and set the container on the

table in front of Phyllis.

"You can do the honors," he told her.

She took the lid off, revealing twenty-three cupcakes. Two dozen — minus the one Barney McCrory had eaten. They were quite pretty, with the bits of red and white crushed candy cane sprinkled on the white icing. She was pleased with the way they had turned out.

She slid the open container onto the center of the table and said, "Help yourselves, gentlemen."

The three men reached into the container and took out cupcakes. They peeled away the paper baking cups and threw them in a wastebasket at the end of the table.

After taking a bite, Whitmire made a pleased sound and said, "Those are really are good."

"Yes, they are," D'Angelo added.

"This is my third one today," Sam put in. "You know I like 'em."

Phyllis didn't really have much of an appetite at the moment, so she didn't take one of the cupcakes. Instead she said, "You wanted to ask us about what happened before the parade started, Chief?"

Whitmire had to swallow before he could say, "That's right. Start from where you saw McCrory on that sleigh . . . carriage . . .

whatever you want to call it."

"I was the one who spotted him first," Sam said. "Phyllis had never met him before, so she wouldn't have known him."

Whitmire looked at Phyllis and asked, "Is that right?"

"Yes," she said. "Tonight was the first time I ever met Mr. McCrory."

Sam resumed the story, and for the next few minutes he and Phyllis took turns talking, telling the chief as much as they could recall about everything that was said and done in the few minutes before the parade began.

At one point Whitmire interrupted their recounting to ask, "What did McCrory say about his daughter and son-in-law?"

"Well, he said they were fine, I think," Sam replied with a slight frown. "He mentioned that they hadn't made him a grandpa yet. Nothin' unusual about that."

Hoping that she wasn't doing the wrong thing, Phyllis said, "When Sam first mentioned them, I thought that Mr. McCrory looked upset for a second. But it was just a momentary reaction."

"Uh-huh," Whitmire said, not seeming to think any more about it. "Go on with your statements, please."

Phyllis wasn't sure the chief's reaction was

as casual as he tried to make it seem. She recalled what Allyson Hollingsworth had said about having a fight with her father before the parade began, how she didn't want the last words she ever spoke to him to be angry ones.

Unfortunately, in most cases, people didn't get to determine what their last words to a loved one would be.

Death wasn't that considerate.

When Sam reached the point in the story where the parade had begun and he and Phyllis had started up the street toward the square, Whitmire turned to Phyllis and said, "You weren't watching the carriage just then, is that right?"

"I wasn't paying attention to it, no," she said. "In that crowd, I was watching where I was going."

"How about you?" Whitmire said to Sam.

"I was lookin' all around, I guess," Sam replied with a shrug. "I remember thinkin' how pretty the lights were on the courthouse and around the square. I saw one of 'em pop — burned out, I guess — and then I saw Barney start to stand up, and I knew something was wrong. A second later, he dropped the reins and collapsed, and those horses took off. I did the only thing I could think of to stop 'em."

"And risked your life doing it," Phyllis said. Something Sam had just said stuck in her mind. She was about to ask him when Chief Whitmire beat her to it.

"You said you saw one of the Christmas lights pop, Mr. Fletcher?" the chief asked.

"Yeah, I guess that's what it was. It was a little flash, anyway."

"Where was that?"

"Somewhere up on the square. Hard to say for sure. There were a *lot* of lights. Why's that important?"

"Because it might not have been a lightbulb exploding that you saw," Whitmire said heavily. "It might have been the muzzle flash from a gun. You may have seen Barney McCrory's murderer fire the fatal shot."

CHAPTER 5

That same sobering thought had occurred to Phyllis. And after Whitmire put it into words, none of them had an appetite for more cupcakes. Phyllis asked the three men, to be sure, and when they shook their heads, she replaced the lid on the plastic container.

"Is there anything else you need from my clients, Chief?" D'Angelo asked.

Whitmire shook his head as he turned off the little recorder.

"No, I don't think so. I'll have these statements typed up tonight, and, if you don't mind, you both can come by here tomorrow and sign them."

"Why don't you send them over to my office?" D'Angelo suggested. "I'd like to review them. I'll see to it that they're signed and promptly returned to you."

Whitmire looked a little annoyed at that, but he nodded and said, "All right, if that's the way you want to do it. Surely by now, though, you can see that I don't suspect Mrs. Newsom and Mr. Fletcher of anything."

"It's just procedure," D'Angelo said.

Since Whitmire had used that same argument earlier in the evening, he couldn't very well dispute it now. He told Phyllis and Sam, "You're free to go. You'll keep yourself available if we need to talk to you again?"

"Within reason," D'Angelo said before either of them could answer.

He picked up his briefcase and ushered them out of the interrogation room. Whitmire followed and pointed to a door.

"You can go out there, so you won't have to go back through the lobby," he said.

Phyllis suspected that was the way Clay Loomis and Allyson and Nate Hollingsworth had left the police station when Whitmire finished questioning them, since she hadn't seen them come through the lobby while she and Sam were waiting there.

"Good night, Chief," she said to him.

Whitmire grunted and said, "I think the chances of that went away about an hour ago."

They stepped out into the chilly night air and followed the walk along the side of the building back to the parking lot. D'Angelo stopped at his car, which, appropriately enough, Phyllis thought, was an expensive luxury sedan.

"I'll call you tomorrow when I've had a chance to look over those statements," he said. "I don't think Chief Whitmire would try to slip anything underhanded into them, but it never hurts to be suspicious of the cops." He grinned. "Spoken like a true defense attorney, right?"

"You and my friend Carolyn would get along splendidly," Phyllis said.

"I know. I got that feeling when she called me tonight."

"So you admit that she's the one who got you here."

"Attorney-client privilege works both ways, you know."

Phyllis smiled, shook her head, and said, "I don't think it does."

Sam said, "You keep callin' us your clients, but we haven't actually hired you."

"Nonsense. After that business earlier this year, you each paid me a retainer to serve as your attorney if the need ever arose. I have the paperwork to prove it."

Phyllis and Sam exchanged a glance in the yellow glow of the sodium lights that illuminated the parking lot. They both knew that wasn't the case. It seemed like a little harmless fudging of the facts to Phyllis, though.

"All right," she told D'Angelo. "Thank you."

"I'll see you tomorrow," the lawyer said as he got into his car.

Phyllis and Sam walked on toward the pickup. Sam was carrying the cupcakes. He said, "We'll be eatin' on these for a while, I guess. That part of it's fine, but I sure wish the rest of it hadn't worked out like it did."

"I know," Phyllis said. "Who in the world would have wanted to shoot Mr. McCrory?"

"I don't have any idea," Sam said as he shook his head. "As far as I know, he didn't have any real enemies. But like I told you, Barney could be a mite rough around the edges, especially when he didn't get his way. I found that out when I didn't take some of his suggestions about how I ought to coach the team. Somebody could've been holdin' a grudge against him that I didn't know about. It's not like we've seen each other a lot since I moved down here from Poolville."

Sam unlocked the pickup and opened the passenger's door for Phyllis. Before she could get into the vehicle, however, two doors slammed on a nearby car and a woman's voice called, "Coach."

Phyllis turned to see Allyson and Nate Hollingsworth walking quickly toward them. Allyson's tears were dry now, but her face was pale and drawn in the lights. Nate's expression was equally grim.

"I'm sorry, kids," Sam said as they came up to him.

"We're not kids anymore, Coach," Allyson said.

"Yeah, I . . ." Sam's voice trailed off. Clearly, he didn't know what to say that would do any good at a moment like this.

Nate said, "Coach, we waited out here to see if we could talk to you." He looked at Phyllis. "To both of you."

"Well, sure," Sam said. "I guess." He looked puzzled by the request, but he wasn't going to refuse, Phyllis knew. He was too fond of his former students to deny them anything, especially at a time like this.

Before they could start peppering them with questions, Phyllis said, "We don't have to stand out here in the cold wind to talk. Why don't you come over to my house? I'll put on some coffee, and" — she looked at the container in Sam's hands — "we have cupcakes."

Nate looked at Allyson, who nodded her agreement. He said, "All right. But I don't know where we're going."

Phyllis told him the address, then added, "You can follow us over there."

"Sounds good," Nate agreed, and the Hollingsworths went back to their car.

"Do you have any idea what this is about?" Phyllis asked Sam as they got into the pickup.

"Not really. I reckon they're upset about Barney and just want to talk. I'm not sure why they're not doin' it with friends or family, though. It's not like I'm that close to 'em."

Phyllis had an idea, but all she said was, "I suppose we'll find out."

It didn't take them long to get to her home. Nate pulled up at the curb as Sam turned the pickup into the driveway.

As the four of them walked up to the porch, Phyllis couldn't help but think about how murder had struck close to home the past few holiday seasons. Violent death had taken place next door and then right on Phyllis's front porch.

Though murder had reared its ugly head again, Phyllis supposed she should be grateful it hadn't occurred in her own living room. The way things had been going, such a tragedy wouldn't have surprised her all that much.

Carolyn must have been watching for

them, because she opened the door before they reached it. She said, "Oh. I didn't know there would be company."

"Allyson and Nate wanted to talk to us," Sam said.

"Have the police arrested anyone?" Carolyn asked.

Phyllis said, "Not yet. The investigation has just barely gotten started."

"Hmph. That's never stopped them from jumping the gun before." Carolyn suddenly looked sorry for her choice of words. "I mean . . ."

"That's all right," Phyllis said, as they all moved into the foyer and started taking off their coats. "Would you mind making some coffee?"

"Not at all." Carolyn looked relieved to have some excuse to bustle off toward the kitchen.

Phyllis led the way into the living room and motioned for Sam to set the cupcakes on the coffee table.

"Please make yourselves comfortable," she told Allyson and Nate.

Now that she could get a better look at them, she saw they weren't quite as young as she originally had taken them for. They were in their late twenties, she estimated, which meant it had been about ten years since Sam had been their basketball coach at Poolville.

Allyson and Nate sat on the sofa. Phyllis and Sam settled into the two adjacent armchairs. Phyllis began, "I really am sorry about Mr. McCrory. Both of you have my deepest sympathy."

"Thank you," Allyson said with a sigh. "It's going to take a lot of getting used to. Him being gone, I mean. He was such a . . . a big part of our lives."

"We owed him a lot," Nate said. "Literally."

"What do you mean by that?" Sam asked.

"Well, I worked for him. I managed all his business affairs."

"I didn't know what you'd wound up doin'," Sam said. "Reckon I sort of lost track over the years."

Allyson smiled faintly and said, "You can't be expected to keep up with what all your former students are doing, Coach. There must be thousands of them. That would be impossible."

"Yeah, I suppose so. You two were pretty memorable, though. You were all-district forward your senior year, weren't you, Nate?"

Nate nodded as a look of nostalgia came over him. He said, "Yeah, I was."

"And I was never more than a second-string point guard," Allyson said.

"Yeah, but you were a valuable part of our bench," Sam said. "You were a gutty little ball hawk. I knew I could count on you for some defense anytime I put you in. You never minded givin' a hard foul or two, either."

"Only way to play," Allyson said. "Full speed."

"Barney taught you that, I expect. That's one thing he and I agreed on when it came to coachin'."

Phyllis wasn't sure if there was a point to this reminiscing. She had a hunch that wasn't why Allyson and Nate had come here. But if it made them feel better at this terrible time, she supposed it was worth it.

Sam turned to Nate and said, "So, you went to work for Barney after you got out of college, did you?"

"That's right. He helped me get my MBA. You remember, my folks never had much money . . ."

"I remember," Sam said. "I know Barney never begrudged helpin' you out, Nate. Even before you and Ally got married, he looked on you like the son he never had. I know that for a fact."

"Thank you," Nate said softly. With a visible effort, he struggled to control the emotions he was feeling and continued. "He asked me to work for him, to put that degree to good use, and I couldn't say no. Not after all the help he'd given me."

"And the job wasn't charity," Allyson said. "My father . . . well, you know, Coach. He didn't exactly have a real head for business."

Sam said, "I wouldn't really know one way or the other about that."

"Take it from me," Allyson said, "Dad always struggled with that part of running the ranch. No one was better at raising cattle, but making good business decisions . . . That just didn't come natural for him. He got better rates for feed, handled the taxes and the insurance and the employees better . . . The ranch was a lot more successful once Nate took over that part of the operation, and I know Dad appreciated that."

"I just did the best I could," Nate said.

Allyson clasped his right hand in both of hers and told him, "You're good at what you do, you know that. And so did Dad. He always appreciated your advice."

"Well . . . maybe not always."

Now they were getting closer to the reason for this visit, Phyllis sensed. Something was on Nate's mind, and on Allyson's, too, and it had to do with Barney McCrory's murder.

Before they could get into that subject, though, Carolyn reappeared carrying a tray with cups of coffee on it. She set it on the table, along with a crystal bowl that held packets of sugar, artificial sweetener, and creamer. For the next few minutes, everyone was busy fixing their coffee the way they liked it. Carolyn took a cup for herself and sat down at the desk in the corner, where Phyllis's computer was.

Sam passed around the cupcakes. This time Phyllis took one. She had started to get a little hungry. Between the sugar and the coffee, she might be awake all night, but at her age she seldom slept well anyway, so she supposed it didn't really matter.

For a few minutes, it felt like this was a homey, almost pleasant gathering, despite the shadow of death that hung over it. Phyllis had always believed that the term *comfort food* had a lot of truth to it. Being a good Baptist, she knew very well how food and mourning went hand in hand. There was never a funeral without a good meal either before or after, usually at the church's fellowship hall, with covered dishes brought in by ladies of the congregation. It was almost like an Irish wake — without the drinking, of course.

Tonight, Barney McCrory's loss was still too recent and painful for the healing to begin, but the cupcakes and coffee offered a brief respite, anyway.

But such respites couldn't last, and after a few minutes Allyson said, "We really wanted to talk to you tonight, Mrs. Newsom. That's why we waited at the police station." She smiled sadly at Sam. "No offense, Coach."

"None taken," he told her. "I'm sure if there's anything Phyllis can do to help you, she'd be glad to. And so will I."

"What is it, Allyson?" Phyllis asked, feeling that under the circumstances she could address the young woman by her first name, even though they had never met until tonight.

"I . . . we . . . well, Nate and I have read about the way you've been involved in murder cases before. We thought you might be able to help us."

Grimly, Nate said, "I still think you're overreacting, Ally. There's no point in getting ahead of ourselves —"

"Yes, there is," she told him. She looked at Phyllis again and said, "We need your help, Mrs. Newsom, because I'm afraid the police are going to arrest Nate for my father's murder."

Chapter 6

Allyson's worried statement hung in the air for a moment before anyone said anything. Finally, Phyllis broke the tense silence by asking, "Why do you think that?"

"She doesn't," Nate interrupted. "Not really. She's just upset, and who can blame her?"

With a hint of the steel that she had developed over decades of facing classrooms full of junior-high students, Phyllis said, "I believe I asked Allyson."

The young woman drew in a deep breath, then said, "It was the argument we had with Dad earlier today. He and Nate got really angry with each other."

"For God's sake, Allyson!" Nate burst out. "Are you *trying* to throw me under the bus?"

Sam said, "Take it easy, son. Nobody's tryin' to do anything except understand what's goin' on here."

"All right." Nate leaned forward and

clasped his hands together between his knees. "I'll start from the beginning and tell you the whole thing."

"I think that would be a good idea," Phyllis said.

"I told you I work as Barney's business manager. Well, a few months ago a man came to see me in my office here in town and had a proposition for me. He was a landsman. Do you know what that is?"

"A fella who scouts up property for oil and gas leases and gets the owners to sign," Sam replied.

"Exactly. This man, Frank Holbrook, was interested in putting a gas lease on Barney's ranch. He gave me all the details and some legal documents for Barney to sign. But when I took the papers out there and told Barney about the deal, he took one look at them and refused to sign."

"Why?" Phyllis asked. "A gas lease is a good thing, isn't it? I know the boom in this area isn't nearly as big as it was a few years ago, but people are still making money off their leases, aren't they?"

"According to Holbrook, they are," Nate said, "and Barney's ranch is a prime location because there hasn't been a lot of drilling around there. The geologists who work for the company Holbrook represents say there's still a lot of gas down there. But he still refused. He said he wasn't going to have a bunch of gas wells ruining the land where he'd raised cattle for more than forty years."

Carolyn said, "I don't blame him. All that fracking they do while they're drilling — it causes earthquakes, you know."

"I'm not sure they've ever proven that —," Sam began.

"Oh, it's just common sense! You remember what happened up in Azle a while back. A bunch of gas wells were put in, and they started having two or three earthquakes a week!"

Phyllis remembered the stories on the news and in the paper, and knew that Carolyn was right, at least to a certain extent. There had been a number of earthquakes in a fairly short period of time in the northeastern part of the county, and the residents of the area had blamed the proliferation of gas wells.

But whether there was any truth to that cause and effect, Phyllis didn't know. She was no geologist or seismologist or whatever kind of -ologist it was who studied such things.

"The thing is," Nate went on, "it was a fair deal, and there was a good chance it would have made Barney quite a bit of money. And as his business manager, it was my duty to advise him to take it. When he refused . . . Well, maybe I got a little stubborn about it."

Allyson said, "And when somebody gets stubborn with my dad, he gets — got — stubborn right back."

"Yeah, that sounds about right," Sam agreed. "No offense, Ally."

She shook her head and said, "No, you're right, Coach. I know better than anybody else how downright muleheaded he could be!"

Tears were shining in her eyes again. She didn't cry, though. Instead she said, "Nate's the same way. He and Dad went around and around about those stupid gas wells, until Dad finally said he didn't want to hear another word about it!"

"It was his decision to make," Nate said. "I tried to respect that — I really did. I didn't say anything about it for a while. Then Holbrook dropped by the office today to see if I'd made any progress with Barney, so I thought I'd give it one more try."

"And he blew up in your face about it, didn't he?" Sam said.

Nate sighed and nodded.

"Yeah. What made it worse, though, was that Ally was there this time."

"I've tried to stay out of it," Allyson said. "But after some of the things Dad said to Nate, I just couldn't. I — I told him he was just being a stubborn old fool who didn't realize when somebody was trying to help him, and — and . . ."

This time she couldn't hold back the tears. She buried her face in her hands and sobbed as Nate put his arm around her and drew her close to him on the sofa. He said, "Shhh," and stroked her hair and tried to comfort and calm her. It didn't seem to be doing much good.

They all sat there in silence for a while, but eventually, as Allyson's sobs quieted, Phyllis asked, "Did you tell all of this to Chief Whitmire when he questioned you?"

"We had to," Nate said. "He heard what Allyson said on Main Street — about the fight with Barney, I mean — and he asked us about it. I wasn't going to lie to the cops. That would just make things worse."

Carolyn looked like she was going to say something disparaging about the police, but Phyllis caught her eye and with a tiny shake of the head warned her to hold her tongue. At this point, comments like that weren't going to help anything.

"It — it's all my fault," Allyson hiccupped. "If I hadn't said anything . . ."

"It's not your fault," Nate insisted. "I'm not mad at you. You were just upset and scared, and anyway, I don't have anything to hide."

Phyllis asked, "Did Chief Whitmire say that he suspected you of your father-in-law's murder, Nate?"

"Well, no. But he'd keep that pretty close to the vest if he didn't have any real evidence, wouldn't he?"

Phyllis nodded and said, "More than likely. He's smart enough to know that motive alone isn't enough to make a case on."

"Yeah, but he's got motive on me, that's for sure," Nate said with a glum look on his face. "With Barney gone, Ally owns the ranch now. She can sign that gas lease and collect all that royalty money."

Sam said, "Then it seems to me like she's the one who's got the motive." Quickly, he added, "I'm sorry, Ally. I'd never believe for a second you'd ever do such a thing. I'm just talkin' about what the chief might think."

"My guess is that Allyson has an alibi," Phyllis said. "Don't you, dear?"

"Ally was with several friends of ours until after the parade had started," Nate said when Allyson didn't speak up. "They can vouch for her whereabouts the whole time."

"But you weren't there, were you?"

Nate sighed and said, "I went up to my office for a few minutes. It's on the second floor of one of the buildings right there in the square. I still had all those documents Holbrook gave me from the trip out to the ranch earlier in the day. I wanted to drop them off. By the time I got back to where Ally and our friends were on the courthouse lawn, all the commotion had broken out. We could tell something was wrong with her dad's carriage, so we got down there as fast as we could, and then we found out . . ."

He couldn't go on, but there was no need to. They all knew what he and Allyson had found: Barney McCrory had been murdered.

"You explained all this to the chief, too?" Phyllis asked.

"Yeah. Like I said, we figured it was best just to tell the truth. But then we got to thinking about how it might look."

They were the ones who'd needed Jimmy D'Angelo there to represent them, Phyllis thought. She asked, "Did Chief Whitmire advise you of your rights before he questioned you?"

"I . . . I think so," Nate said. "I'm pretty sure he did. I didn't think anything about it at the time. We were still so upset about

Barney."

Phyllis was confident that Whitmire had followed proper procedure, and he would have the two of them waiving counsel on tape, too.

Sam was frowning in thought. He asked, "You said your office is on the square, Nate?"

"Yeah. On the second floor of the Cranmoor Building."

"That's on the northeast side of the square, isn't it?"

"That's right."

Phyllis said, "You're thinking about that flash you saw, aren't you, Sam?"

"Yeah," he admitted. He sounded like he didn't want to take the next step in what he was thinking.

It was unavoidable, though. Phyllis asked, "It came from that part of the square, didn't it?"

For several seconds, Sam didn't answer. Then he said, "Yeah, it did. And it was up high enough that it could have come from a second-floor window, too. That's why I thought it was one of the lights strung up on a building."

Allyson let out a new wail of dismay.

Nate's face was set in grim lines as he tried to comfort her. He said, "After Chief

Whitmire let us leave, we sat in the car and talked about it, and that's when Allyson started worrying. We knew you and Mrs. Newsom were there, Coach, and Ally said the two of you solved crimes or something like that. I remembered reading about that, too. She said maybe you could help us."

"By findin' out who really killed Barney, you mean."

"Isn't that the best way to clear my name?"

"It is," Phyllis said, "and it's the only way to make sure a cloud of suspicion doesn't hang over you from now on, even if the police can't make a case against you."

"Could we, like . . . hire you?"

Sam started to speak up, but Phyllis said, "No." She looked at him and added, "We're not private detectives, Sam." She turned back to Nate and Allyson. "But you can hire a lawyer we know named Jimmy D'Angelo. If the police do try to charge you with anything, he can help you. And we can help Mr. D'Angelo."

"Well, it's kind of the same thing, seems like, but if that's the way you want to do it . . ."

"For right now it's the best way to proceed."

"All right. Thank you."

Allyson wiped away tears with the back of

her hand and added, “Yes, thank you. I’m just so scared they’re going to try to take Nate away from me, too, when I’ve already lost my dad.”

“You’ve still got friends,” Sam said gruffly. “Don’t ever forget that.”

She managed to smile a little as she told him, “Thanks, Coach.”

Phyllis had one of D’Angelo’s cards on the desk. She got it and handed it to Nate.

“Call him first thing in the morning, and tell him that Sam and I suggested it,” she said. “I’m sure he’ll want to talk to you right away.”

Nick looked at the card and nodded.

“His office is close to mine,” he said. “That’ll make it easier. Despite everything that’s happened, I still have to keep the ranch running as smoothly as possible. That’s my responsibility now, for Allyson — and for Barney.”

They left a few minutes later, after thanking Phyllis not only for promising to help them but also for the cupcakes and coffee. Sam started gathering up the empty cups to take them back to the kitchen.

Carolyn asked, “What do you think of their story, Phyllis? Do you believe they’re telling the truth?”

Instead of answering, Phyllis turned to

Sam and said, "What do you think?"

He straightened with the tray in his hands and gave her a solemn look.

"I believe every word they told us," he said. "I coached both of 'em for four years. I don't think they ever lied to me that whole time. Not about anything important, anyway." He smiled. "Maybe about makin' out under the bleachers in the gym."

"That was a long time ago," Phyllis pointed out. "Ten years. People can change in that amount of time."

"I know it. But I don't think those two have. I think they're still the same good kids they always were. They've just gotten a raw deal all the way around in this mess, especially Ally. It's hard enough on her, losin' her dad like that, without havin' her husband locked up to boot."

"Maybe that won't happen."

Carolyn said, "Do you really believe that? Goodness knows I like to stick up for the underdog, but it sounds like the police might actually have a case against that boy."

"If they do," Phyllis said, "Mr. D'Angelo will sort it all out. And we'll help as much as we can, won't we, Sam?"

"Darn straight we will."

Carolyn looked at Phyllis and frowned.

"What's gotten into you?" she asked.

"Usually you have to be dragged kicking and screaming into these cases. You always insist that you're just a retired schoolteacher, not a detective."

"Why fight it?" Phyllis said with a sigh. "The world seems determined to prove otherwise. Besides, I like those two. I want to help them if I can."

Her eyes narrowed slightly as she thought about Barney McCrory's murder and how close Sam had come to dying, and how other innocent people might have been hurt or even killed. She thought about all the families who had turned out on a crisp winter evening to enjoy a parade and a Christmas-tree lighting to launch a wonderful holiday season, only to have it turn into screaming chaos.

Then she said, "And I don't want whoever did this to get away with it."

Chapter 7

When Phyllis woke up the next morning, the world was new again, as it usually was, and for a moment there was no room in her head for thoughts of murder.

That didn't last long, though, as memories of what had happened the night before came flooding into her brain.

Sometimes that first rush of thought brought with it possibilities that she hadn't considered before. That wasn't the case this time. She was just as baffled by Barney McCrory's murder as she had been when starting out. Mentally, she examined everything she had seen and heard, and didn't spot anything that would prove Nate Hollingsworth was innocent.

Conversely, though, there was nothing else to point to him as the killer, other than what he and Allyson had talked about downstairs in the living room as they ate cupcakes and drank coffee.

It was early — Phyllis never slept in anymore; that ability seemed to have deserted her — but Eve was already in the kitchen when Phyllis came in. Eve seldom attempted to cook anything, but she had the coffee on already. She sat down at the table with the cup she had just poured and said, "Carolyn tells me you're going to investigate that murder at the parade last night."

"It's possible," Phyllis admitted as she got her cup from the drainer by the sink.

"I'm sorry I didn't join you when there was company here. I was all wrapped up in something and didn't even know about it until I ran into Carolyn in the hall later."

Phyllis filled her cup and said, "That's all right. Were you working on something?"

"Oh, just a little hobby I've taken up. Nothing important."

Phyllis hadn't heard anything about a hobby and was curious about what Eve was up to, but her friend didn't seem to want to talk about it, and Phyllis wasn't going to press her. It wasn't like she was nosy or anything.

That thought brought a smile to her face. *Nosy* was probably one of the milder words some people might use to describe her. She didn't see it that way, but she could understand why others would.

She preferred to think of her activities as digging for the truth. Like an archaeologist.

Eve said, "I'm sure Sam is worried about that situation. It was an old friend of his who was killed, after all."

"It seems like these things always hit too close to home," Phyllis said with a sigh. Eve knew that as well as anyone, since she'd had her own run-in with murder, nasty business that had landed both her and Phyllis behind bars for a while.

"Well, if you want to talk about it anytime, I'd be glad to listen. I'm no detective like you are, but my ear is always available."

"Thanks," Phyllis said. Eve's attitude was a little puzzling. She had never taken that much of an interest in the cases Phyllis investigated unless they affected her personally.

Interrupting her thoughts, Carolyn came into the kitchen and said, "I wouldn't expect Sam to be down anytime soon, the way he's sawing logs up there. I could hear him out in the hall when I passed his room."

Phyllis smiled and said, "I'll cook some bacon. That smell always has amazing rejuvenating powers where Sam is concerned."

Carolyn sat down at the table with her

cup of coffee and asked, “Have you decided what your first column is going to be about?”

The question sounded casual, but Phyllis suspected that it wasn’t. A few months earlier, she had won a recipe contest sponsored by their favorite magazine, *A Taste of Texas,* and the editor had surprised her by asking her to write a monthly column featuring a new recipe. The deadline was looming, and Phyllis knew she had to come up with something soon.

“I was thinking about combining a couple of things I like,” she said, then hesitated. Over the years, she had gotten into the habit of being rather closemouthed about recipe ideas around Carolyn, since they were usually competing in one contest or another. Phyllis didn’t think for a second that Carolyn would actually steal one of her recipes, but just knowing what Phyllis was considering might give her an advantage in making her own plans.

This time, however, there was no competition involved. Indeed, Carolyn had seemed to be nothing but pleased and supportive about Phyllis’s column.

“Combinations are usually a good idea,” Carolyn said now. “As long as you don’t try to combine things that really don’t go together. Those oddball mixtures are usually awful."

Phyllis wasn't so sure about that. How were you supposed to know what went together well if you didn't try them out?

But she let that go and said, "I think these will be just fine. I'm going to make some baklava macarons and see how they turn out."

"Oh, that does sound good," Eve said.

"Yes, it does," Carolyn agreed. "If I can give you a hand, just let me know." She paused, then added, "You wouldn't even have to mention me in the magazine."

Phyllis took a sip of coffee to keep from laughing. Eve wasn't that restrained. She smiled sweetly and asked, "How's the fishing, dear?"

"Fishing?" Carolyn frowned. "What are you talking about?"

Phyllis didn't know if Eve's pointed comment had really gone over Carolyn's head, or if Carolyn just chose to pretend not to understand. Either way, the conversation had gone far enough. She stood up and headed for the cabinet to get out a frying pan and start on that bacon.

As Phyllis had predicted, about ten minutes after the smell of frying bacon filled the big old house, Sam walked into the kitchen in his bathrobe. By that time, Carolyn had mixed up some blueberry muffins and had them in the oven, and the aroma in the kitchen was even more delicious.

As the four friends sat around the table eating, Carolyn asked, "Are you and Sam going to start investigating this morning, Phyllis?"

"I imagine we'll wait to hear from Mr. D'Angelo's office," Phyllis said. "We're supposed to go by there sometime today to sign those statements we gave Chief Whitmire last night, and he'll be talking to Nate this morning, too. It's possible Mr. D'Angelo may think the police don't have a strong enough case to charge Nate, so the whole thing could turn out to be moot."

Carolyn frowned and said, "But what about that cloud of suspicion you mentioned last night? If the real killer isn't caught, some people will always believe that Nate shot his father-in-law."

"I suppose that's true. I'm not sure the general public will ever hear enough about the case to form such an opinion, though."

"Are you joking?" Carolyn asked. "A murder at a Christmas parade, a runaway Santa Claus sleigh, and who happens to be on hand to stop it and save lives? You two!"

She shook her head. "I'll bet the story is all over the Internet already. Those — what do you call 'em? — fan sites will be buzzing about this."

Phyllis frowned. She hadn't thought about that. As farfetched as it seemed to her, as difficult as it was for her to believe, she knew there were true-crime websites devoted to the cases she had solved. She didn't have any connection to any of them, and she scrupulously avoided commenting on them, no matter how outlandish they got, but she knew they were out there.

And she knew Carolyn was right: Barney McCrory's murder would be prime blog fodder.

Sam said, "Nobody who knows Nate very well would ever think he was a murderer. He was always a good kid, and grew up to be a good man."

"You know that," Carolyn said, "and the rest of us will certainly take your word for it. But what about everybody who doesn't know him? He's going to be the prime suspect in everyone's mind, Sam. There's no getting around that."

Sam grimaced and shrugged. He knew there was no point in arguing with Carolyn, especially when she was right.

After breakfast, once they had cleaned up

the dishes and gotten dressed, Sam fed his Dalmatian, Buck, who had been part of the family since Sam had adopted him several months earlier. Phyllis went to the computer in the living room and turned on the monitor. She checked her e-mail — nothing important, not even a message from a Nigerian prince — and then opened one of the true-crime websites in her browser. She didn't want to admit it to Carolyn, but she had bookmarked several of them.

She winced as she saw the title of the first post: WEATHERFORD, MURDER CAPITAL OF TEXAS — AND PHYLLIS NEWSOM'S HOMETOWN. There was a picture of the big crowd gathered on the courthouse lawn for the previous year's Christmas-tree lighting, since it had never taken place this year.

The person who had posted the story had included a photograph of Barney McCrory, too. It had been taken somewhere outside, probably on his ranch, and Phyllis thought it made him look like the Marlboro Man. Of course, there was no mention of that, since not many members of the Internet generation would even be aware of who the Marlboro Man was.

There was a picture of Clay Loomis, too: a professional portrait showing his sleek, silver-haired good looks and plenty of white teeth bared in a politician's smile. The story explained that he was the local official who'd been playing Santa Claus in the parade.

Not only that, but there were also pictures of attractive young women in elf costumes that were even skimpier and more suggestive than the ones the cheerleaders had actually been wearing. The story made it sound as if the women in the photos were the high school girls who had been on the carriage, even though they really weren't.

As she skimmed through the story, Phyllis had to admit that despite its overall sleazy tone, the basic facts as presented by the website were correct. She clicked on the bookmarks again and went to another site.

This one was more restrained, although one of the commenters on the post had written in all caps, NEVER GO TO THE OPERA WITH PHYLLIS NEWSOM! She wasn't sure what *that* meant. She hadn't been to the opera in years. She didn't even *like* opera.

Then she frowned and said, "Ohhhh," as the light dawned. The idea was ridiculous, of course. She went to plenty of places where murders never took place.

Sam came into the room behind her and she gave a little guilty start, as if she'd been looking at something she shouldn't. She started to close the browser, then decided not to. She wasn't doing anything wrong.

"Carolyn was right, eh?" Sam said. "The story's already out there?"

"Yes, but there's really not much about Nate and Allyson." She let out a ladylike little snort. "They're too busy making snide comments about how dangerous it is to be around me."

"Maybe I'd better keep that in mind," Sam drawled. "These days, I spend more time around you than anybody else, so I reckon I'm in the most danger."

"Don't be —" She was going to say *ridiculous,* but then she turned and saw that he was grinning. "You're just giving me the business."

"Maybe." He grew more serious as he came to stand beside her. "Did you see anything that gave you ideas?"

"Unfortunately, no. There's nothing in-depth in any of the stories. We need to sit down with Nate and Allyson again, maybe with Mr. D'Angelo there, and go over everything they can tell us about Mr. McCrory and his business. There has to be something somewhere to justify someone taking a shot at him."

"Unless it was just a random shooter,"

Sam said.

"If that were true, isn't it more likely he would have kept shooting? Maniacs like that generally don't stop with one shot."

"That's true. The way the whole thing played out makes it look like he was just after Barney. When he made his first shot, that was the end of it."

Phyllis frowned. She said, "How do we know it was his first shot?"

"Well, nobody else was hurt . . ."

"Maybe his first shot missed. Maybe his first two or three shots. The police need to go over that carriage very carefully and look for bullet holes. I wonder what happened to it."

"My guess is that the cops impounded it. It'll be in the police garage. I don't see what some extra shots would prove, though."

Phyllis sighed.

"Neither do I," she admitted. "The case has barely gotten started, and I'm already grasping at straws."

"You're gatherin' information and considerin' possibilities," Sam said. "I wouldn't call that graspin' at straws."

"Maybe not, but —"

The ringing of the doorbell interrupted her.

"You expectin' anybody?" Sam asked.

"No," Phyllis replied with a frown. She turned off the computer monitor and stood up. A glance out the living-room window showed her an unmarked van parked at the curb in front of the house. The van might not have any words written on it, but the presence of a small dish antenna attached to the vehicle's roof was a dead giveaway.

The TV people had arrived — and they were just about the last people Phyllis wanted to see.

Chapter 8

Sam had come up beside Phyllis to peer through the window. He muttered, "I don't like the looks of that."

"Maybe if we just ignore them, they'll go away," she suggested.

"Maybe," Sam said dubiously, "but I doubt it. Anyway, there'll just be some more along later."

The doorbell rang again. Carolyn came up the hall from the kitchen and said, "Goodness, isn't someone going to answer that?" She started toward the door herself.

Phyllis waved her back and said in resignation, "I've got it."

She opened the door to find three people standing on her porch: two burly men in Windbreakers and blue jeans, one carrying a video camera and the other some sort of equipment Phyllis didn't recognize, and a young woman with artfully tousled chestnut hair and perfect makeup. She held a microphone and wore a blue blazer and a scandalously short skirt that showed off sleek, nylon-clad legs.

"Mrs. Newsom," she said quickly, without any preamble, "I'm Felicity Prosper from *Inside Beat.* I'm sure you've seen our program. What can you tell us about this latest murder case you're investigating? Have you zeroed in on the killer yet?"

"I'm sorry," Phyllis began, "I really can't comment —"

"You *are* Phyllis Newsom, aren't you?" the young woman went on. "Texas's Elderly Angel of Death?"

That question left Phyllis so shocked, she couldn't find any words. While she was standing there speechless, Sam moved up behind her, rested a hand on her shoulder, and said through the screen door, "Listen here. You folks just get on out of here. You've got no business comin' around and upsettin' people —"

"You're Sam Fletcher," Felicity Prosper said. "Mrs. Newsom's *friend.*" Her tone of voice put a leer in the word. "What's it like to be romantically involved with a woman who catches killers for a living?"

Phyllis finally found her voice again. She burst out, "I don't catch killers for a living. I'm a retired schoolteacher!"

"A retired schoolteacher who's responsible for nearly a dozen murderers being behind bars, even though the incompetent authorities in this town had no idea they were guilty," Felicity Prosper went on smoothly. Phyllis wondered crazily how the woman could talk so fast without ever stopping to take a breath. "That's true, isn't it? In every one of those cases, the police arrested the wrong person and claimed that he or she was the killer. Including one of your very best friends."

The torrent of words threatened to overwhelm Phyllis. She thought about slamming the door in Felicity's face, but before she could do that, Sam said angrily, "I've seen that *Inside Beat* show of yours, miss. It's pure trash. Nothin' but sordid celebrity gossip and the most lurid crimes you can dig up. Well, there's nothin' for you to see here. Nothin'!"

Sam stepped back, bringing Phyllis with him, and took care of slamming the door. In fact, he slammed it so hard, it shivered in its frame.

"Dang," Sam muttered. "Hope I didn't knock anything outa line."

"Good grief," Carolyn said from behind them. "I don't think I've ever seen you so angry, Sam."

"I just hate to see those . . . those buzzards peckin' around in the tragedy of a good man's death."

The doorbell rang again. Phyllis's only response was to reach up and turn the dead bolt, making sure it was closed. Then she went back into the living room and pulled the curtains shut over the picture window.

Felicity Prosper gave up trying to wear out the doorbell after a while and went back to the van, trailed by the two men, who hadn't said a word. A few minutes later the phone rang, and when Phyllis answered, the first thing she heard was the young woman's voice saying, "Mrs. Newsom, if you'd just give me an interview —"

Phyllis thumbed the button to end the call. It went against the grain for her to hang up on someone — her generation had been raised to be polite — but she didn't want to talk to the tabloid-TV reporter.

A few minutes later Felicity was back on the porch, ringing the bell.

"Would it do any good to call the police?" Eve asked. She had joined Phyllis, Sam, and Carolyn in the living room.

"I'm sure the police could tell them to get off the property," Phyllis said, "but then they'd just sit out there in their van. That's not against the law."

"Maybe it should be," Carolyn said. "It ought to be illegal to harass law-abiding citizens in their own homes."

"It's the information age," Sam said, "and information wants to be free. Or so all the anarchists will tell you. That's not what the young lady and her associates are after, though."

"What do you think they want?" Phyllis asked.

"Ratings." Sam rubbed his right thumb against the fingertips of that hand. "Money. Moolah."

Phyllis had to laugh.

"I don't think I've heard anybody use that word in ages," she said. "Thank you, Sam. You've lightened the mood."

"Maybe so, but I don't reckon it'll take Miss Short Skirt out there long to darken it again."

Phyllis raised an eyebrow and said, "You noticed the skirt, did you?"

"Hard not to. My bones may creak, but my eyes still work pretty good."

It was a long morning. Felicity Prosper went back and forth from the porch to the van, ringing the doorbell each time, and she called on the phone at least half a dozen times. Phyllis let both of them ring.

Finally, though, on one of those calls, the

phone displayed the name of the law firm where Jimmy D'Angelo had his practice. That one Phyllis answered right away.

"Good morning," D'Angelo said.

"I'm not so sure about that," Phyllis told him.

"Oh? What's wrong?"

"There's a reporter from some tabloid TV show camped out on my front porch. She wants to talk to me about Mr. McCrory's murder." Phyllis paused. "She called me Texas's Elderly Angel of Death."

D'Angelo made a noise on the other end of the connection. She couldn't tell if he was trying to be sympathetic — or trying not to laugh.

But he managed to sound properly outraged as he said, "That's terrible. I can try to get a restraining order against them. It might not be easy, though. I'm sure the show has plenty of lawyers on retainer, ready to start yelling about the freedom of the press."

Phyllis sighed and said, "I wouldn't waste any time and energy on that. This reporter is persistent, and I'm sure there'll be others. I'm just going to try to ignore them."

"You can always say *no comment,* no matter what they ask you," D'Angelo said. "Do you think you can get out without them following you?"

"It's doubtful, but I can try. Do you want to see me?"

"You and Sam. I've got those statements for you to sign. Also, Nate Hollingsworth was here earlier. I think it would be worthwhile for all of us to sit down with him and his wife to talk about the case. They're supposed to be here at two this afternoon. Can you and Sam make that?"

"We'll be there," Phyllis promised. "We may have a TV crew in tow, but we'll be there."

Felicity Prosper and her cohorts must have taken a break for lunch, because their van disappeared from the curb in the middle of the day. Phyllis hoped they would be gone until after she and Sam left for Jimmy D'Angelo's office. She didn't want the TV people following them there. That would tip them off that D'Angelo was involved and might lead them straight to Nate and Allyson.

In fact, once the housemates had finished eating lunch themselves, Phyllis said to Carolyn and Eve, "Do you two mind cleaning up? I think it might be best if Sam and I went on downtown now, while Miss Prosper and her friends aren't out there, spying on us."

"That's a good idea," Carolyn said. "Of course Eve and I can take care of things here."

"That's right," Eve seconded the statement. "You two should go ahead while you've got the chance."

"We'll be early," Sam pointed out as he stood up from the kitchen table, "but I suppose we can wait in Jimmy's office, or maybe walk around the square."

Phyllis thought that was a good idea. They could walk by the Cranmoor Building, where Nate had his office, and see how the second-floor windows lined up with the trajectory of the shot that had killed Barney McCrory.

Quickly, they got ready to leave. Instead of taking Sam's pickup this time, they got into Phyllis's Lincoln inside the garage. The garage door was closed, so they couldn't be seen from the street. Phyllis opened the door, backed out quickly, and turned toward the downtown area.

They had gone less than a block when she noticed something odd in the rearview mirror.

Someone was following them on a bicycle.

The schools hadn't dismissed for Christmas vacation yet, since Christmas was still more than two weeks away, so there shouldn't have been any kids out and about on a weekday. Well, not many anyway, Phyllis thought. These days there were always a few homeschooled children around.

The person on the bicycle didn't look like a child, though. He appeared to be a grown man, and a rather large one at that. In fact, he was so big, he looked ridiculous perched on the bicycle seat.

He seemed to be having trouble controlling the bike, too. He wobbled and weaved back and forth nearly from one side of the street to the other as he pumped hard on the pedals. It was a good thing there was no traffic right now.

Then Phyllis exclaimed, "Oh, dear!" as she saw the cyclist lose control of the bike and fall over. It was a classic wipeout, the sort of crash that left a rider with skinned elbows and knees, if not worse.

"What's wrong?" Sam asked, as Phyllis slowed down.

"There was a man back there on a bicycle," she explained. "He wrecked it."

"Kind of a chilly day to be out ridin' a bike," Sam said, as Phyllis turned into a driveway and began to back up and turn around. "Sure it's not a motorcycle?"

"It would be just as cold on a motorcycle as on a bicycle, wouldn't it?"

"Well, yeah, I guess it would," Sam said with a shrug. "A bicycle just seems colder somehow."

"Anyway, this fellow looked familiar. I want to make sure he's all right."

Phyllis hadn't realized until just then that there *was* something familiar about the man. I must have noticed it subconsciously, she thought as she drove toward him.

By the time she reached him, he was sitting up and shaking his head like he was groggy. He wasn't wearing a helmet. She hoped he hadn't hit his head on the pavement and seriously injured himself.

The curb was empty, so she parked there even with the man and the overturned bicycle. He was an overweight young man with a shock of curly dark hair and thick lenses set in black plastic rims. He wore jeans and a University of North Texas sweatshirt with a lightweight Windbreaker over it.

The knees of the trousers were torn. It looked like he had skinned his knees, although his elbows appeared to have escaped the crash unscathed.

Phyllis got out of the car and asked, "Good heavens, are you all right? That was quite a tumble you took."

The young man's glasses had slipped down on his nose. He pushed them up and said, "Yeah, I — I guess so. It knocked the wind out of me pretty good."

Sam had gotten out of the Lincoln, too. He came around the front of the car and said, "I know you. You're one of the fellas who was with that reporter gal. Miss Prosper."

The young man looked down, seemingly embarrassed.

"Yeah," he mumbled. "I'm one of Felicity's interns."

"You were following us, weren't you?" Phyllis said sternly.

"She told me to, okay? I'm sorry, but she's the boss. She calls the shots." Under his breath he added, "Boy, does she ever."

Sam said, "She left you behind to keep an eye on us, didn't she?"

"Yeah. She and Nick went to get something to eat. They said they'd bring something back for me." The young man blew out his breath. "Nick said I could go longer without eating because I've got plenty of fat stored up."

"Well, that was rude," Phyllis said.

"Yeah, maybe, but it's true." The young man pushed up his glasses again. "They left me the bicycle. Felicity carries it around with her so she can get in her ten miles a day." He groaned. "If she finds out I wrecked it, she'll kill me! I told her I wasn't any good on bikes."

Sam went over to the bicycle and righted it.

"Doesn't look damaged to me," he said. "Anyway, wouldn't she be more worried about you?"

A bitter laugh came from the young man. He said, "You don't know Felicity."

"And I don't think I want to," Phyllis said. "If you're all right, we need to be going."

"Before they get back, huh? I don't blame you. Go ahead. I won't try to follow you. I'll say I lost you at a light."

"Won't that get you in trouble?" Sam asked.

The young man shrugged and said, "Felicity will be mad. She'll get over it, though. She's really not a bad person. She's just . . . *driven.*"

"What's your name, son?"

"Josh Green."

"We're obliged to you, Josh. Did you say you're an intern?"

"Yeah, that's right."

"So that means you put up with that gal bein' mean to you, and you don't even get paid for it?"

"It'll all be worth it someday," Josh said, "when I'm an award-winning TV news producer."

"You hang on to that dream, son. Hope it works out for you. Just not today."

Sam pushed the bike up onto the sidewalk and lowered it carefully onto its side. He extended a hand to Josh Green and helped the youngster to his feet. Then, while Josh stood there brushing off the seat of his pants, Phyllis and Sam got back into the Lincoln.

Phyllis turned around in another driveway and they headed for downtown again, leaving Josh standing there on the sidewalk in a slump-shouldered attitude of despair.

CHAPTER 9

Christmas decorations were up on the buildings and streetlights around the square, and the tall Christmas tree, covered with lights and ornaments, stood proudly on the courthouse lawn. Everything was starting to look festive, Phyllis thought.

"Poor kid," Sam said, clearly referring to Josh Green, as Phyllis was parking. "Sounds like that TV gal is sort of a dragon lady to work for."

"That doesn't surprise me," Phyllis said, "but it's his choice to be her intern." She looked around suspiciously. "He didn't hop back on that bike and follow us, did he?"

"I don't think so. Fact is, it looked to me like it was all he could do not to start cryin' like a kid who'd fallen off a bike. It must've hurt like the dickens when he landed in the street."

Phyllis agreed. She had seen that same look of stubborn stoicism on her son Mike's face when he was growing up. In fact, he had wrecked his bike on the same stretch of street more than once.

But it was up to Josh to escape from Felicity Prosper's clutches if he wanted to. For now it was more important that she and Sam had given him the slip. She pointed and said, "There's the building where Nate's office is."

"Yeah. We don't know where his office is situated inside the building, though, or which way the windows face," Sam pointed out. "If they're on this side . . ."

He didn't have to finish the sentence for Phyllis to know what he meant. She turned her head, looking from the office building back to the south.

There appeared to be a clear line of sight past the eastern face of the courthouse and on down South Main to the spot where the parade had assembled. Someone would have to be a pretty good marksman to make such a shot, but it didn't strike her as being impossible by any means.

"Was Nate a good shot in high school?" she asked.

Sam shook his head and said, "I don't have any idea. I seem to recall him talkin' to some of the other fellas about goin' huntin', but there wouldn't have been anything unusual about that. Plenty of the boys went deer huntin' or dove huntin' every year. Some of the girls, too."

Phyllis understood that. Even though she wasn't a hunter herself, she knew the tradition was still strong in Texas. These days, youngsters had to be more careful about certain aspects of it — they couldn't have deer rifles or shotguns in their pickups at school, as had been an everyday occurrence when she was growing up — but they still learned how to handle firearms and how to shoot.

So at this point she had no way of knowing if Nate Hollingsworth could even make such a shot, but she certainly couldn't rule it out.

The encounter with Josh Green had delayed them enough that it wasn't long until their appointment with Jimmy D'Angelo. They walked down the street to his office, where his receptionist greeted them with a friendly smile.

"Jimmy said for me to tell you to go on into the conference room," she said. "He'll join you in there shortly."

Phyllis and Sam had been in the firm's conference room before. It was just what you'd expect from such a place: a lot of dark wood and rich leather and portraits of the firm's partners on the wall. D'Angelo was an associate, not a partner, but Phyllis wouldn't be surprised if he wound up running the place someday.

She and Sam sat down at the mahogany table. Sam leaned back in the plushly upholstered chair and said, "Every time we come in here, I feel like there ought to be cigars and whiskey. Maybe some retired brigadier with a white handlebar mustache sittin' in the corner readin' the *London Times.*"

"I'm just thankful there aren't any smelly cigars."

"How about the whiskey?"

Before Phyllis could answer that, one of the other doors opened and Nate and Allyson came into the conference room, followed by Jimmy D'Angelo. The young couple took seats on the other side of the table, and the lawyer sat at the end. He had a dark blue folder with him.

"Thanks for coming in," he said. "You don't mind that Nate and Allyson are here, do you?"

"Of course not," Phyllis said.

"And you two are all right with Phyllis and Sam being here, right?"

"Yes, that's fine," Allyson said. She didn't look happy, but Phyllis didn't think it was because she and Sam were there.

"First things first," D'Angelo said. He opened the folder and took out two documents. There were two sheets in each one, held together by a paper clip. He pushed them down the table to Phyllis and Sam and instructed, "Look those over, please, and if they're accurate statements, you can sign them." He took a pen from his shirt pocket and passed that down to them as well.

Phyllis looked over her statement while Sam was reading his. It was exactly what had been said at the police station the night before, so she nodded to D'Angelo and picked up the pen, saying, "Everything looks all right to me."

"Me, too," Sam said.

Phyllis signed first and handed the pen to Sam, and then, when he had signed his statement, he picked up both documents and handed them back to the lawyer, along with the pen. D'Angelo replaced the documents in the folder.

"I'll have these delivered to the police," he said. "Now what we all need to talk about is what happened last night."

Allyson said, "We've been over it and over it. I don't see why we have to keep repeating the same things."

"Because sometimes when you're going

through a series of events, new memories crop up. We have to be sure we have every possible fact at our disposal."

Nate said, "Wouldn't it be better to do this *after* I've been arrested? Rehashing it now is just upsetting Allyson, and there may not be any need."

"You're not going to be arrested," Allyson said. "How can the police arrest somebody for something they didn't do?"

It's a good thing Carolyn isn't here, Phyllis thought. She would have an acerbic comment or two in response to that question.

D'Angelo said, "Unfortunately, it happens all the time. The cops just go by their interpretation of the evidence they have."

"There can't be any evidence saying that Nate killed my father, because he didn't do it."

"There's evidence establishing that he had a reason to, whether he did or not," D'Angelo said bluntly. "That argument over the gas wells, along with the value of your father's estate — those things go right to motive."

Nate said, "Yeah, but just because something looks bad doesn't mean that the police will arrest somebody. How many high-profile murders have there been over the years where the identity of the killer seems obvious to everybody, but the police never arrest anyone?"

"It happens," D'Angelo admitted. "Not very often, but when it does, we remember it because, like you say, those are high-profile cases. This one doesn't have any movie stars or professional athletes involved in it, but it's going to draw some interest anyway."

It already has, thought Phyllis. She had told D'Angelo about the people from the *Inside Beat* TV show, but the lawyer might not have mentioned that to Nate and Allyson, so Phyllis didn't say anything about it, either.

D'Angelo went on. "This case has got sexy girls, a cowboy, and Santa Claus mixed up in it. If it hasn't gone nationwide yet, it will before too much longer. And the more publicity it gets, the more pressure the DA will put on the cops to make an arrest. This DA, he doesn't like pressure."

Phyllis knew that from experience . . . the experience of looking out through the iron bars of a jail cell.

"So, we have to be ready," D'Angelo said, "and if we wait to make our preparations, it'll just be harder then. Let's go through all of it, starting with the visit the two of you paid to Mr. McCrory's ranch yesterday afternoon."

Nate sighed and said, "Frank Holbrook came by my office yesterday morning. I hadn't talked to him in a while. He said he just wanted to touch base with me and see if maybe Barney had reconsidered the lease offer. I told him that he hadn't, but that I'd go out and check with him one more time, just to be sure. This was right before Allyson came in. We were meeting at the office so we could go to lunch together."

"Allyson, had you met this man Holbrook before?" D'Angelo asked.

She shook her head and said, "No, although I'd certainly heard plenty about him from Nate. He seemed like a nice man. I asked him to come to lunch with us, but he said he had another meeting."

"What did you do then?"

"We went to lunch," Nate said.

"And while we were at the restaurant, I decided to ride out to the ranch with Nate," Allyson said. "I hadn't really tried to convince Dad that it might be a good idea to sign the lease, so I thought I'd talk to him about it."

"Where was he when you got there?"

"My dad? He was out in the barn. He had a cow about to calve, so he was keeping an eye on her."

"Was anybody else around?"

"A couple of the men who worked for him — Fred Harriman and Matt Gonzales."

"So there were witnesses to the conversation."

Nate said, "You mean, were there witnesses to the argument? Yeah, there were. We went off a little ways to talk, but when Barney got worked up, like he did yesterday, he could be pretty loud. Fred and Matt wouldn't have had any trouble hearing every word he said."

"And they could hear what the two of you said, too?"

"Yeah, I guess so."

"I know they heard me," Allyson said, looking embarrassed. "I got . . . pretty loud and angry. Daddy acted like Nate was somehow betraying him, just because Nate thought the gas lease was a good business deal. It made me mad at him for treating Nate like that."

"So, the two of you left the ranch on bad terms with your father?"

"Barney calmed down a little after I promised I'd let the subject drop," Nate said. "I told him I'd call Holbrook and tell him it was no deal. After that there was sort of a truce declared, I guess you'd say. I think there were still some hurt feelings on both sides, though."

"We told Dad we'd see him at the parade last night," Allyson said, her voice catching with emotion as she did so. "I was looking forward to seeing him driving that carriage with Santa in it . . ."

She didn't sob, but tears welled up in her eyes and rolled down her cheeks. Nate reached over and rested a hand on her shoulder. Allyson caught her bottom lip between her teeth in an obvious effort to control her emotions.

D'Angelo turned to Phyllis and Sam and said, "That brings us to yesterday evening, when you saw Mr. McCrory at the parade and went over to talk to him."

"Wait a minute," Phyllis said. Since Allyson was upset, she asked Nate, "What time was it when the two of you left the ranch yesterday afternoon?"

He frowned and said, "Oh, I guess it was about three o'clock."

"And it was six when Sam and I were talking to Mr. McCrory. The parade was supposed to start at six, but I remember thinking it was running a few minutes late, as usual. It's hard to get something like that coordinated and started exactly on time."

"I see what you're getting at," D'Angelo said. "There's three hours in Mr. McCrory's life we haven't accounted for. What was he doing during that time?"

Phyllis said, "Nate, do the men who work for your father-in-law live on the ranch?"

"Some of them do. There are some little houses out there where the hands live with their families." Nate hesitated. "Barney used to hire . . . well, illegals. When I started running the business end of the operation, I talked him into putting a stop to that. There haven't been any undocumented aliens working on the ranch for several years." He looked at D'Angelo. "That can't get us in any trouble now, can it?"

"You personally didn't break any immigration laws," D'Angelo said. "I can't guarantee that some overzealous federal prosecutor might not try to make something out of it, if he found out about it, but nothing said in here is going to leave this room. Privilege applies to me because I'm your attorney, and it extends to Mrs. Newsom and Mr. Fletcher because they're working for me as investigators. For all practical purposes, you don't have to worry about that." He paused, then added significantly, "Just don't go around talking about it. Don't volunteer that information to the police, and if they ask you about it, tell them to talk to me."

Nate nodded and said, “All right. Barney always treated his employees very well, though, whether they were legal or not. He never tried to take advantage of anybody. That’s just not the sort of man he was.”

“I can vouch for that,” Sam said. “There was never a fairer man than Barney McCrory.”

D’Angelo clasped his hands together on the table in front of him and said, “So, we ought to be able to talk to the guys on the ranch and find out what Mr. McCrory did during those three hours.”

“I think so,” Nate said. “It’s pretty obvious, though. He hitched up the team and drove that carriage from the ranch down to town for the parade.”

“He did?” D’Angelo said with a surprised frown. “He didn’t, like, put it on a truck or something and bring it in that way?”

“No,” Nate replied with a smile. “Barney was the old-fashioned sort. He drove the team in.”

“We ought to be able to check on that, too,” D’Angelo said. He turned back to Phyllis. “That’s good thinking, though, covering that window of time. Now, about the conversation that the two of you had with Mr. McCrory . . .”

For the next few minutes, Phyllis and Sam

went over everything that had happened. D'Angelo had said that such sessions sometimes prompted witnesses to remember things they hadn't recalled before, but Phyllis knew that wasn't going to be the case here. All the details were clear in her mind, and nothing new was going to emerge.

However, she did bring up the possibility she had raised with Sam earlier, saying, "We were wondering whether the killer might have fired more than one shot."

She saw Allyson wince slightly at the word *killer* and wished she had phrased things a bit more considerately. They were talking about cold-blooded murder, though, and it was hard to put any sort of pretty face on that.

"If he did, the other bullets had to go somewhere," D'Angelo mused. "I wish I could get a look at that carriage. The cops won't let me anywhere near it, though, unless they charge Nate. Even then they'll stonewall. Anything I get out of them, I'll have to force it."

"What difference does it make whether there was one shot or several?" Nate asked.

"It helps us know just how good a shot the guy really is. One shot, in a crowd like that, he's got to be a real sharpshooter."

A frown creased Phyllis's forehead as

something occurred to her. She leaned forward and said, "Unless he's really not a good shot at all."

"How can you say that?" Sam asked. "He hit what he was aimin' at, and no matter how you look at it, it was a hard shot."

"Unless," Phyllis said, "he wasn't aiming at Mr. McCrory at all."

CHAPTER 10

Silence reigned around the table for a long moment. Then Allyson said, "You're saying you think . . . whoever it was . . . *didn't* mean to kill my father?"

"I'm not saying I think that, no," Phyllis replied. "We don't have anything to make us believe that Mr. McCrory wasn't the target. But it's *possible* that whoever fired that shot meant it for someone else. There were a lot of people around, after all, as we've mentioned several times."

D'Angelo leaned back in his chair and looked intently at her.

"That's right," he said. "With a crowd of people like that, until we know who pulled the trigger, we can't be sure who they were aiming at. There was even a politician right behind McCrory. Maybe *he* was the intended victim."

"Wait a minute," Allyson said. "You mean my father may have died by *accident*?"

Her voice had a ragged edge of hysteria in it.

"It's just a possibility," Phyllis said, keeping her own voice level and calm. "Something else that could be a good idea to investigate."

"I agree," D'Angelo said. "Let's face it — the cops aren't going to think that far outside the box. They're only going to concentrate on the obvious, and that means finding out who had a motive for wanting Barney McCrory dead, which brings them right back to Nate."

Allyson shuddered.

Nate squeezed her shoulder again and said, "If the man was really after somebody else, why did he stop shooting?"

"Because he realized he missed," Sam said. "That could've shaken him up some. And once those horses took off like they did, there was no way he could take another shot, no matter how good a marksman he was."

Phyllis nodded and said, "As a theory, it holds together. But that's all it is: a theory."

"We'll start with the guy in the sleigh," D'Angelo said. "The . . . county judge?"

"County commissioner," Phyllis said. "Clay Loomis."

"Not exactly a real big shot, is he?"

"You'd be surprised how hot and heavy some of those election campaigns get, even on the county level," Sam said. "To some people, bein' a big fish in a small pond is still worth fightin' over."

"Not to mention sometimes there's a considerable amount of money in play when it comes to county contracts," Phyllis added. "I'm not saying it's a motive for murder . . ."

"But sometimes it doesn't take much," D'Angelo finished for her. "How about those girls? Santa's slutty little elves?"

"They were high school girls," Phyllis said, a little sharper now.

D'Angelo shrugged and spread his hands. "Passions sometimes run pretty high at that age," he said.

Phyllis couldn't argue with that statement. She had taught at the junior-high level, where hormones first started really affecting students, and she had seen how much havoc those runaway emotions could wreak. In her more cynical moments, she had believed there might be some basis in fact to the theory that all seventh- and eighth-graders were clinically insane.

Still, she thought it made more sense to start with Clay Loomis, and she said as much.

D'Angelo nodded and said, "I agree. Look

into his background and see if there's anything that would make somebody want to shoot him. If there's not, we can always move on to the other people who were right around there."

There didn't seem to be anything left to say. Phyllis was glad they'd had this meeting. She knew it had been difficult, especially for Allyson, but now she had a better picture of what had happened before the parade.

She also had a hunch that by now the police would have been out to Barney McCrory's ranch to talk to those two men who had overheard the argument the day before.

That and the fact that Nate doesn't have an alibi are enough to make the police consider him the primary suspect, she thought.

She was afraid it was only a matter of time before Nate was arrested.

As they all stood up to leave, D'Angelo said, "Phyllis, Sam, if you guys could wait a minute so we can talk some more . . ."

"Of course," Phyllis said.

D'Angelo shook hands with Nate and said, "We'll be in touch. In the meantime, go on about your business and keep your head down, kid. And if any cops show up to talk to you, don't say a word. Even if they take you in, don't say anything except that you want to talk to me. As long as you stick to your guns, they can't do a blasted thing about it."

"All right." Nate sighed. "It's hard, though. I was raised to respect and cooperate with the police."

"Yeah, that's fine . . . except when it's your head on the line."

Both Nate and Allyson looked worried as they left the conference room. Once the door was closed, D'Angelo waved Phyllis and Sam back into their seats.

"What do you think?" he asked them. "Any chance the kid did it?"

"Not a chance in the world," Sam answered without hesitation. "He idolized Barney McCrory, over and above Barney bein' his father-in-law."

"Didn't sound much like it, from the description of that argument."

"Shoot, everybody gets hot under the collar now and then, even with folks they love and respect. It doesn't mean you're ready to go and shoot somebody."

"What do you think, Phyllis?"

She took her time about answering, then said, "I never knew any of these people until yesterday, so maybe I'm a little more objective about the situation than Sam is."

"Wait a minute," Sam objected. "Are you sayin' you think Nate is guilty?"

"Not at all. You didn't let me finish. I'm saying that even looking at it objectively, I don't think Nate shot Mr. McCrory. Yes, he might have motive, but I don't think it's strong enough. And he seems genuinely upset about his father-in-law's death. He seems like a young man who's lost a loved one."

"I hope you're both right," D'Angelo said.

Phyllis's eyes narrowed. She said, "You sound like you have some doubts."

The lawyer grimaced. He reached inside his coat and took out a folded piece of paper.

"I didn't want to bring this up, especially in front of Allyson," he said. "I got to thinking about something and looked into it a little while ago. I've got a buddy in the ATF who does me a favor now and then. I asked him to check on something for me. I got this e-mail from him just before Nate and Allyson got here."

He unfolded the paper, which was a printout of an e-mail, and slid it in front of Phyllis and Sam. Phyllis leaned forward to read it, her frown deepening.

"This doesn't really prove anything," Sam said.

"It's a gun registration," D'Angelo said, even though both of them could see that for themselves. "It proves that Nate Hollingsworth owns a high-powered hunting rifle . . . just the sort of thing you'd use if you wanted to put a scope on it and shoot somebody several blocks away."

Sam had a disheartened look on his face as he and Phyllis left the lawyer's office a short time later.

"This doesn't mean Nate's guilty, you know," she told him. "There are probably hundreds of people in the county who own hunting rifles like that one. Maybe thousands."

"Yeah, but why didn't he come clean about it?" Sam said. "He knows something like that could be important. He should know, anyway."

"I imagine he's scared. With everything else already weighing against him the way it is, he might think that if he admitted owning such a rifle, it would be the last nail in his coffin."

"Yeah, but if D'Angelo knows about it, you can bet the cops do, too. Isn't it better to be prepared for something like that that they could use against you?"

Phyllis couldn't argue with that logic. Sam

was right. Nate should have told D'Angelo about the rifle.

"I wonder where it is now," she said as they walked toward the spot on the square where she had left the Lincoln.

"Well, let's say Nate used it last night to shoot Barney. I don't believe that for a second, mind you, but let's just say that. What would he do with it afterward?"

"He couldn't carry it out of the building," Phyllis said. "There were too many people around for that. Someone would have noticed. It might have even caused an uproar, someone walking around in a crowd like that, carrying a rifle."

"So he would've had to leave it in his office, or at least somewhere in the building."

"Chief Whitmire probably wouldn't have been able to get a search warrant until this morning," Phyllis said. "That would have given Nate time to go back last night, after the parade and tree lighting were canceled and everyone was gone, to get the rifle and dispose of it somehow."

Sam shook his head and said, "I sure don't like talkin' like this. I know we're just speculatin', but somehow it feels like we're bein' disloyal to Nate."

Phyllis didn't feel any particular loyalty to Nate Hollingsworth, other than the fact that

Sam liked and trusted him, but she knew what he meant. She had felt the same way whenever one of her friends was suspected of murder. She didn't like to even consider the possibility that they might be guilty.

"Right now, let's devote our efforts to that other theory," she suggested.

"That the killer really meant to shoot somebody else?" Sam nodded. "I like that idea."

Before they had a chance to discuss it more, however, they came in sight of Phyllis's car.

And waiting beside it, microphone in hand, was Felicity Prosper.

Phyllis stopped short. She felt the impulse to turn around and go the other way, but it was too late. Felicity had seen them and started striding toward them, moving fast for someone wearing high heels. Josh Green and the other man — Nick, Phyllis recalled — trailed her. Nick, a stocky, red-haired man, had the video camera perched on his shoulder.

"Mrs. Newsom," Felicity said. "If I could just have a word with you?"

"The young fella ratted us out," Sam said under his breath.

"He didn't know where we were going," Phyllis pointed out. "All he could have done was tell her which direction we went. She must have figured out the destination herself."

"Mrs. Newsom," Felicity said as she came up to them, "I take it you've been conferring with noted defense attorney Jimmy D'Angelo on how to proceed with the Nate Hollingsworth case."

Phyllis tried to hide how surprised she was by the fact that Felicity knew they were connected to D'Angelo and also that Nate was a suspect in Barney McCrory's murder. She wasn't sure how the reporter could have discovered either of those things.

Of course, Phyllis's involvement with the case where they had first met D'Angelo was no secret, and it had happened fairly recently. Felicity could have dug that out of newspaper and Internet accounts of the case.

As for Nate's involvement, maybe that was sheer speculation on Felicity's part, or maybe she had a source in the Weatherford police department. It wasn't hard to imagine someone who looked like her being able to persuade some male cop to divulge information he shouldn't.

It didn't really matter how Felicity got any of her information. What was important was that they didn't give her any more, Phyllis reminded herself. She said, "No comment."

"That goes for me, too," Sam added.

Felicity pouted a little and said, "You don't want to do that. When you say *no comment* it looks like you're trying to cover something up. You don't want our millions of viewers to think that you have something to hide, do you?"

Phyllis wasn't sure a syndicated tabloid show like *Inside Beat* had millions of viewers. Hundreds of thousands, though, more than likely. But right now their opinions didn't really matter.

"Your viewers can think whatever they like," she said. "I still have no comment."

"I got a question for you," Sam said. "How'd you find us?"

Felicity smiled and said, "A good reporter always knows how to sniff out a story."

"Or snoop around where she ain't wanted."

Sam was letting the annoyance he felt make him talk too much. Phyllis put a hand on his arm and said, "Let's go."

She urged him around the three TV people. Felicity kept yammering questions at them, but Phyllis ignored the young woman. As they passed Josh, Phyllis glanced at him and saw him mouth the word *Sorry.*

She wasn't the only one who saw that.

Felicity noticed, too, because she exclaimed, "Sorry? Why are you telling them you're sorry, you little weasel? Are you sorry you have a glamorous job working in television?"

From what Phyllis had seen, Josh's job wasn't even remotely glamorous, and since he was an intern, it certainly wasn't high-paying.

But as he stammered a response to Felicity's angry questions, at least it served as a distraction, and Phyllis was grateful for that. She and Sam reached the Lincoln and got in quickly. The slamming doors made Felicity's head jerk around. She started toward them, but Phyllis was already backing out of the parking place. As soon as she could, she shifted into drive and pressed down on the gas.

That left Felicity behind them, stomping one expensively shod foot in frustration.

"Poor kid," Sam said. "But better him than me."

"Amen," Phyllis said.

CHAPTER 11

When Phyllis and Sam got back to the house, Carolyn and Eve wanted to know how the meeting with D'Angelo, Nate, and Allyson had gone. Eve seemed especially interested in the details, which was unusual for her. She didn't have much to occupy her days, though, Phyllis thought, so it wasn't really surprising that she would try to distract herself this way.

When they had gone over what had happened in D'Angelo's conference room, Phyllis concluded by saying, "When we got back to the car, that lady reporter was waiting for us again. I'm not sure how she found us, but she was there, ready to pounce."

"The one who's parked in front of the house again?" Carolyn asked as she nodded toward the front window.

Phyllis stepped over there, looked through the gap between the curtains, and sighed as she saw the now-familiar van. She pulled the curtains a little more tightly closed and said, "I'm just going to ignore them. Maybe they'll go away."

"I wouldn't hold my breath waitin'," Sam said.

Phyllis went over to the computer and said, "I'm going to see what I can find out about Clay Loomis."

"On the theory that he may have been the intended target?" Eve asked.

"That's right."

"Believe I'm gonna go sit out on the back porch with Buck," Sam said. "We'll keep an eye out and make sure that Felicity gal doesn't try to sneak around and peep in the windows."

"And I've got some potatoes cooking for potato salad," Carolyn said. "I need to check on them."

That left Eve in the living room. She said, "I'll keep you company, Phyllis. If you need to use me as a sounding board for the case, feel free."

"All right," Phyllis said. She had never talked much about her investigations with Eve before — except when her friend was the subject of one of them — but sometimes it was helpful to lay out a theory in words.

First, though, she did some searching online. It wasn't difficult to find references to Clay Loomis in the archives of the local newspaper. Most of them were mundane stories about the activities of the county commissioners, but the county-government website had a biography page for each of them, and Phyllis went to the one for Loomis.

From it she learned that Loomis owned a commercial trucking business and that he was married. That gave Phyllis two more trails to follow. Those trails converged, however, when Phyllis's searching led her to a story about the trucking firm, Cross Timbers Transport. It was a publicity piece in a newspaper supplement about the Parker County Chamber of Commerce and the businesses located in the county. The businesses covered in feature stories were actually the ones that had bought a display ad in the supplement.

Of the most interest to Phyllis was the photograph accompanying the story, which showed Loomis, his two partners, and their wives all standing in front of an eighteen-wheeler emblazoned with the company logo. Loomis had his arm around the shoulders of a strikingly attractive Hispanic woman identified in the caption as his wife, Serita.

Loomis's partners were named J. D. Ridgely and Phil Hedgepeth. Their wives, respectively, were named Willa and Lindsay. Both women were pretty enough, Phyllis thought, but not as stunning as Serita Loomis. As her husband embraced her, he wore the self-satisfied smirk of a man who was rich, successful, and married to a beautiful woman.

Another picture with the same article showed some of the employees of Cross Timbers Transport, also smiling into the camera as they stood in front of one of the big eighteen-wheelers: head mechanic Grant Freel; mechanics Jimmy Dempster, Wally Lomax, and Joe Patton; drivers Ed Paddock, Henry Miller, Bob Wygand, and Mac McHale; and the lone woman in the group, office manager Jaycee Fallon, a blonde with a brilliant smile.

Those were a lot of names to remember, and in all likelihood none of them had any connection with the case. Phyllis filed them away in her memory, anyway. It was impossible to predict when something might turn out to be important.

From the sofa, Eve said, "My, you spend a lot of time just looking at things on the computer, Phyllis. And you seem so intent on them."

Phyllis repeated the thought she'd just had. "You never know when something will turn out to be important. Right now I'm trying to find out as much as I can about Clay Loomis's life. If he has an enemy who hates him enough to shoot at him in the middle of a Christmas parade, something about it might turn up in the information about him on the Internet."

"How did sleuths find out about such things before there were computers?"

Phyllis frowned and said, "That's a good question. I suppose they had to go to newspapers and physically search through all their old archives."

"The morgue, you mean."

Phyllis nodded.

"Yes, I think that's what they call it. It's a lot easier this way. They'd have to go around and talk to people who know the person they're investigating, too."

"You and Sam do that. I've heard you talk about it. I've even seen you doing that."

"Yes, but I like to find out as much as I can beforehand," Phyllis said. "That helps me know which questions to ask so I'm not just wasting my time."

"I understand," Eve said, nodding.

Phyllis smiled and said, "It almost sounds like you're thinking about becoming a detective yourself."

"Me?" Eve looked genuinely shocked.

"Oh, goodness, no! I could never do that. I'm just curious about how you go about doing the things you do."

"Half the time I don't believe I know that myself," Phyllis said with a little laugh. "I just muddle along, asking questions until things start to make sense."

"The world is so crazy I would think that when something actually makes sense, it might stand out a little."

"You know," Phyllis said, nodding slowly, "that's true."

Eve seemed satisfied for the moment, so Phyllis went back to her searching. She turned her attention next to Loomis's political career, beginning with his most recent reelection campaign. She wasn't sure any of his political opponents would be holding a grudge against him that went back any farther than that.

As Sam had indicated, any political campaign could become heated. That had been the case this election season, when Clay Loomis had run for reelection to the commissioner's court against a man named Gene Coyle. Phyllis found a newspaper story about a candidates' debate between the two men in which Coyle had accused Loomis of using his position for personal gain. Loomis had denied that, of course, and challenged Coyle to come up with specifics.

Coyle hadn't done so at the debate, but a few days later the story had broken that Cross Timbers Transport had leased trucks to a company that provided gravel for a major road-expansion project carried out by the county. Clay Loomis hadn't benefited directly from the road-construction deal, but indirectly his company had made quite a bit of money.

Not so coincidentally, Gene Coyle was in the sand-and-gravel business, and his company had lost out in the bidding war for the contract on the road-expansion project. Clearly, he believed that Loomis's alleged conflict of interest had cost him the lucrative contract.

In follow-up stories, an angry Loomis had denied that charge and was able to prove that he had recused himself from the bidding process just so there wouldn't be a conflict of interest. Everything about the deal was a matter of public record, he insisted. The company that got the contract — the company to which Cross Timbers Transport had leased trucks — had submitted the lowest bid, plain and simple.

Of course, it was easy enough for Loomis to *say* he recused himself from the bidding process. Phyllis had no doubt he had done so.

Still, he had served with the other commissioners for quite some time, and there was a good chance they were all friends. He could still wield some subtle influence on their decisions, even though he didn't do so openly.

But a low bid was a low bid, Phyllis supposed, and it was hard to get around that.

A few days after *that* story had broken, another one came out, this time concerning Gene Coyle. The newspaper had received an anonymous tip that when Coyle lived in central Texas a number of years earlier, he had been in trouble with the law over both drugs and domestic violence.

Lack of evidence after a lengthy investigation had led the police to drop the drug charges, and Coyle's clearly battered first wife had refused to press charges against him. She had divorced him, however, claiming mental and physical cruelty.

When interviewed by the newspaper, a livid Coyle had declared vehemently that all the allegations against him were false, that Clay Loomis was responsible for dragging up all this old dirt — a pack of lies, Coyle called it — and that Loomis would be sorry he had resorted to such tactics.

The election had been less than two weeks later, and Loomis had won handily, taking nearly sixty-five percent of the ballots.

Phyllis sat back and took a deep breath as she stared at the monitor. It seemed to her that a perfectly feasible motive for Clay Loomis's murder was staring right back at her.

Coyle had even hurled the classic "You'll be sorry!" threat at Loomis.

She wondered if Chief Whitmire knew about any of this . . . and if Gene Coyle owned a rifle.

"You look like you've found something," Eve said eagerly. "You just solved the case, didn't you?"

"No, not at all," Phyllis said. She pointed at the screen. "But this could cast some definite doubt on Nate's potential guilt."

She reached for the mouse to see what else she could find.

A search of court records for the county turned up something almost right away. A lawsuit had been filed against Loomis a month earlier by his partners, Ridgely and Hedgepeth. The information available online didn't include anything other than the date of filing and the fact that the suit was still pending.

Phyllis went back to the picture of the

three men standing in front of the truck with their wives. Everyone looked happy in that photo, but the newspaper supplement in which it appeared had come out six months ago. Obviously, a lot had changed during that interval.

So there was a business dispute and an ugly election controversy that could have caused a great deal of bad blood among the parties involved and anger directed toward Clay Loomis. Phyllis clicked back over to the window containing the court records and continued her search.

It didn't take long for her to discover that Serita Loomis had filed a petition for divorce from her husband three weeks earlier, not long after the election.

Other than being reelected, it has been a bad autumn for Clay Loomis, Phyllis thought.

A spouse was usually the first suspect in a murder or attempted murder, especially an estranged spouse seeking a divorce. Phyllis couldn't find anything to indicate that the Loomises had children, so maybe there wasn't a custody battle going on, but Loomis had a successful business. Surely Serita would be seeking a piece of that, and Loomis would be trying to keep it out of her hands.

So, in less than an hour of searching on the Internet, Phyllis had turned up what she considered to be four perfectly feasible suspects: Gene Coyle, J. D. Ridgely, Phil Hedgepeth, and Serita Loomis.

The problem was that they would be perfectly feasible suspects only if Clay Loomis was the person who'd been killed.

He was still alive, Barney McCrory was dead, and it was nothing but sheer speculation that Loomis had been the real target.

Phyllis sat back and sighed.

"What's wrong?" Eve asked.

Quickly, Phyllis laid out the information she had uncovered, then said, "But none of this really does Nate much good at this point. Chances are, the police won't take any interest in it. They'll only investigate people who have a motive for wanting Mr. McCrory dead. The theory that Loomis was the intended victim and that Mr. McCrory was killed by accident might impress a jury, and all this other stuff could help to create reasonable doubt, but to reach that point the case would have to come to trial. I'd rather it didn't ever get that far."

"Then it comes down to finding proof that whoever pulled the trigger was aiming at Loomis," Eve said. "You'll have to put them there, on the scene, with a rifle in their hands and a reason to kill that man."

"Yes," Phyllis said. "It's as simple as that."

"So, you'll need to get out there and do some good old-fashioned legwork."

Phyllis nodded and said, "You're right. That's what being a detective is all about."

"Of course, you always say that you're not really a detective," Eve pointed out.

"Sometimes, though, it's foolish to fight the inevitable," Phyllis said.

If Nate Hollingsworth is innocent, and if anyone is going to save him, it will have to be me, she thought.

With good old-fashioned legwork, as Eve had put it.

CHAPTER 12

It was too late in the afternoon to go out and do any investigating today, Phyllis decided, and there was also the matter of the tabloid-TV crew lurking outside. If she left now, Felicity and her cohorts would follow her. Phyllis didn't want the reporter interfering.

So she went into the kitchen instead and put together the ingredients for the filling in the baklava macarons. It had to chill overnight, so once that was done and in the refrigerator, Phyllis strolled out onto the back porch and joined Sam and Buck in enjoying what was a mild afternoon for December. The sun was shining, and the air was just pleasantly crisp without being cold. The yard was covered with a dense carpet of fallen leaves from the tall post oaks. Phyllis knew they needed to be raked, but Buck enjoyed playing in them, racing back and forth and sending the leaves flying into the air.

Right now Sam was sitting in one of the rocking chairs, reading an old Western paperback, while Buck lay at his feet, head resting on paws. The Dalmatian stood up as Phyllis came out onto the porch. He walked over to her to get his ears scratched as she sat down in the rocker next to Sam's.

Marking his place in the book with a finger, Sam asked, "Did you find anything?"

"Quite a bit, actually." Phyllis scratched behind Buck's floppy black ears as she told Sam what she had discovered on the Internet. He sat up straighter, obviously interested.

"Shoot, from the sound of it, Loomis might've had half a dozen folks gunnin' for him," he said when Phyllis was finished.

"Well, not quite that many, at least not that we know about. But there are definitely people out there who might have wanted to kill him."

"I'd say it's a lot more likely he was the target than Barney. Barney didn't have any real enemies that I know of."

"It might not hurt to look into that," Phyllis said, "but I agree with you. Loomis is where we need to concentrate our efforts right now. Those cheerleaders from the high school were in the carriage, too, but it seems pretty far-fetched to me that somebody would want to shoot one of them."

Sam grinned and said, "Unless it was some other cheerleader's mama. This *is* Texas, you know."

"And sometimes the stereotypes are true," Phyllis said, nodding. "So we can't rule them out, but we'll investigate the more likely theory first."

"Sounds like a plan," Sam said.

Even here on the back porch, they heard the doorbell ring in the house. Carolyn appeared at the back door a moment later and said, "I didn't answer it, but I looked out and that woman from the TV show is ringing the bell again. I think we should call the police and complain."

"She'll give up eventually," Phyllis said.

Sam shook his head dubiously and said, "I'm not so sure about that. She looked mighty determined to me."

"Well, then," Phyllis said, "we'll just ignore her."

That proved to be easier said than done. Felicity Prosper rang the doorbell and called on the phone the rest of the afternoon, off and on. The housemates tried to pretend they didn't hear, but it was a challenge.

Phyllis tried to distract herself by cooking,

which had often worked in the past. She made a tomato and mozzarella salad and put that in the refrigerator. Then she started preparing a crustless spinach and bacon quiche for supper. It hadn't been easy getting Sam to admit that he liked quiche, especially one without a crust, but over time he had come around.

Carolyn had finished making her potato salad, but, like the filling for the baklava macarons, this particular recipe was better if it was refrigerated overnight. It was chilling so they could have it for lunch the next day.

While they were eating, they talked about Phyllis's article for *A Taste of Texas* rather than the McCrory case. She hoped to start writing it this evening so she could e-mail it to the magazine's editor in the next couple of days . . . assuming the macarons turned out all right, of course.

"Would you be willing to look it over for me when I'm done with it, Eve?" she asked. "You were the one who taught English all those years, not me. I'm afraid my writing skills may not be up to snuff anymore."

"I'd be glad to," Eve said. "I don't think you have anything to worry about, though. I've always thought your spelling and grammar were just fine."

"Maybe so, but I'd feel better if somebody who knows what she's doing checked it before I send it in."

"Of course. Just e-mail the file to me whenever you're ready."

That made Phyllis glance around the table at her friends. When you considered how old they all were, herself included, she thought they were fairly computer literate. Carolyn was the only one who didn't use the computer much, and she could when she needed to. Sam was practically addicted to YouTube, like a kid. He mostly watched clips of old sports highlights — "Back when the Cowboys were actually, you know, good," as he phrased it — rather than music videos, though.

The thing was, none of them believed that just because they were retired, it was time to stop learning things. Phyllis enjoyed taking it easy now and then and figured she had earned that privilege, but she couldn't think of anything worse than just sitting and doing nothing for the rest of her life.

Of course, she had never dreamed that catching killers would turn out to be her retirement hobby, but life took some odd twists, no doubt about that.

The doorbell hadn't rung for a while, Phyllis realized. Neither had the phone.

Phyllis hoped that meant Felicity Prosper had given up and gone away. She didn't really expect that to be the case, but it would be nice if it turned out to be true.

Almost as soon as that thought went through Phyllis's mind, the sound of the doorbell filled the house again. She gave a mental groan. She had jinxed it.

"Just ignore her," she said. "I won't have that woman in my house."

After a minute of persistent ringing, the doorbell fell silent again. Then Phyllis's cell phone rang.

That was a surprise. Felicity had been calling the landline all day, leading Phyllis to suspect that was the only number the reporter had. When she slipped the phone out of her pocket and looked at the number, she recognized it as the cell phone belonging to her son, Mike.

"Hello?" she said.

"Mom, why aren't you answering the door?" Mike asked. "You're here, aren't you? The lights are on."

Phyllis came quickly to her feet and said, "Yes, we're here. Hang on just a minute."

She hurried up the hall to the front door, flipped on the porch light, and looked out the narrow side window. Sure enough, Mike stood there in his deputy's uniform with a look of concern on his face.

Phyllis opened the door and told him, "Come on in. I'm sorry you had to stand out there. We, ah, haven't been answering the door today."

"Why not?" he asked as he stepped into the foyer.

Phyllis looked past him and saw that the TV van was gone from the curb again.

Mike noticed that. He was naturally observant and his job had made him even more so. He said, "Does not answering the door have anything to do with the van that drove off as soon as I pulled into the driveway?"

"It does," Phyllis said as she closed the front door. "The sight of your patrol car must have scared them off. Although they were probably getting pretty tired and hungry, too, after being out there most of the day."

"Who?"

Sam, Carolyn, and Eve had followed Phyllis from the kitchen. It was Sam who answered Mike's question by saying, "TV vultures. A gal reporter and some fellas from one of those tabloid shows."

Mike frowned.

"They were trying to interview you about the McCrory case?" he asked.

"That's right," Phyllis said, heaving a disgusted sigh. "The woman referred to me as Texas's Elderly Angel of Death."

Mike still wore a concerned frown, but the corners of his mouth twitched a little.

"Oh, go ahead and laugh!" Phyllis told him. "It's completely ridiculous."

Mike allowed himself to smile, but he didn't actually laugh. He said, "Yeah, it is sort of ridiculous. You know what those shows are like, though. They go way over the top about everything. They're just trying to get bigger ratings."

"Well, come on in and sit down. We were just finishing up supper. I think there's one piece of quiche left."

"No, that's all right, I can't stay. Maybe if you've got any of those famous cupcakes left, though, I could take one with me."

"You mean the candy cane cupcakes? How do you know about them?"

"Isabel mentioned them. I think Chief Whitmire must have told her about them. He said something about sitting around and eating cupcakes in the interrogation room. That's not something that happens every day."

"I see," Phyllis said. She had wondered before if she ought to worry about Mike's friendship with Isabel Largo, who was a detective on the Weatherford police force. There didn't seem to be anything between them except the camaraderie of fellow law-enforcement officers, although they worked for different agencies. But Isabel was a young, attractive single mother, and Mike was a healthy young man . . .

A healthy young man who seemed to be quite happily married to his wife, Sarah, the mother of their son, Phyllis's grandson, Bobby. Phyllis told herself not to be so suspicious. She needed to save that for ferreting out murderers.

That thought prompted her to ask, "Is Detective Largo handling the McCrory case now?"

"It's still the chief's case officially, but he's got her covering some of the bases." Mike looked over at Sam and said, "I'm sorry about your friend."

"Thanks. We're gonna get whoever's responsible."

Mike frowned again, looked at Phyllis, and said, "You're looking into this, Mom? I thought you and Sam were just witnesses."

"It's a little more than that," Phyllis admitted. "How much has Detective Largo told you about the case?"

"Not much. Isabel isn't a strictly by-the-book cop, but she doesn't bend the rules too far, either. I know what the public knows." He shrugged. "And maybe a little more, like the lab got some pretty good ballistics results from the bullet that killed Mr. McCrory. If they recover a suspected murder weapon, they shouldn't have any trouble determining if it matches up with the bullet."

"If you've got a few minutes, I'll get those cupcakes out and pour you a cup of coffee, too," Phyllis suggested.

"I'll make the time," Mike said without hesitation. "I want to hear about this."

The five of them sat down around the kitchen table. Over candy cane cupcakes and coffee, Phyllis and Sam recounted everything that had happened so far.

When they had covered all that she could remember, Phyllis said, "So, you see, Mike, it's not really like those other times. We're working for Mr. D'Angelo, so we have a right to investigate the case."

"I don't know," Mike said slowly. "It seems a little iffy to me. This guy Nate hasn't been charged with anything yet."

"People who think they may fall under suspicion of a crime have a right to hire a lawyer, don't they?"

"Sure. But that also makes them look a little more guilty."

Carolyn said, "Why should it? People have figured out by now that they have to look out for their own best interests when it comes to the legal system. No one else will."

In the past, Mike had taken polite exception to some of Carolyn's adversarial attitudes about the law. This time he said to Phyllis, "I just don't want the two of you getting into any trouble." He shrugged. "Although by now I guess you ought to know what you're doing. Do you have any suspects of your own?"

Phyllis and Sam exchanged a glance; then Phyllis said, "We've been wondering if Barney McCrory wasn't really the murderer's intended target."

Mike cocked his head a little to the side and said, "Now, that's an interesting idea. I didn't get the impression from Isabel that they were considering anything except a straightforward investigation of McCrory and anybody who might have reason to want him dead. But it was a long rifle shot — several hundred yards. It's certainly possible the killer could have just missed." Mike paused. "But who was he aiming at?"

"Clay Loomis," Phyllis said.

Mike's eyebrows arched in surprise. As an employee of the county, he definitely knew who Loomis was. He said, "Loomis was sitting behind McCrory in the carriage, wasn't he?"

"That's right. At that distance, the killer's aim wouldn't have had to be off by very much for him to hit Mr. McCrory instead of Clay Loomis."

"Who would want to shoot a county commissioner? They're a pretty innocuous bunch most of the time."

Phyllis explained about the mudslinging election campaign, the divorce petition, and the lawsuit by Loomis's business partners. Mike began to nod, almost as if against his will.

"You put together a pretty strong case for somebody wanting Loomis dead," he admitted. "Several somebodies, actually. But since he *wasn't* the victim . . ."

Sam said, "All the police have against Nate is a possible motive, just like those other folks have possible motives to kill Loomis. All it would have taken was for the killer's aim to be off a little bit."

"Is there any chance you could bring this up with Detective Largo?" Phyllis asked.

Mike said, "She'd think I was meddling in her case — a case where I don't have any jurisdiction. And she'd be right. I don't know how kindly she'd take it." He leaned back in his chair at the kitchen table. "But if I could approach it just right, like we were just shooting the breeze and talking about how a case sometimes looks like it's about one thing but turns out to be about something entirely different . . . Well, maybe. I might be able to plant a seed. But it'd be up to her whether she wanted to follow it up."

"Of course," Phyllis said. "If there's anything you can do to help, we'd appreciate it."

"Sure." Mike grinned down at the few crumbs left on the saucer in front of him, all that was left of two of the cupcakes. He grew more serious as he went on. "Just be careful. You've been pretty lucky in the past."

Carolyn said, "I don't think luck had anything to do with Phyllis solving all those crimes."

"Solving them, no, probably not," Mike said. "Surviving the confrontations with those killers . . . Well, that's another story."

CHAPTER 13

Before Mike left, he promised to call a friend of his on the Weatherford force who worked patrol and ask him to swing by the house a few times during the evening. If Felicity Prosper tried to come back, the police presence might scare her off again.

Phyllis went upstairs to her bedroom to work on the column for *A Taste of Texas* on her laptop. Even though she hadn't made the baklava macarons yet, she wanted to get a rough draft of the recipe written. That way if the cookies were good — and she certainly hoped they would be — she would have some of the work done already.

Her door was open, so Sam looked in later to say good night. He reported, "No sign of that van out front. Looks like Miss Prosper gave up."

"Gave up for today, maybe," Phyllis said. "It wouldn't surprise me if she was back tomorrow, though."

"Well, no. Me neither." Sam leaned a shoulder against the doorjamb. "How's the column writin' comin' along?"

"All right, I suppose. I'm still not sure I'm cut out to be a writer. There are too many words in the world to choose from!"

Sam grinned and said, "You'll do fine. Not to change the subject, but I thought I might go see Gene Coyle in the morning and talk to him about gettin' a load of dirt or gravel or some such."

"And maybe get an idea of whether he'd be capable of shooting someone if he were angry enough?"

"That's the plan," Sam said.

"Be careful. If he really is a murderer, he might not take kindly to someone poking around in his business."

"Yeah, well, I could say the same to you," Sam pointed out. "I've got a feelin' you'll be doin' some diggin' of your own. You know I'm always willin' to go with you."

"I know," Phyllis said. "We'll wait and see."

Sam nodded and said, "All right. Good night, then."

"Good night, Sam," she said fondly. He was a good man, and she knew she was lucky to have him for a friend.

■ ■ ■ ■

The next morning over breakfast, which consisted of excellent sausage egg muffins made by Carolyn, Phyllis told Sam she was going to be working on the macarons for a while.

"You go see Gene Coyle, and we'll investigate another angle this afternoon," she said.

"Sounds like a plan," he told her.

After getting dressed, he went out to feed Buck, and looked up at the sky while the Dalmatian was eating. Clouds had moved in during the night, and the air was chillier. A front had come through. Sam didn't keep up with the weather as closely as he once had, but he wasn't surprised by this change. Christmas was less than three weeks away, so it was time for some cold weather.

Buck had already eaten his canned food and was crunching on his dry food now. Sam filled the water bowl and told the dog, "You'll probably need to stay inside tonight, but you ought to be all right out here today. If the wind gets too brisk, you can curl up in your doghouse."

Buck looked up as if he understood. Sometimes Sam thought his dog was smarter than a lot of people he knew, himself included, more often than not.

He put on his sheepskin-lined denim jacket and looked out the picture window in the living room. The curb in front of the house was still empty, with no sign of the van belonging to the TV crew.

Phyllis was passing by in the hall and said, "They're not out there, are they?"

"I don't see 'em. Of course, that doesn't guarantee they're not parked down the street somewhere out of sight, just waitin' to follow us if we go anywhere."

"Keep an eye out behind you."

"I will," he promised. "Maybe it's too cold out there for them today."

"As short as Miss Prosper likes to wear her skirts, I wouldn't be surprised."

Sam grinned and said, "Yeah, that could be a mite, ah, chilly on the nether regions."

Phyllis just sniffed disdainfully as she headed for the kitchen.

Sam had looked up Gene Coyle's business, which was not-so-imaginatively called Gene's Sand and Gravel, and found that it was located on the interstate between Weatherford and Fort Worth, less than a mile west of the old racetrack.

As he drove out there, he changed the station on the radio several times, not in any mood to listen to folks argue about sports or politics, before he settled on a station playing classic country. Since he was by himself, he didn't worry about the fact that his voice sounded like somebody pulling rusty nails from an old two-by-four as he warbled along with the lonesome strains of George Strait's "Amarillo by Morning."

He didn't notice a van or any other vehicle following him.

Coyle's office was a cinder-block building with a metal roof that sat at the top of one of the rolling hills along the highway. Behind it was a huge gravel pit gouged out of the earth. As Sam parked the pickup in front of the office and got out of it, he saw numerous small mountains of earth and rock scattered around the property. Bulldozers moved here and there, as did tractors with front-end loaders attached to them.

The wind was even colder on this hilltop. Sam was glad to get out of it as he went inside.

He found an office with a counter running across it, a small waiting area in front, and a larger space behind it where a couple of desks sat. Each desk had a computer on it, but there was a pair of old-fashioned filing cabinets against one wall. No matter how much the world tried to go digital and paperless, it was hard to run a business without generating some printed documents.

The place had a plain, functional look about it. A calendar hung on the wall of the waiting area, along with an advertising poster listing the high school's football schedule for the recently concluded season. Someone had written in the final score for each game with a black marker.

A man in a baseball cap and a flannel shirt with the sleeves rolled up a couple of turns over his brawny, black-haired forearms sat at one of the desks behind the counter, squinting at the monitor at front of him. His big, powerful-looking hand dwarfed the mouse he was using. He didn't look up from the screen. His concentration was so fierce, it seemed like if he broke it he would forget what he was doing.

The woman at the other desk stood up and came to the counter, though. She was a pleasant-looking woman in her forties, wearing jeans and a Western shirt with pearl snaps instead of buttons. Her graying brown hair was short and curly. She smiled and asked Sam, "Can I help you?"

"Yes, ma'am. I think I'm gonna find myself in need of some loads of gravel."

"Of course. How many?"

Sam pretended to think for a couple of

seconds and then said, "I figure we're lookin' at six. Maybe a few more."

"Well, we can certainly handle that. Do you want me to figure up a price for you?"

"That'd be good, but what I'd really like to do is talk to the boss man." He nodded toward the man at the other desk. "No offense, I just always like to deal with the top dog."

He figured a man from his generation could get away with a little political incorrectness.

The woman seemed more amused than offended. She said, "That's not the boss man. That's Lou, one of our drivers."

Lou grunted but didn't otherwise acknowledge that the conversation was going on.

For a split second Sam worried that the woman on the other side of the counter was Gene Coyle. Then he reminded himself that couldn't be right. The name was spelled wrong for a woman, and, besides, Phyllis had done her research and hadn't said anything about Clay Loomis's opponent in the election being a woman.

"I'll see if Mr. Coyle has a minute," the woman in the Western shirt went on. She walked over to a door in the office area, opened it without knocking, and went inside. She reappeared a moment later and crooked a finger at Sam.

He went to a swinging gate at the end of the counter and pushed past it. The woman moved out of the doorway and motioned for him to go in.

He stepped into a private office that was considerably fancier than the one outside. The cinder-block walls had dark wood paneling over them, and the floor was covered with carpet instead of tile. An expensive oak gun cabinet with several rifles and shotguns in it sat on the wall to Sam's right. On the wall to his left were mounted the heads of four deer, good-looking bucks with lots of points on their antlers.

Directly in front of him was a large desk. A man rose behind it and extended his hand.

"Gene Coyle," the man said. "Pleased to meet you."

Coyle wasn't what Sam expected. He was a head shorter than Sam, a wiry little fella who carried himself with an attitude that was bound to be described by most people as feisty. He wore a Coyle Sand and Gravel gimme cap, and looked at Sam through rimless, wire-framed glasses. He had a good grip, though, Sam found when he shook hands with the man.

Without thinking, Sam said, “Sam Fletcher.” He wasn’t used to introducing himself as anybody else. He hoped Coyle wouldn’t connect his name with Phyllis and remember that the two of them had been involved in investigating several murders in the past.

Of course, it probably won’t matter if Coyle isn’t actually a killer, Sam reminded himself.

Coyle didn’t show any reaction to the name, just waved Sam into the chair in front of the desk and said, “I hear you need some gravel.”

“Yeah, I’m puttin’ in some culverts on a piece of property I own outside of town. Gotta put in some roads so I can break it up and sell it in smaller lots.”

Coyle nodded and said, “If you’re building roads, you’ll need more than half a dozen loads.”

“Yeah, I know. I’m just startin’ with the culverts. I figure the whole project’ll take a while.”

“How big is the property?”

“Fourteen acres,” Sam said. He had worked out some of this in his head on the way out here and was coming up with the rest of it on the fly. “Thought I’d break it into twenty lots for houses. Those’ll be pretty good-sized lots this day and age."

"That's true," Coyle agreed. "The housing market's not great right now, though."

"It is what it is," Sam drawled. "I don't see it gettin' a lot better anytime soon, and I hate to see property just sittin' there. You know what I mean?"

That put a thin-lipped smile on Coyle's face. He said, "Yeah, I do. You're a go-getter like me, aren't you, Sam? You need to be accomplishing something all the time, even if the circumstances aren't the best for it."

"That's about the size of it."

"You're going to need, oh, forty or fifty loads before you're through." Coyle pulled a calculator over to himself, turned it on, and pushed some buttons on it. "I can give it to you for, let's see, a hundred and seventy-five a load. That's eighty-seven fifty . . . call it eighty-five hundred. How does that sound?"

"Pretty good," Sam said. "Pretty good. You don't mind if I mull it over a little, do you? I wasn't figurin' on linin' up the whole project at once."

Coyle leaned back and waved a hand. "Sure," he said. "I can't guarantee how long that price will be good, though. This business is pretty volatile."

Sam wasn't sure why the price of sand and

gravel ought to fluctuate that much, but he wasn't an expert on the subject, either.

"I'll get back to you pretty quick," he promised, even though he had no intention of doing so. He looked around at the gun cabinet and the mounted heads and said, "You look like you're quite a hunter."

A proud smile immediately lit up Coyle's face. He said, "I like to think so. Not a one of those bucks is less than ten points, and I've bagged a bunch of 'em almost that good. I've got a lease over in the Palo Pinto Mountains. You hunt?"

"Not as much as I used to. These bones of mine are gettin' too old to be trampin' around in the cold and the damp."

"I love it. There's nothing like it. Man pitting himself against nature."

It seemed to Sam that man had an unfair advantage most of the time, but he didn't say that. Instead he told Coyle, "You must be a pretty good shot."

"See that twelve-pointer?" Coyle pointed at one of the mounted heads. "I knocked that son of a gun down from five hundred yards."

Sam let out a low whistle of admiration. "That's some pretty good shootin'," he said.

"I've got a good eye, if I do say so myself."

"Well, I'm mighty glad I came in here today, Gene. I can call you Gene?"

Coyle nodded.

"I've got a feelin' you and me are gonna hit it off," Sam went on. "Makes me even gladder I voted for you in that election. It's just a damn shame you didn't win."

Coyle's narrow face darkened with anger. He made a slashing motion with his hand and said, "Ah, I should've known better than to ever get mixed up in politics! They're all a bunch of crooks, if you ask me."

"Especially that fella Loomis," Sam said, shaking his head. "I don't see how he keeps gettin' reelected. You'd think folks'd catch on to what a varmint he is."

"He's good at fooling people, and he knows how to cheat and get away with it. He slung so much mud at me during the campaign, it's a wonder I didn't drown in it."

"Well, it'll catch up to him one o' these days. A fella can't just keep goin' through life like that, hurtin' people, without gettin' his comeuppance sooner or later."

Coyle snorted and said, "It can't be soon enough to suit me." He put his hands flat on the desk and went on. "But that's over and done with. I've put it behind me."

Sam doubted that. It looked to him like the election campaign and subsequent defeat at the ballot box were still eating at Coyle pretty fiercely.

"You think you might run again sometime?"

"Maybe. You never know."

"Well, you'll have my vote if you do."

"I appreciate that." Coyle got to his feet and held out his hand to shake again. "Now, if you'll excuse me, Sam . . ."

"I understand." Sam stood up, too, and gripped Coyle's hand. "I reckon we've both got work to do. I'll give you a call later today or tomorrow."

"That's fine. Thanks for coming by."

Sam left Coyle's private office and waved at the woman in the Western shirt on his way out. Lou was still hunched over the other desk, peering at the computer screen as if it were the most fascinating thing in the world. From this angle Sam could see that the man was playing solitaire.

He got in the pickup and headed west on the interstate again. Phyllis was going to be mighty interested in what he'd found out, he thought.

If the killer's target really had been Clay Loomis, then Gene Coyle was about as perfect a suspect as you'd ever find.

CHAPTER 14

Phyllis spent the morning making the macaron shells and filling them with the baklava mixture that had set overnight in the refrigerator. With that done, the finished cookies went back in to chill more. Like a fine wine, they needed to mature to be at their best. In this case, that would take another twenty-four hours in the refrigerator.

From time to time she checked the curb in front of the house, which had remained empty. She was glad that Felicity Prosper seemed to have given up, but at the same time she was surprised. The young woman had seemed quite determined to get the story she wanted. Actually, *stubborn as a mule* might be a better way to put it, Phyllis thought.

Sam came in later in the morning, and Phyllis could tell from the look on his face that he was pleased with the results of his visit to Gene Coyle.

"You must have been able to talk to him," she said.

"I did," Sam replied. They went into the kitchen, where Sam poured himself a cup of coffee to warm up. When Phyllis offered him one of the remaining cupcakes and he declined, she knew that he must be excited about the case.

They sat down at the table, and he told her about his conversation with Coyle. When he was finished, Phyllis said, "He sounds like an unpleasant man."

"Yeah, I didn't like him, but just about everything he said pointed right to him as a possible killer. If he wasn't just braggin' about what a good shot he is."

"Do you think he might have been doing that?"

Sam frowned in thought, then shook his head.

"No, I reckon he was tellin' the truth. Not that I'd trust him about much of anything, but he didn't have any reason to lie about that. As far as he knew, I was just another good ol' boy he figured on doin' some business with."

"Was that a good price he quoted on the gravel?"

Sam held out a hand, wobbled it, and said, "Not really. Not for the number of loads we were talkin' about. He could've come down a little more, I think."

"Then it's a good thing you don't really need fifty loads of gravel."

"Don't know what I'd do with it if I had it," he said with a grin.

They had fried chicken and potato salad for lunch. Sam commented that it was almost like a picnic, except for the fact that they were inside and it wasn't summer.

Afterward, Phyllis said, "I'd like to find out more about Clay Loomis's business, but I'm not sure how to go about it. It was believable that you might want to buy some gravel from Gene Coyle, but I don't think we come across as the sort of people who'd be leasing trucks."

"Well, there's really no tellin'," Sam said. "We could have something that needed transportin' from one side of the country to the other, I suppose."

"Maybe," Phyllis said, but she didn't sound convinced. "There's also the problem that Loomis might recognize us from a couple of nights ago. He would have seen us talking to Mr. McCrory before the parade started and then, of course, after all the commotion, too."

"After the murder, you mean," Sam said grimly. He gave a little shake of his head, as if trying to put that part of it out of his mind. "I'm not sure how much attention Loomis paid to us. Before the parade, he was too busy oglin' those teenage elves, and afterward he was pretty shook up."

"Still, if he knows who we are, he might not be willing to talk to us. We need to find a time to visit his company when he's not there."

Carolyn had come into the living room while they were talking. She said, "I can help you with that."

Phyllis and Sam turned to look at her.

"What would you do?" Phyllis asked.

"Why don't I call the place and ask for this man Loomis? If he's not there, you'll know it's safe to pay the place a visit. If he is and they start to put me through to him, I'll just hang up."

"All right. That might work," Phyllis said. "Use your cell phone, so my name won't come up on the caller ID."

"Neither will mine," Carolyn said. "I pay to have it blocked when I call someone. I don't want anybody stealing my identity."

Phyllis wasn't sure how that would help prevent identity theft, but paranoia sometimes came in handy, she supposed.

It took only a couple of minutes online to find the number of Cross Timbers Transport. Carolyn called it, waited for an answer, then said in a brisk, businesslike tone, "Clay Loomis, please. Joan Dawson from the Texas Department of Transportation."

Phyllis's eyes widened at her friend's audacity. She hadn't expected Carolyn to pretend to be an official from the state government.

"He isn't, eh?" Carolyn went on. "When do you expect him back? No, that's all right. I'll give him a call again tomorrow. It's nothing important — just routine."

She broke the connection, turned to Phyllis and Sam, and said, "He's out of the office and won't be back until tomorrow."

"Thanks," Phyllis said. "But you can't go around impersonating a state official like that! You could get in trouble."

"I just said the first name that came to my mind. Anyway, I thought they'd be more likely to cooperate if they believed they were dealing with some bureaucrat," Carolyn said. "And I was right."

"You had the act down, too, except for one thing," Sam said.

"What's that?"

"When you said the call wasn't important. Every government bureaucrat I've ever run across, from the Feds on down, thinks what they're doin' is the most important thing in the world."

The headquarters of Cross Timbers Transport was located on Highway 51 north of Weatherford, on the way to Springtown. It was a pretty bleak-looking place, especially on a gray, chilly day like today. Situated on several acres surrounded by a high chain-link fence, the business was housed in a brick building with a small parking area in front. The rest of the property was paved with asphalt, and two dozen trucks were parked on it. Some of them were just the cabs, while others had trailers attached to make them true eighteen-wheelers. Several tall, shedlike metal buildings were ranked behind the brick office building.

Three cars were parked in front of the office, Phyllis saw as Sam drove his pickup through the open double gates in the chain-link fence and followed a short driveway to the parking lot.

"The place doesn't look very busy," she commented.

"No, that's quite a few rigs to be just sittin'," Sam agreed. "Of course, we don't know how many trucks Loomis has in his fleet. Could be he's got hundreds of 'em leased out."

"That doesn't seem likely."

"Probably not."

Sam parked and they went inside. The heat was turned up to an almost uncomfortable level, Phyllis noticed immediately.

The only person in the outer office was a birdlike gray-haired woman who wore one sweater and had another draped over her shoulders as she sat at a desk. She has to be the one in charge of the thermostat, Phyllis thought, but even with the heat cranked up as high as it is, the woman still seems cold.

"Hello," she said. "Can I help you?"

"We're with the Lions Club," Phyllis said. She and Sam had cooked up the story on the way out here. "We're going around to the businesses in the area asking for donations to help fund the Angel Tree we always have at Christmastime."

"Oh, yes, that's a fine thing that you do," the woman said. "But I thought people were supposed to take the angels from the tree and provide presents for them."

"That's right," Phyllis said, "but there are always angels who don't get picked. People can only do so much these days, you know, especially with the way the economy is. So the club always provides for those children."

Phyllis felt a little bad about using such a good cause as part of their cover story, but if they actually got a donation, they planned to turn it over to the Lions Club, along with a donation of their own, so it actually would do some good.

"That's wonderful," the woman said. "Let me get my purse."

"Actually," Phyllis said quickly, "we're handling corporate donations, so if we could speak to the owner . . ."

She knew from Carolyn's call that Clay Loomis wasn't there — unless he had returned unexpectedly. So she held her breath a little as she waited to see how the woman would react.

"Oh, Mr. Loomis isn't here this afternoon. I'm sorry. My, that man's popular today."

Sam had brought a clipboard with him. He looked at the paper on it, which was a printout of the TV schedule for that evening, and said, "How about his partners? Mr. Ridgely and Mr. Hedgepeth?"

The woman's eyes widened slightly as she said, "Oh, they're not here anymore. I mean, they still own part of the company, I suppose, but there's some sort of legal trouble between them and Mr. Loomis, so they don't come into the office anymore."

"Really? We've still got 'em down on our records."

"Well, like I said, technically they're still partners." The woman lowered her voice to a conspiratorial tone. "But they're suing Mr. Loomis."

"That's terrible," Phyllis said. "I suppose business partners fall out from time to time, though."

The woman said primly, "They do when two of them believe that the other one has been embezzling funds from the company." Then she put a thin, long-fingered hand with almost transparent skin to her mouth. Blue veins showed through the back of the hand. "Oh, my goodness. I shouldn't have said that."

"You don't have to worry about us," Phyllis assured her. "We're not interested in anyone's personal business."

"Neither am I, but it's hard not to hear things when you work here."

Phyllis remembered something, and reached over to take the clipboard from Sam. She pretended to look at it, then said, "We also have Jaycee Fallon listed as the office manager. Is that you?"

She remembered the photograph she had seen in the newspaper supplement and knew that unless Jaycee Fallon's appearance had changed dramatically, this woman wasn't her.

"Goodness, no. Jaycee left, too. I used to work here part-time, and now I'm filling in for her, I guess you could say."

"Did she leave to take another job?"

"She left because she broke up with Mr. Loomis."

"Oh," Phyllis said. "I didn't know —"

"I shouldn't be talking out of turn, but it was like something from a TV show. I mean, poor Mr. Loomis left his wife for Jaycee, and then she turned around and left him. You should have heard all the yelling when she broke it off with him." The woman sighed and shook her head. "It's just been such an uproar around here. I'll be glad when things just settle back down."

Phyllis tried to sound sympathetic as she said, "I imagine so. A lawsuit, a divorce, and an angry mistress. It *does* sound like a TV show."

The woman frowned a little and said, "I didn't mention anything about a divorce."

"Well, I just assumed that Mr. Loomis was divorcing his wife," Phyllis said quickly. "Since you said he left her, I mean."

"Actually, she's the one who filed for divorce. I don't know why people can't just stay married. I mean, you don't have to be *happy* to be married to someone. I know. I was married for forty years."

Phyllis didn't want to listen to the woman's life story, so she said, "Do you think if we came by another time, we could talk to Mr. Loomis about donating?"

"I don't know if he could afford it or not." The woman lowered her voice again and whispered, "Things are pretty tight around here right now." In a normal tone, she went on. "But let me get my purse. I'd like to give something."

Sam said, "That's nice of you, ma'am."

The woman went back to her desk, moving slowly, reached under it to pull out a big purse, and rummaged around in it for a minute before she came back with a five-dollar bill.

"There you go," she said as she handed it to Sam.

"That's mighty generous," he said. "We'll have to, uh, mail you a receipt . . ."

"Oh, that's all right. I don't need a receipt. It's for a good cause."

"Yes, ma'am. Thank you."

"Thank you," Phyllis said as well. Sam slid the bill under the clip on the clipboard, and they headed for the door.

"People should just stay married, like you two," the woman called after them. "It's so much simpler."

As Sam closed the door behind them, he said, "Whew."

"She was a character, wasn't she?" Phyllis said.

"Reminded me of my grandma. Fine, upstandin' woman who'd be mortified if you called her a gossip, but eager to spill the dirt just the same."

"People like that come in handy for us," Phyllis said as they got into the pickup. "We have another suspect."

Sam raised an eyebrow.

"Jaycee Fallon," Phyllis said. "Loomis's mistress. She must have had a good reason for breaking up with him after she'd ruined his marriage."

"A good enough reason for her to want him dead?"

"It's possible."

"That makes five, if I'm countin' right. With that many folks mad at him, I'm sort of surprised ol' Clay's lasted this long."

As Sam drove away from the place, Phyllis thought about the way the woman had assumed the two of them were married. She supposed they came across that way. They were certainly comfortable enough with each other to be an old married couple, and she knew that both of them had thought about it . . .

Her cell phone's ring tone interrupted those musings. She took it out, looked at the caller's number, and told Sam, "It's Mr. D'Angelo."

"I won't hold my breath waitin' for good news," Sam muttered.

Neither would Phyllis. She answered the call and heard the lawyer say, "Mrs. Newsom, I'm headed for the jail. The police have just arrested Nate Hollingsworth."

Chapter 15

D'Angelo wanted them to meet him at his office. Since they didn't know how long it would be before they got home, Sam asked Phyllis to call Carolyn and ask her to go ahead and bring Buck in. The Dalmatian had a bed in the utility room where he liked to curl up, and he was generally well-behaved when he was inside.

When Phyllis had done that, Sam asked her, "What else did D'Angelo have to say?"

"Just that he didn't really know much yet. Evidently the police showed up at Nate's office with a search warrant, along with a warrant for his arrest on murder charges."

"Don't they usually carry out their searches first, before they actually arrest somebody?"

"Usually," Phyllis said, "unless they consider the suspect a flight risk. Then they'd want to go ahead and place him in custody."

Sam snorted and said, "Nate's not a flight

risk. And he's sure as heck no murderer."

"When they took him to jail," Phyllis went on, "he called Allyson, and she's the one who called Mr. D'Angelo. He told her not to worry, that he'd see about arranging bail and would get Nate out of there as soon as possible."

"I didn't really expect 'em to move quite this quick."

"Neither did I." Phyllis's expression was grim as she added, "They must have some evidence we don't know about."

When they reached the lawyer's office, the receptionist told them, "Mr. D'Angelo isn't back yet. He wanted me to ask you to wait in the conference room. Is that all right?"

"Of course," Phyllis said. A part of her wanted to go to the jail, but she knew they couldn't really do any good there, and they might just be in the way.

"Can I get you something to drink? There are soft drinks and coffee."

"Some coffee would be good," Sam said. Phyllis nodded in agreement.

A few minutes later, they were settled in the comfortable chairs in the conference room with mugs of excellent coffee on the inlaid table in front of them.

"I hate to think about Nate bein' locked up," Sam muttered. "I reckon he can take care of himself, though."

"He probably won't be in there for long," Phyllis said. She was trying to be encouraging. But at the same time, she knew the police could hold Nate for a while before charging him, and there were other ways to drag the process out even more when they wanted to keep a suspect behind bars longer.

When Jimmy D'Angelo came into the conference room twenty minutes later, he was alone. Phyllis's heart sank a little when she saw that. She had hoped that Nate would be with D'Angelo.

As Phyllis and Sam stood up, the lawyer set his briefcase on the table and heaved a sigh.

"More bad news," he told them as he waved them back into their chairs. "Nate's bail hearing won't be held until tomorrow morning. I won't be able to get him out today."

"Dadgummit!" Sam exclaimed. "I was afraid of that."

"Why did they take him into custody?" Phyllis asked. "Did the search warrant turn up anything?"

"Warrants, plural," D'Angelo said. "They served the first one at the house where Nate and Allyson live. They were looking for

Nate's rifle. I was pretty sure they'd get around to that sooner rather than later."

"But they didn't find it," Phyllis guessed.

D'Angelo shook his head and said, "No, so then they went to his office, and they took an arrest warrant with them because they were afraid Allyson would warn Nate they'd been at the house, and he would run. They had a warrant for the whole Cranmoor Building, in case Nate hid the rifle in one of the maintenance areas or even in another office."

"Did they find it?" Sam asked.

"No. It's still missing. And Nate followed my advice. He wouldn't tell them anything, including where the gun is."

"But he told you," Phyllis said.

D'Angelo grimaced.

"He claims he doesn't know where it is. He says it should have been at the house. The only thing he can come up with is that somebody must have broken in and stolen it without him or Allyson being aware of it."

Sam frowned and said, "That's a mighty weak story. I might not be able to swallow it, and I *want* the kid to be innocent."

"Yeah. A jury won't buy it, that's for sure. They never reported a burglary or anything like that. The prosecutor will make it look like Nate got rid of the rifle somehow, because he knew it would incriminate him, and without knowing what happened to it, we won't be able to prove otherwise."

Phyllis said, "Is that all they have — the fact that the rifle is missing?"

"I gather they've talked to several of the hands who work out at the McCrory ranch," D'Angelo said, "not just the two who were there the day before yesterday. Evidently this whole conflict between Nate and his father-in-law over the gas wells went back further, and was worse than Nate made it sound. There were a lot of shouting matches over it. They almost came to blows a few times, is what I'm hearing."

Sam shook his head and said, "I don't believe that. Barney could get pretty hot under the collar, sure, but Nate was always too levelheaded to let his temper get the best of him."

"I'm sure he was when you knew him," Phyllis said. "But you have to remember, Sam, that was ten years ago. People can change. Goodness, I was a much different person ten years ago than I am now."

That is true in some ways, she thought. Her husband, Kenny, had still been alive then. Mike had been a young sheriff's deputy, dating Sarah but not married to her yet, and of course there was no Bobby. She and Carolyn had been friendly acquaintances, but she barely knew Eve at that time. And she was still years away from meeting Sam.

Yes, a lot had changed . . . but was *she* really all that different? It was hard to say. Back then, she never would have set out to solve a murder, no matter what the circumstances. At least she didn't think so . . .

D'Angelo said, "They've got testimony about a bunch of arguments. That gives Nate a motive, and he can't establish exactly where he was when the shot was fired. And along with the missing rifle, the cops think that's enough. To be honest, I think it's probably enough for the grand jury to indict him, too. Whether a trial jury would convict him right now, I couldn't say." D'Angelo's heavy shoulders rose and fell. "But I think we'd better start trying to come up with as much evidence as we can to create reasonable doubt."

Phyllis leaned forward and said, "That's what we've been working on."

For the next few minutes, she and Sam went over what they had learned about Gene Coyle and about Clay Loomis's business. While they talked, D'Angelo took a legal pad from his briefcase and scrawled notes on it.

"You're right," he said when they were finished. "This guy Loomis practically has a target painted on him. I can get a ballistics expert to testify as to what tiny degree of difference it would take for the bullet to hit McCrory instead of Loomis. We've got Coyle's own admission that he's a good enough marksman to attempt a shot like that. We've got a scorned wife, and they're always good for reasonable doubt. We need to find out more about the girlfriend and about Loomis's business partners. If any of them had access to a rifle of the right caliber, we can throw suspicion on them, too."

Phyllis frowned and said, "Of course, even if one of those five turns out to be the killer, that means the other four are innocent. We'll be tarring them all with the same brush."

D'Angelo spread his hands and said, "That's the way it works. I don't like casting a shadow over people who haven't done anything wrong, but, in the end, all that matters is convincing those jury members that the prosecution didn't make its case."

That is the difference between being a lawyer and being a detective, Phyllis thought. D'Angelo would be satisfied with an acquittal.

But Phyllis wanted the truth.

"What about the ballistics report on the bullet that killed Barney?" Sam asked. "I reckon the police know what caliber it was by now?"

"They must," D'Angelo said. "And it must match the caliber of the rifle that's registered to Nate — otherwise they wouldn't be looking so hard for it."

"There could be a bunch of rifles like that."

"Exactly."

"What do you want us to do?" Phyllis asked.

"I was hoping you'd talk to Allyson," D'Angelo said. "She's supposed to be on her way here. You're an old friend of the family, Sam. Maybe she'll be more comfortable talking to you."

"You don't believe what she's told you so far?" Sam said.

"I just want her to open up more about how things really were between Nate and her father. They downplayed the whole gas-well thing before. We need to know how bad it really was."

Sam nodded slowly and sighed.

"I'll talk to her," he said. "I don't know if she'll tell me any more than she already has, though. I don't know if there's anything more to tell."

D'Angelo put the legal pad back in the briefcase and said, "If there is, we need to get ready to deal with it. I'll have her brought in when she gets here, if that's all right."

Sam nodded again. D'Angelo stood up and bustled out of the conference room.

Phyllis reached over and rested her left hand on Sam's right.

"Just remember you're trying to help Nate," she told him, "even though it may not always seem like it."

"I know. I just hate to think of the boy bein' behind bars."

It was another fifteen minutes before the receptionist led Allyson into the conference room. The young woman's eyes were red from crying, but she seemed fairly composed at the moment. She was even able to summon a faint smile as she said, "Hello, Coach."

Sam was on his feet. He put a hand on Allyson's arm and steered her into one of the chairs. The receptionist asked, "Can I get you something to drink?"

Hesitantly, Allyson said, "I . . . maybe a Dr Pepper?"

The receptionist smiled and said, "You got it. I'll be right back."

Sam sat down again and said, "I know this

is a mighty bad time for you, Ally —"

"Yes. My father is dead and my husband's in jail. It's a really bad time."

"But we'd like to help if we can," Phyllis finished. "That's why we're here."

"I know that, Mrs. Newsom, and I appreciate it — I really do. It's just that my life has been turned upside down. I . . . I don't even know what to hope for anymore."

"Hope that we get Nate home to you safe and sound before too long," Sam told her.

"And that we find out who's really responsible for what happened to your father," Phyllis added.

Allyson was able to nod. She said, "All right. What . . . what can I do to help?"

"Tell us about the trouble between Nate and your father over the gas wells," Phyllis said.

Allyson frowned and said, "I already told you. Nate told you. It didn't really amount to that much —"

"That's not what the fellas who work on your dad's ranch say, Ally," Sam broke in. Phyllis could tell by the look in his eyes that he hated doing it. "They say Nate and Barney were fightin' about it hammer and tongs for a long time. They even came close to goin' to Fist City over it."

Allyson sat back in her chair. Her eyes

widened as she shook her head.

"No, I don't believe that! Nate and my dad loved each other. Nate was like a son to him. They might have argued, but they wouldn't have fought."

"Some of the worst brawls I've ever seen have been between brother and brother, and father and son," Sam said. "I reckon a father-in-law and son-in-law is close enough to count."

"Sometimes when you love someone, you get even angrier *because* you care about them so much," Phyllis put in.

Stubbornly, Allyson shook her head again. "No, Nate and Dad wouldn't have done that."

Phyllis said, "You weren't with them most of the time when they were talking about the gas lease, were you?"

"No, just . . . just the one time. Day before yesterday. Actually, they got along so well when it came to running the ranch that I didn't want to get involved. I was afraid I would mess things up."

The receptionist came in then with a can of Dr Pepper for Allyson. She asked Phyllis and Sam, "Can I get you some more coffee?"

"I'm all right, thanks," Phyllis told her, and Sam said, "Same here."

When the three of them were alone again, Allyson took a sip of the soft drink. Her hand trembled as she lifted the can to her mouth.

"Where's Mr. D'Angelo?" she asked. "He's Nate's lawyer. Shouldn't I be talking to him?"

"He's working on some other aspects of the case," Phyllis said. "He hoped you wouldn't mind talking to us."

"I don't." Allyson smiled slightly. "I was always able to talk to Coach. All of us who played for him were."

"And that's the way I wanted it," Sam said. "My office door was always open to you kids — even though I might've wanted to shut it on your folks every now and then."

"My dad could be pretty hot tempered, couldn't he?"

"To tell you the truth," Sam said, "I thought he was gonna take a swing at me a time or two."

"I guess he could have gotten mad enough to take a swing at Nate, too. I hate to say that, but it's true. But Nate never would have hit him back. And he certainly wouldn't . . . never would have . . ."

Her voice trailed off with the unsaid words hanging in the air.

Never would have shot him.

Phyllis sensed that Allyson was a dead end as far as the long-standing disagreement between Nate and McCrory over the gas lease. Nate had probably kept his own counsel about the matter, and by her own admission, Allyson had tried not to meddle in her father's business affairs. All she would know was what Nate told her, and it was unlikely he would have come home and revealed that her father had tried to punch him.

It might be better to change tacks, Phyllis thought. She asked, "What about Nate's rifle, Allyson?"

"I don't know anything about it. I thought it was still in the guest-bedroom closet until the police came to look for it and didn't find it. That's where Nate always kept it."

"Did you tell them that before they started looking?"

"Noooo . . ." Allyson looked a little scared now. "You understand, I knew why they were looking for it. I didn't want to *help* them. But there was nothing I could do to stop them. They had a search warrant."

Sam said, "You did the right thing by co-operatin'. Wouldn't have done Nate a bit of good for you to get in trouble, too."

"When they didn't find the rifle, did you tell them where it was supposed to be?"

Phyllis asked.

"I did. I said someone must have broken in and stolen it without us ever noticing. But that's not very likely, is it?"

Phyllis shook her head and said, "I'm afraid it's not."

"Did Nate go huntin' a lot?" Sam asked.

"No, not really. Sometimes he took the rifle out to the ranch and helped my dad chase off the coyotes. And they went deer hunting a time or two, but Nate didn't really care for it." She paused. "He didn't like to kill anything, you see."

"But he was a good shot?" Phyllis said.

"He was on the ROTC rifle team in college."

Phyllis and Sam exchanged a glance. This was looking more damning for Nate as time passed.

"Do you remember the last time he took the rifle out of the house?" Phyllis asked.

Allyson frowned in thought, then said, "It was about a month ago, I think. He took it to the gunsmith to have some work done on it. I don't know enough about it to tell you what it was. But he brought it back, and it was there in the closet ever since. I'm sure of it."

Which brings us back around to the mysterious "burglary," Phyllis thought. It just wasn't believable that someone would break into the Hollingsworths' home so skillfully that the intrusion wasn't even noticed and then steal only a single rifle. As D'Angelo had said, no jury was going to believe that.

It appeared that the answers they were looking for just weren't there.

The door of the conference room opened, and Jimmy D'Angelo came in. He rested his hands on the back of the chair at the head of the table and said, "I'm sorry, Allyson. I've been making some calls to see if there's any way to speed up Nate's bail hearing and get him out of jail today, but it's not going to happen. He'll have to stay there overnight. But I give you my word that I'll have him out of there first thing in the morning."

Allyson nodded and said, "Thank you. Will . . . will he be all right?"

"I'm sure he will be. They have him in a cell by himself. No one will bother him."

"Well, that's good, anyway."

"Why don't you go on home and try to get some rest? I know that won't be easy, but it's the best thing you can do right now."

"I don't think I'll ever sleep again," Allyson said. "I'm afraid if I close my eyes, all I'll see is Nate and my father . . . And I'm just so scared."

She put her hands over her face and started to cry again.

D'Angelo looked distinctly uncomfortable. He said, "Uh . . . I'm not sure she should be alone right now. Do you know if there are any relatives or friends she could stay with?"

"Nate's folks moved down to South Texas, I think," Sam said. "I don't know about anybody else."

Phyllis didn't hesitate. She said, "Allyson can come stay with us tonight. There's an extra room, and it won't be any trouble."

Allyson looked at her and asked between sobs, "Are . . . are you sure?"

"I'm certain," Phyllis said. She reached over to put her hand on Allyson's shoulder and give it a reassuring squeeze.

They all stood up and moved toward the conference-room door. D'Angelo said, "I think this is a good idea." He gave Phyllis a look behind Allyson's back, and Phyllis understood what it meant.

Pump her for all the information you can get.

That hadn't been the motivation for Phyllis to extend the invitation, but she supposed it wouldn't hurt to find out as much as they could while Allyson was at the house. Without making her feel like she was being interrogated constantly, of course.

The group stepped into the hall and then into the firm's lobby, with D'Angelo leading the way. He stopped short and said, "What the —"

The receptionist stood behind her desk, stiff and angry. She said, "I'm sorry, Mr. D'Angelo — these people refused to leave. Do you want me to call the police?"

Phyllis looked past the beefy lawyer and saw Felicity Prosper standing there, along with her two partners in journalistic crime.

CHAPTER 16

Holding a cordless microphone, Felicity started toward them. She said, "Mrs. Hollingsworth, could I get a comment? How does it feel knowing that your husband has been arrested for murdering your father?"

"Hey, now — ," D'Angelo started to say.

"He didn't do it!" Allyson cried. "Nate didn't hurt anybody!"

Felicity smirked and said, "I don't think the police would have taken him into custody if they didn't have some pretty solid evidence. Do you think he'll be convicted? Do you think he'll get the death penalty? The viewers of *Inside Beat* want to know —"

Nick was crowding up with his video camera, trying to get a close-up of Allyson's tear-streaked face. Sam got between them, and at the same time D'Angelo interposed his considerable bulk between Allyson and Felicity.

"My client has no comment," he snapped. "The three of you are trespassing. Leave immediately, or I'll call the police and file charges against you."

"I'm sure, as a lawyer, you've heard of freedom of the press, Mr. D'Angelo," Felicity said. "You have no right to suppress the truth. You can't kick us out —"

"This is private property, and I *can* kick you out," D'Angelo said. "But I'll call the cops and have them do it for me."

Nick tried to sidle around Sam with the camera. Sam said, "Watch it, buddy. You're treadin' on thin ice."

"Are you threatening my cameraman, Mr. Fletcher?" Felicity demanded. "Be advised that we have a video record of it."

Phyllis took Allyson's arm and began edging backward, toward the still-open door to the hallway.

"Maybe we'd better go back inside," she suggested.

"Mrs. Hollingsworth!" Felicity called. "Tell us how it feels being married to a killer!"

Sam and D'Angelo were backing up, too, trying to shield Allyson and Phyllis from the tabloid-TV vultures. D'Angelo told the receptionist, "Helen, call the cops! Tell them we have trespassers here who refuse to leave."

They all backed into the corridor, and D'Angelo slammed the door in Felicity's face.

"I'm sure that's not the first time somebody's done *that,*" he muttered.

Phyllis put her arms around the sobbing Allyson. She was furious with Felicity Prosper. Allyson had barely calmed down from being questioned earlier, and now Felicity had upset her again.

"Why don't you take Allyson back into the conference room?" D'Angelo suggested. "I'll make sure those jerks get what's coming to them."

Sam ushered Phyllis and Allyson out of the hallway and into the conference room. Phyllis got the young woman to sit down at the table. Allyson wasn't sobbing anymore, but she sat there shaking her head with a look of despair.

D'Angelo came into the room a few minutes later and said, "They'd already taken off by the time I got back out there. Guess they didn't want to wait for the cops. But I'm going to file harassment charges against them, anyway."

"Will that do any good?" Phyllis asked.

"Probably not. Chances are the charges

will be tossed. But I need to do it, because it'll help establish a precedent for requesting a restraining order against those three. I don't want them coming anywhere near Allyson — or Nate, either, once he's out."

"She thinks he's guilty," Allyson said in a shaky voice. "She called him a murderer. Everybody else is bound to feel the same way."

Sam said, "Nobody who really knows Nate will believe that. Your friends'll stick by you, Allyson. Wait and see."

"I hope you're right, Coach. But I don't think so. Even if he's not convicted, everybody's always going to believe that Nate killed my dad."

Not if we find the real killer, Phyllis thought.

When Allyson had calmed down again and said that she was ready to go, Sam said, "I'll take a look outside first and make sure that woman and her friends aren't hangin' around anywhere watchin' for us."

"Maybe you could get the pickup and pull up right outside the building," Phyllis suggested.

"Good idea. I'll do that."

He hurried out, and Phyllis followed with Allyson. D'Angelo went outside to stand on the sidewalk and keep an eye out. When he saw Sam's pickup coming, he looked through the glass door and beckoned to Phyllis and Allyson.

The curb was a no-parking zone, but Sam stopped there only long enough for D'Angelo to open the door so Allyson and Phyllis could climb in. The pickup had a bench seat. Allyson slid in first, to sit between Phyllis and Sam. He waved at D'Angelo and pulled away.

"You didn't see them anywhere?" Phyllis asked, as Sam circled the courthouse to head out on South Main.

"Nope. Of course, that doesn't mean they won't be staked out at the house, waitin' for us when we get there."

"They had better not be," Phyllis said grimly. "I'm getting tired of this."

Thankfully, the van wasn't parked in front of the house when they got there, nor did Phyllis see it anywhere else along the block. However, that didn't make her think that Felicity Prosper had given up being a troublemaker. She wasn't sure the reporter even had that ability.

Carolyn and Eve were both in the living room when Phyllis, Sam, and Allyson came in. So was Buck, who lifted his head and wagged his tail at the sight of Sam.

Allyson smiled and said, "What a cute

dog." Phyllis was glad to see something put a smile back on the young woman's face, even if it probably wouldn't last long.

"His name's Buck," Sam said. The Dalmatian came over to him and stood there happily while Sam bent and scratched behind his ears. "Named after Buck Jones, the cowboy actor, who I expect you've never heard of."

"Of course I've heard of him," Allyson said. "My dad watched every Western movie ever made, I think, including the really old ones from the fifties and sixties."

Carolyn rolled her eyes, but Allyson had bent over to pet Buck, too, and didn't see her. Phyllis thought her friend could have shown a little more restraint with that reaction, but she understood it. Sometimes it seemed to her that the current generation considered everything from before their own lifetimes to be incredibly ancient.

"Allyson's going to be staying here tonight," Phyllis explained to Carolyn and Eve.

Allyson straightened and said, "Mr. D'Angelo can't get Nate out of jail until tomorrow morning. I hope I'm not going to be too much of an imposition."

"You won't be an imposition at all, dear," Carolyn said.

"Not at all," Eve added. "To tell you the truth, it'll be nice to have someone young in the house for a change."

"The best any of us can do is bein' young at heart," Sam said.

Phyllis was glad to see that Allyson seemed to be coping better with the situation now. The human spirit was resilient, especially in the young.

Allyson said, "I'll need some things from my house, though. I wish I'd thought of that sooner."

"I'll take you out there," Sam said. "Won't be a problem."

"Why don't the two of you do that?" Phyllis said. "And by the time you get back, we'll have some supper ready. We'll all feel better once we've had a good meal."

Sam nodded and said, "Sounds like a plan. Is that all right with you, Allyson?"

"Yes. I'm just sorry to be so much trouble."

"Stop apologizin'," Sam told her. "It's no trouble at all. You ready to go?"

"Yes, I suppose so."

"We'll be back," Sam said to Phyllis. "So long, Buck."

The Dalmatian wagged his tail and followed Sam and Allyson to the door. Allyson smiled down at him and said, "He looks like he wants to come with us."

"He likes ridin' in the pickup, all right. You mind him comin' with us?"

"Not at all. You're the one doing me the favor, Coach. Anything you want is fine with me."

"Come on, then, Buck," Sam said as he got a leash and harness from a shelf in the coat closet. Seeing them, Buck ran around in circles in his excitement. Once Sam had the harness on him and clipped the leash to it, the three of them left.

Phyllis turned toward the kitchen, running possibilities through her mind for supper now that they had company.

Buck sat in the middle of the front seat this time. Allyson looped her left arm around him and held him close to her. Buck didn't seem to mind, Sam noted. He didn't take to strangers that well, but since Allyson had come into the house with Sam and Phyllis, Buck had obviously accepted that she was all right.

"You'll have to tell me where we're goin'," Sam said. "I know you live somewhere north of town, but that's all."

"The house is in one of the developments off Peaster Highway," Allyson said. "It's not hard to find." She paused, then asked, "Do you keep in touch with any of the other players from your old teams, Coach?"

"Oh, not really. I run into some of 'em in town from time to time and always enjoy catchin' up on what they're doin' now, but that time of my life is sort of in the past. You know what I mean?"

"I was sorry to hear about your wife."

"Thanks. It was a rough time. You figure when you get to be my age, you're gonna have lost a lot of folks from your life. But, even so, it's never easy." He glanced over at her. "I don't reckon anybody's immune from losin' the ones they love, no matter what age they are."

"No," she said softly as she shook her head. "No, they're not."

They rode in silence for a few minutes; then Allyson said, "You and Mrs. Newsom seem to be really good friends."

That made Sam grin.

"You wouldn't be pryin' a little bit, would you?" he asked.

"I just think you deserve to be happy, Coach."

"I am," Sam said. "Happier than I've been for a good long while. Reckon I got that way by not questionin' how I wound up where I am and just acceptin' it for what it is. There's all kinds of good things and bad things in life, Ally. The secret is to be grateful for the good ones and not sit around broodin' over the bad ones. I know people who can't do that, and I always feel a little sorry for 'em."

"It's hard not to brood sometimes."

"Well, you've got sort of special circumstances to deal with right now. Times like this, you do what you have to in order to get through 'em, and hope that things will get better."

"I think with you and Mrs. Newsom on our side, there's at least a chance of that."

"I hope there is," Sam said. "I surely do."

Allyson gave him directions to the house, which was easy to find, as she'd said. It was on a paved side road in an area that was half-country, half–housing developments, but there were no curbs — just bar ditches with culverts at the driveways.

The sight of that reminded Sam of the yarn he'd spun for Gene Coyle that morning. This was just the sort of housing development he had talked about with Coyle, although these lots were bigger than the imaginary ones he'd mentioned, probably close to two acres each. That gave people enough room to keep a horse or maybe some goats.

The houses weren't the McMansions

found in so many suburbs, either. They were nice-looking brick structures but had some age on them, having been built probably thirty years earlier. The size of the trees around them, mostly cottonwoods and fruitless mulberries and live oaks, agreed with that estimate, Sam thought. The trees had had some time to grow since they'd been planted.

A number of the houses along the street had aboveground pools in the backyards, covered at this time of year. Others had chain-link fence around the backyards, with wood and sheet-metal sheds in them for those horses or goats Sam had thought about as he started along the road. He had to swallow hard, because this was exactly the sort of neighborhood where he and his late wife had lived for more than twenty years.

"What's wrong, Coach?" Allyson asked.

"Nothin'," Sam said. "It's just been, uh, kind of a long day, and I'm not as young as I used to be."

"See, I told you I was being too much trouble."

"Nope, not at all. I'm fine. Which house is yours?"

"Up there on the left. The one with the camper parked beside the garage." Now it was Allyson's turn to have her voice catch a little. "Nate and I used to take it on vacation trips sometimes."

"And you will again," Sam assured her. "You'll see — everything's gonna be fine."

He wished he could guarantee that. He had complete faith in Phyllis, and in his own efforts, too, but he knew what a close thing it had been in some of the other cases on which they'd worked. If things had gone a little differently, an innocent person easily might have been convicted of murder in those cases.

Sam parked in the driveway in front of the garage.

"Hang on to Buck until I get out and take his leash from you," he told Allyson.

"I've got him," she said as she tightened her arm around the Dalmatian. Sam slid out of the pickup and then reached back across the seat to take the leash. Buck jumped out right away, and Sam could tell he was eager to explore. He hurried to the shrubs that ran along the front of the house next to the walk and started sniffing them.

Allyson went to the front door and unlocked it. Sam tugged on the leash and said, "Come on, Buck." Reluctantly, Buck abandoned his intense examination of the bushes.

"You and Buck come on in, Coach," Allyson said as she went inside. "It won't take me but a few minutes to grab the things I need."

"Take your time," Sam told her. "We're in no hurry."

He stood in the living room, holding Buck's leash as Allyson disappeared elsewhere in the house. She'd flicked the lights on when they came in, so he was able to look around. The house had a fireplace, and the first thing he noticed was a small trophy on the mantel over it. He had to take a closer look.

"Bi-district champs," he said aloud as he read the inscription on the gold plate attached to the trophy's base. The trophy itself was a representation of a basketball. "Look at that, Buck. One of our championship seasons."

There were framed photos on the wall above the fireplace, too, one of the boys' team and one of the girls' team. He had no trouble picking out Nate and Allyson in the pictures, ten years younger, and each of them grinning with the innocent exuberance of youth.

Sam started trying to remember the names of the other players in the photos, but to his dismay there were some he couldn't recall.

Their faces were familiar, but he just couldn't dredge the names out of his brain.

That was sad, and worrisome in a way, too. He had seen too many people his own age and even younger fall prey to fading memories. It was almost like a plague, he thought sometimes. He dreaded winding up that way himself. That was one reason he tried to keep as mentally active as he could, reading and watching movies and using the computer and always trying to learn new things.

And helping Phyllis solve murders, he reminded himself. Keeping up with her would give the ol' noggin a workout, that was for dang sure.

"All right. I think I've got everything," Allyson said as she came back into the living room carrying a small overnight bag.

"Tell me somethin', would you?"

"Of course, Coach. What is it?"

Sam pointed to one of the players on the girl's team and asked, "Who's this?"

Allyson laughed as she looked at the photo.

"Why, that's Carly Smithson. You don't remember her?"

"Played forward. Averaged eight boards and just under eleven points a game. Good player." Sam felt relieved that with a little nudge, he was able to recall that much.

"That's right," Allyson said. "She has four kids, and she's working on her third marriage."

Sam made a clucking sound and said, "Too bad. Not about the kids, but I'm sorry to hear that her marriages didn't work out too good."

"Did you remember everybody else in those team photos?"

"No, but I reckon we might as well leave the past where it is. Dealin' with the present and the future is enough to keep us busy right now."

"Yes, it is."

They stepped out of the house, Allyson locking the door behind them, and started along the walk that ran in front of the house over to the driveway. As they approached the pickup, Sam glanced along the road and saw two SUVs with sheriff's-department logos on the doors and lights on the roof coming toward them. A Weatherford police car followed the sheriff's vehicles. The sight put a frown on his face.

"What in the world?" Allyson said. She had seen the official vehicles, too, and she sounded worried.

"They're probably not comin' here —," Sam began, then stopped short as the first of the SUVs pulled to a stop along the street in front of the house. The other two vehicles followed suit.

Buck growled deep in his throat as he stood stiffly beside Sam.

A woman with long dark hair got out of the police car. She wore a black leather coat that came down to her knees. As she walked along the driveway toward them, Sam recognized Detective Isabel Largo.

"Mr. Fletcher," she greeted him. "I didn't expect to find you here."

"What do you want?" Allyson asked. Her voice was tight with fear and anger.

"I'm here to serve another search warrant," Detective Largo said.

Chapter 17

"Another search warrant?" Allyson repeated. She went on raggedly, "You've already searched the house. In fact, you practically tore it apart."

"The officers and I put everything back the way we found it," Isabel said coolly. "But this warrant isn't for the house." She nodded toward the camper. "We weren't aware that you had this vehicle when the first warrant was drawn. Now we're going to search in there, too." She reached up and tried the door, then said, "You'll need to unlock it for us."

"And if I don't?" Allyson asked.

Isabel shrugged and said, "We'll break the lock. We're within our rights to do that, but you can check with your attorney first, if you'd like to."

"I'll get the key," Allyson said through clenched teeth. "It's in the house."

"Go ahead. We'll be here."

Allyson glanced at Sam and said, "I'm sorry, Coach."

"No need to apologize," Sam told her. "This isn't any of your doin'."

Allyson unlocked the front door again and went inside. Detective Largo stood with her hands in the pockets of her coat and asked, "What are you doing here, Mr. Fletcher?"

"Is that an official question?"

Isabel smiled faintly and shook her head. "Just a curious one," she said. "Actually, I shouldn't be surprised to find you here. I know you and Mrs. Newsom have an indirect connection to this case."

"I wouldn't call it indirect. Phyllis and I were only a few yards away when Barney McCrory was killed."

"Yes, that's true."

"And I've known these kids for a long time, too."

"You mean Nate and Allyson Hollingsworth?"

"That's right."

"They're hardly kids," the detective said. "They're my age."

Sam managed not to point out that to him, she seemed like a kid, too. Practically everyone under the age of forty did. Sometimes fifty.

"They're responsible for their own actions," Isabel went on.

"Nobody said they weren't," Sam drawled.

Isabel looked down at the dog and said, "This must be Buck."

"Yeah. How'd you know his name?"

"Mike mentioned it. And Buck was mixed up in a murder case not that long ago, too, wasn't he?"

"Sort of," Sam admitted. "But that really *was* an indirect connection."

Isabel started to reach out toward the Dalmatian, but Buck growled again.

"He's not a dangerous dog, is he? He's not going to interfere with our search?"

"I'll put him in the pickup," Sam suggested. He didn't want any of the cops to get worried about Buck and decide to shoot him.

"Good idea," Isabel said.

Sam felt better once Buck was in the pickup, with the doors and windows closed. On a chilly day like this, with the sky overcast, there was no chance it would get too hot for him to stay in there for a while.

Isabel was starting to look and sound impatient as she said, "Mrs. Hollingsworth has been inside for a while."

"She hasn't tried to run away," Sam said. "You would've seen her if she did. Anyway, she wouldn't do that."

"She's not the same person who played ball for you ten years ago, Mr. Fletcher," Isabel said, revealing that she had done her homework about Allyson. "You don't know what she would or wouldn't do."

"I reckon I can make a pretty good guess," Sam said.

At that moment, Allyson emerged from the house again, carrying a small ring of keys.

"I'm sorry," she said. "I had a little trouble finding the key. We haven't used the camper in a while."

She fitted one of the keys into the door and unlocked it. As Allyson swung open the door, Isabel said, "You and Mr. Fletcher step back now, please."

She climbed up into the camper. A couple of the uniformed officers followed her. One of them carried a computer tablet, which he held up in front of him, evidently to record the search.

Sam and Allyson moved off to the side and stood there waiting. Allyson shifted her feet awkwardly, as if she didn't know what to do with them.

"Why are they doing this?" she said quietly to Sam. "What are they looking for?"

"You know what they're lookin' for. That rifle."

"They won't find it. I don't think Nate's ever had the rifle in the camper."

"They're just doin' everything they can think of," Sam said. "Coverin' all the bases."

"It still feels like . . . like we're being persecuted."

Sam looked over at the pickup, where Buck was watching them through the side window. The Dalmatian looked like he wanted to bite somebody.

Sam knew the feeling.

Several minutes stretched by. They seemed to Sam like they were longer than they really were. And poor Allyson is even antsier than I am, he thought. When he glanced over at her, she had her lower lip caught between her teeth and was chewing at it.

"Try to relax," he told her. "It'll be —"

He saw her eyes go wide with horror. Her body stiffened as if an electric shock had just passed through it. Sam turned toward the camper, afraid of what he was going to see.

Detective Largo was coming down the steps, holding a rifle in one of her blue-gloved hands. The other cops followed her, the one with the tablet still recording.

"No!" Allyson screamed. She started to lunge toward Isabel, but Sam moved fast and clamped his hands on her shoulders to hold her. "No! That's not Nate's! You planted it!"

"Every second of the search is documented digitally," Isabel said, "and the recording will stand up to any technical tests to prove it wasn't doctored. Mrs. Hollingsworth, is this your husband's rifle?"

Allyson strained against Sam's grip. She said, "No, I told you. That's not Nate's."

"You're not under oath," Isabel said. "You can't be prosecuted for lying to me. But if you are, it won't help your husband. This rifle has serial numbers on it that can be checked against his gun registration. We'll know who it belongs to. So I'll ask you again —"

"It . . . it looks like Nate's rifle," Allyson broke in. "But it can't be! It just can't."

Sam asked, "Where did you find it, Detective?"

Isabel just smiled and shook her head. It was clear that she was asking the questions, not answering them.

One of the sheriff's deputies came over, also wearing blue gloves. Sam knew the sheriff's department handled forensics and ballistics for the Weatherford police. The deputy took the rifle from Isabel, who turned back to Sam and Allyson and started pulling the gloves from her hands.

"Thank you for your cooperation, Mrs. Hollingsworth," she said.

"Nate didn't do it," Allyson said, her voice low and menacing. "I don't care what you found or what you think. He didn't do it."

"That's not up to me to determine. I just gather the evidence and build the case. That camper's going to be sealed now, until a forensics team can go through it. There'll be an officer here to see that you don't disturb anything about it."

"She's not gonna disturb anything," Sam said. "She's comin' back to Phyllis's with me."

"Good." The detective permitted herself another thin smile as she said to Allyson, "I'll know where to find you."

Sam might have been mistaken, but he thought that sounded like a threat.

Phyllis and Carolyn almost had supper ready by the time Sam and Allyson got back. Phyllis was putting the finishing touches to the potato soup, and Carolyn was taking the ham-and-cheese sliders out of the oven. It was getting dark outside. The shortest day of the year, the official first day of winter, even though the weather was already chilly, would soon be here.

Phyllis heard the garage door go up. Sam

often came in that way, even though he parked his pickup outside. A moment later the door rumbled back down, and the door between the kitchen and the garage opened.

She knew as soon as she saw Allyson's face that something was wrong. The young woman's eyes were red. She had been crying again. Sam's craggy features had a grim cast to them as well.

"What's wrong?" Phyllis asked as Sam closed the door behind them.

"Let me take Ally in the livin' room so she can sit down," Sam said. He had a hand on her arm as if to steady her. He carried a small overnight bag in his other hand. They went through the kitchen and up the hall toward the living room, as Phyllis and Carolyn exchanged worried looks.

Sam was back a moment later, still carrying the bag. He sighed and said, "Detective Largo and some other cops showed up just as we were fixin' to leave Ally's house. They had a warrant to search the travel trailer that was parked there. Ally said her and Nate sometimes take it on vacation."

"And they found the rifle hidden inside there," Phyllis guessed. It didn't take much of a leap.

"Yep. Ally swore it wasn't Nate's rifle and said he'd never had it in the trailer, but I reckon the cops will be able to determine pretty quick whether or not it is."

Phyllis nodded. Unless the serial numbers had been filed off the rifle, the police would be able to check it against the registration. They could also fire a test bullet from it and compare that to the bullet that killed Barney McCrory, as well as check the gun for fingerprints and any other forensic evidence.

The problem there was that Nate had never denied owning a rifle. If the weapon found in the travel trailer was his, of course his fingerprints would be on it.

And though that won't prove anything, it won't look good to a jury, either, Phyllis thought. If she could sense the metaphorical noose tightening inexorably around Nate's neck, then Allyson surely could, too.

Carolyn reached out to take the overnight bag from Sam. She said, "I'll take this up to the spare bedroom. I suppose we should just leave her be for a while and let her sort things out for herself."

Phyllis nodded and said, "That's probably a good idea. Supper will be ready soon, Sam. Do you think she'll feel like eating?"

"I don't know," Sam said with a shake of his head. "I reckon we'll just have to wait and see."

"She should go ahead and eat," Carolyn said. "No problem is so bad that a good meal won't help it a little."

Phyllis felt the same way, although she wasn't sure that was always true. Some things probably were so bad that even good comfort food wouldn't make them better.

"We'll eat here in the kitchen," she decided. "That's more homey, and it's what we'd usually do if we didn't have a guest. I want Allyson to feel like she's welcome here and can stay as long as she likes."

"If Jimmy D'Angelo gets Nate out on bail in the mornin', Nate and Ally will want to go home, I'm sure," Sam said.

"Well, whatever they want, however we can help, that's fine."

Once they had supper on the table, Phyllis sent Sam to the living room to fetch Allyson. Of all of them, he was the closest to the young woman, so Phyllis thought he might have the best chance of convincing her to eat.

Meanwhile, Carolyn brought in an extra chair from the dining room. The kitchen table was big enough for more than four chairs, but normally that was all they had arranged around it.

Sam came back from the living room with Allyson. She was dry-eyed now, and the redness had faded a little. Her face still revealed the strain she was under, though.

"I'm afraid I don't have much of an appetite," she said. "I don't know how much I can eat."

"Well, whatever you can manage is fine," Phyllis assured her. "Just eat however much you'd like."

They all sat down, Phyllis and Sam on the side with two chairs, Allyson across from them, and Carolyn and Eve at the ends. Allyson summoned a weak smile and said, "Everything looks really good."

"Well, dig in," Sam told her. "It never hurts to keep your strength up."

There were bowls of the hot, creamy potato soup at each setting, with a small ham slider on the side of the plate beside the bowl.

Once Allyson started eating, her appetite seemed to improve. Phyllis had seen that happen before. No matter what sort of turmoil was going on in a person's brain, the body craved sustenance. And most of the time it was a good idea to listen to what your body was trying to tell you.

After a while, Allyson smiled again, and the expression seemed more genuine this time.

"I like this," she said as she looked around

the table. "It almost feels like I'm visiting my grandparents' house."

Phyllis let the comment pass, even though she thought that she and her friends weren't quite old enough to have a granddaughter Allyson's age. Or maybe we are, she told herself. It had gotten to the point where it was difficult to keep up with such things. Anyway, she was just glad that Allyson was feeling more comfortable now.

"What does everyone have planned for the evening?" Carolyn asked.

"*White Christmas* is on TV," Eve said. "It's been several years since I've seen it, so I wouldn't mind watching it again."

"Is that a movie?" Allyson asked.

Sam gazed across the table at her in disbelief and said, "You've never seen *White Christmas*?"

"I don't think so, no."

"Well, we'll have to do somethin' about that gap in your cultural education. I'm not the biggest fan of musicals in the world, mind you, but I like this one. Anyway, it's almost a war movie for a few minutes at the beginnin'."

Phyllis said, "Dessert first." She got the plastic container with the last of the candy cane cupcakes in it, opened it, and set it on the table so everyone could help themselves.

Carolyn looked like she was about to say something, and Phyllis was worried that it might be about how one of the cupcakes was the last thing Barney McCrory had eaten, or how she and Nate had eaten them the last time they were there before he was arrested. Phyllis caught Carolyn's eye and gave her a warning frown. Allyson didn't need to be reminded of that. Phyllis hadn't thought about it until she'd put the cupcakes on the table, and then it was too late to do anything about it without calling attention to that uncomfortable fact.

Allyson didn't seem to think anything about it. She took one of the cupcakes, ate it, and said, "That was really good."

"Thank you. I was pleased with the way they turned out."

Sam said, "Well, there's one left, and if nobody else is gonna eat it . . ."

Phyllis laughed and said, "Help yourself."

"I can give you a hand cleaning up," Allyson offered.

"Oh, no. That's not necessary. You're a guest —"

"I'd like to — really. You've all been so friendly to me. I — I just don't know what I would have done without you."

"All right, then," Phyllis said, smiling. "But it's not much trouble. I just have to load the dishwasher."

"Well, then, I'll give you a hand with that."

It was nice working side by side with the younger woman, Phyllis discovered, almost like having a daughter. She still wasn't ready to look on Allyson as a granddaughter. When they had finished up, they went to the living room and found that Sam, Carolyn, and Eve already had the big-screen TV on.

"Movie's about to start," Sam said. He patted the sofa beside him. "Have a seat and enjoy."

Allyson sat on one side of him; Phyllis on the other. As the movie got underway, Allyson said, "I've heard the song 'White Christmas,' of course, but I didn't know it came from a movie."

"Actually, it made its debut in another Bing Crosby movie called *Holiday Inn* —"

"Don't get him started," Carolyn said. "He's like a living DVD commentary."

"All right," Sam said, chuckling. "I'll shut up and let everybody watch the movie."

Bing Crosby and Danny Kaye as GIs had just started to sing a touching song to their hard-nosed but tenderhearted general when the doorbell rang. Phyllis stiffened.

Some instinct warned her this unexpected caller might not be welcome.

Sam muted the TV and got up hastily.

"Let me get it," he said. "Could be those reporters again."

That was what Phyllis was afraid of. She followed Sam to the door, ready to read the riot act to Felicity Prosper and her companions if she had to.

But it wasn't Felicity who stood there when Sam opened the door. It was Jimmy D'Angelo, and, from the look on the lawyer's face, he didn't come bearing good news.

On the TV, artillery shells began to rain down on Bing, Danny, and the rest of the cinematic dogfaces.

Chapter 18

"Sorry to bother you folks this late," D'Angelo said.

"It's no bother," Phyllis told him. "Come on in."

D'Angelo stepped into the foyer. Sam closed the door behind him. The lawyer wore an overcoat, and Sam said, "Let me take that for you."

"Thanks," D'Angelo said as he shrugged out of the coat.

Allyson could see through the arched opening between the living room and the foyer. She was on her feet, and even though she had seemed to relax earlier, she was stiff as a board again now. The tension drew her features taut as she asked, "What is it, Mr. D'Angelo?"

D'Angelo came into the living room, with Phyllis and Sam following him. He said, "I hear you had a visit from the cops again."

"I should have called you, shouldn't I?"

"Yeah, but don't worry about that," D'Angelo told her. "There was nothing I could have done to stop Largo from serving you that search warrant."

"How do you know about it?" Phyllis asked.

"I stopped by the police station to check on Nate. Since his bail hearing is in the morning, they're still holding him there instead of transferring him to the county jail. I ran into Detective Largo, and she seemed to think I knew about the second search and what they found. I guess she thought you'd called me and told me about it. I played along with her and let her spill however much she wanted to spill."

"So, you know about the rifle," Allyson said.

"Yeah. You're sure there's no reason — no innocent reason, I mean — why Nate would have stashed it in that camper?"

"None I can think of. Like I told the detective, I don't think he ever had it out there."

Phyllis asked, "Do you know if they found out anything from it?"

"Not for sure," D'Angelo said. "Largo seemed pretty pleased with herself, though. If I had to guess, the serial numbers match up, they found Nate's prints on the rifle and nobody else's, *and* they got a ballistics match with the, ah, other bullet."

"The bullet that killed my father," Allyson said grimly.

"Well, yeah. But look, I don't know any of that for sure." D'Angelo sighed. "I've talked to a lot of cops, though, and I'd say Largo was acting like one who had just wrapped up a big case. Like she had dotted all the *i*'s and crossed all the *t*'s."

Allyson stood there with a bleak look on her face for a moment, then asked, "What do we do now?"

"Same as before," D'Angelo said. "We concentrate on the bail hearing in the morning and getting Nate out of jail. Then we keep working on his defense. They'll have to turn over all their evidence to me before the case goes to the grand jury."

"How long do you think it'll take for that?" Phyllis asked.

"It'll be after the first of the year," D'Angelo admitted.

Allyson said, "So he'll have that murder charge hanging over him until then. Merry Christmas. Happy holidays."

Phyllis didn't blame her for sounding bitter. Maybe it wouldn't be as bad as what Allyson expected, though.

For one thing, Phyllis was far from giving

up on discovering who had killed Barney McCrory. In fact, she thought, Sam and I are just getting started.

"Do I need to be there for the hearing in the morning?" Allyson went on.

"It can't hurt for the judge to see Nate's wife waiting for him," D'Angelo replied. "I may need to call you to testify that he's not a flight risk, too."

"All right. Whatever needs to be done, I'll do it."

D'Angelo looked at Sam and asked, "Can you be there, too, Mr. Fletcher? To serve as a character witness, if need be?"

"Sure," Sam said without hesitation. "Anything I can do to help, I'm willin'."

"Very good. Allyson, try to get some sleep. I know it may not be easy, but try."

D'Angelo said good night and left. Allyson glanced at the TV, where Bing and Danny were watching Rosemary Clooney and Vera-Ellen perform in some glitzy postwar nightclub. She said, "I'm sorry, Coach, but I don't think I feel like watching any more of the movie."

"Don't worry about that," Sam told her. "You can watch it some better time. It's on a lot around Christmas."

"I'm afraid it's not going to be much of a holiday season for Nate and me."

"Don't give up." Sam glanced at Phyllis, who wished she could look more reassuring. "You might be surprised."

"I think I'd like to just go up to my room now, if that's all right."

"Of course it is," Phyllis said.

As she ushered Allyson out of the room and toward the stairs, she glanced back at Sam, Carolyn, and Eve. The two women looked sympathetic, but Sam wore an angry, determined expression. Phyllis had a hunch he was feeling the same thing she was.

They had a killer to find.

Unfortunately, by the time she got up the next morning, Phyllis had no real idea how to go about doing that. Her optimism and determination from the night before had faded somewhat.

But she had to start somewhere. One place she hadn't visited yet was Nate's office. Over breakfast, she found out from Allyson exactly where it was.

Allyson was picking at a bowl of oatmeal. The dark circles under her eyes were silent testimony to the fact that she hadn't slept much. She asked Phyllis, "What are you going to do?"

"I just want to take a look at the place," Phyllis explained. She didn't go into detail about how she wanted to check the line of sight from the window and make sure it would have been possible for Nate to line up the shot that had killed his father-in-law.

Allyson was smart enough that she might have guessed that anyway. She said, "You'll need a key. I'll give you mine."

"I can go with you to the bond hearing, if you'd rather I do that."

Allyson shook her head.

"There's really nothing you can do there. You don't have any history with Nate, so you can't be a character witness for him like Coach can."

Sam nodded and said, "I can vouch for the boy's character, that's for sure."

"I'd rather have you out looking for something to clear his name," Allyson added to Phyllis.

"That's exactly what I'm going to do," she said.

She just hoped she didn't find more evidence pointing to Nate as Barney McCrory's killer.

The weather remained chilly, but the overcast of the day before had gone away. The sky was mostly clear this morning, with a brisk wind out of the north, as Phyllis parked on the square and walked toward the Cranmoor Building.

Like most of the buildings on the square, it was old, dating back more than a hundred years. Its exterior had been refurbished a number of times during its existence, so it didn't look as old as it really was. Since it was close to the courthouse, most of the offices were rented by legal firms, bail bondsmen, and the like, although there were also some accountants, financial managers, and other professionals who had offices there.

The lobby was small but ornate, with several potted palms and a lot of gilt trim. The floor was smooth tile. Hallways led off to both sides. As she came through the entrance, directly in front of Phyllis was an old-fashioned cage-style elevator. She was sure it was safe enough, but the broad tile staircase with a gleaming, carved wooden banister was more appealing to her. She had never cared much for riding in elevators. A little touch of claustrophobia, perhaps.

She had just started toward the stairs when the elevator cage descended from the second floor and stopped. The door with its metal grate slid back, and Detective Isabel Largo stepped out. She and Phyllis both stopped short at the sight of each other.

The startled pause lasted only a second. Then Isabel smiled, nodded, and said, "Mrs. Newsom."

"Detective," Phyllis said.

"I'd ask what you're doing here, but I'm pretty sure I know. It's the same reason Mr. Fletcher was with Allyson Hollingsworth yesterday afternoon, isn't it?"

"If you mean we feel sorry for that poor girl and her husband and want to help them, then you're right."

"I mean you're investigating the McCrory case," Isabel said. "As for your sympathy, I think you're wasting it, at least where Hollingsworth is concerned."

"Because he's a murderer?"

"That's what the evidence indicates," Isabel replied coolly.

D'Angelo had been right: The detective carried herself as if the case against Nate were sewed up tight. Phyllis didn't want to believe that.

"Why don't I ask you what *you're* doing here," she said.

"No reason not to tell you," Isabel replied with a shrug. "I was just unsealing Hollingsworth's office and taking a last look around. All the investigators have finished their work here."

"So it's not considered a crime scene anymore?"

"I didn't say that."

And she wouldn't say anything about what

the forensics investigators had found, either, Phyllis knew. Isabel was too good a cop for that.

"Talked to Mike lately?" Phyllis asked instead. She tried to keep her voice neutral and casual, but she wasn't sure she'd succeeded entirely.

"It's been a few days."

"I saw him day before yesterday. I need to find out what plans he and Sarah and Bobby have for the holidays. This is a wonderful time of year when you have small children. Quite busy, though."

"I know. I have a son, too, remember?" Isabel paused. "And you don't need to remind me that your son is happily married, Mrs. Newsom. Mike and I are just friends. I have no intention of breaking up his marriage. I *like* Sarah."

"That's not what I meant —," Phyllis began.

Isabel motioned with her head toward the second floor and asked, "Are you going up to Hollingsworth's office?"

"I have his wife's permission," Phyllis said. "Allyson gave me her key."

"Yes, I suppose she's at the hearing right now, isn't she? Did she send you to fetch something, or are you hoping to find evidence that will prove Nate Hollingsworth's innocence? Because you're going to be disappointed if you are."

Phyllis didn't answer the detective's questions. Instead she said, "If the office isn't sealed, there's no reason I can't go in, is there?"

"No reason at all," Isabel said with an annoying, condescending smile. "Help yourself."

Phyllis nodded again, a little more curtly this time, and started up the stairs. She glanced over her shoulder as Detective Largo walked out of the Cranmoor Building.

She told herself she shouldn't be angry with Isabel. The detective was just doing her job. She didn't know any of the people involved in this case. She was an objective observer, just going by the evidence.

And as far as Isabel was concerned, the evidence clearly said that Nate Hollingsworth had killed his father-in-law.

Phyllis reached the second floor and went along the hall to Suite 208. The door had a frosted-glass upper panel with no writing on it, only the numbers to indicate that it was the right one. There was no crime-scene tape on the door, so Phyllis unlocked it and went in.

The outer office, which Nate didn't even

use, according to Allyson, was small and unostentatious. The door to the inner office wasn't locked. Phyllis stepped in, turned on the lights, and saw that the place had a comfortable look to it. There was a desk with a swivel chair behind it, a couple of leather armchairs in front of it, a computer workstation, a couple of low file cabinets, and a love seat. One wall had built-in bookshelves on it, but they were only about half-full of books. The rest of the space was taken up by a number of framed photographs, mostly of Allyson, but also some of Nate and Allyson together. There were even a few with Nate, Allyson, and Barney McCrory in them.

The office was on a corner, so there were two windows on adjoining walls, built that way for ventilation in the days before air-conditioning. Phyllis went to the one that overlooked the square. She pushed back the curtains and raised the venetian blinds to make the view even better.

She could see a little of the courthouse and most of the lawn on the near side of that distinguished edifice. Looking past the courthouse, she had a good view of Main Street stretching off to the south. The Christmas parade had been coming straight in this direction, Phyllis saw.

From here it would have been easy for an excellent marksman to shoot Barney McCrory. The line of sight was perfect. The only real challenge would have been the distance.

Phyllis's heart sank a little. If the rifle found in the travel trailer was Nate's, if the test bullet fired from that gun matched the one that killed McCrory, and if the forensics crew had found any evidence in this room to indicate that a gun had been fired here, then it was easy to see why Detective Largo would be so smug. With the testimony of the ranch hands, along with Nate's own admission that he and his father-in-law had argued, to provide motive, it was no stretch to think that any jury would convict him of murder.

Against that, Phyllis and Sam had only a vague theory that maybe the killer's real target had been Clay Loomis. Proving that was going to be next to impossible, especially since Phyllis didn't see any way of getting closer to Loomis to probe into his life. Sam had already checked out Gene Coyle. It seemed unlikely that Loomis's partners or his estranged wife and mistress would be willing to answer questions.

For the first time since this whole bizarre crime-solving thing had been thrust upon her, Phyllis was completely at a loss how to proceed.

Out of habit, she looked around the office, but found nothing that looked like it would be helpful; only paperwork related to running the business end of McCrory's ranching operation. The books on the shelves were a mixture of popular novels, self-help books, and volumes on business strategies. Nate had an MBA, Phyllis recalled. Nothing unusual there.

She even checked the office's closet and bathroom and drew a blank in those places as well. Phyllis had always thought of herself as determined and persistent rather than stubborn, but she knew when she was beating her head against a brick wall and not getting anywhere.

She left the office, locking it behind her, and went back down the elegant staircase.

Felicity Prosper, the intern Josh Green, and Nick the cameraman were waiting in the lobby.

Seeing them came as no surprise to Phyllis. She had been expecting Felicity to pop up again at any time, like the proverbial bad penny.

But Phyllis *was* surprised that she wasn't upset to see the young tabloid-TV reporter. The sight of Felicity standing there with an eager expression on her face had made an idea form in Phyllis's brain.

Phyllis strode toward the trio. Like it or not, maybe it was time for her to make a deal with the devil.

Chapter 19

"I'm with Phyllis Newsom," Felicity said into her microphone before Phyllis had a chance to speak, "and don't let her appearance fool you. She's not some kindly grandmother. She's a killer's worst nightmare."

Phyllis could have taken offense at that crack about not being a kindly grandmother. She was certainly a grandmother, and she hoped that she was kindly.

But she let it pass. She had more important things on her mind right now.

"We're here in the Cranmoor Building in Weatherford, Texas," Felicity went on, "where murder suspect Nathan Hollingsworth has his office. Let's find out what Mrs. Newsom is doing here. Looking for clues, I expect."

She thrust the microphone at Phyllis. Felicity was clearly waiting for her to say something, so Phyllis cleared her throat and leaned closer to the microphone.

"Um, hello."

Josh Green made a gesture that Phyllis interpreted as meaning she didn't have to talk so loud.

"You were just upstairs in Nathan Hollingsworth's office, weren't you?" Felicity asked.

"That's right."

"You're aware that his bail hearing is underway at this very moment?"

"Yes, and I'm a little surprised you're not there, waiting to get a comment from him."

Felicity smiled and said, "I'd rather talk to you. You're the one who's known as the Elderly Angel of Death —"

"As far as I know, you're the only person who's ever called me that," Phyllis interrupted.

"The woman who seems to have cold-blooded murder following her around," Felicity went on, as if Phyllis hadn't said anything.

Phyllis lowered her voice and said, "Listen, could we talk without the camera and the microphone on?"

"*Inside Beat* never goes off the record. We broadcast the truth, the real, hard-hitting facts. And the fact is, the police have arrested Nathan Hollingsworth for the murder of his own father-in-law, Barney McCrory, and, from what I hear, their case against him is airtight!"

"I don't think it's as conclusive as what you've been led to believe," Phyllis said. "But I'd really like to talk to you privately . . ."

Felicity looked irritated, but she lowered the microphone and nodded to Nick. The red light on the camera went out. Phyllis kept an eye on the man to make sure he didn't surreptitiously turn it back on.

"What's this all about?" Felicity snapped. "Like I told you, I don't do things off the record —"

"Not even to get the inside story?" Phyllis said.

A frown creased Felicity's forehead. She said, "What are you talking about?"

"Nate Hollingsworth didn't kill his father-in-law, and I'm going to prove it. How would you like to be there for every step of the investigation from this point on? I'm talking about more than just an eight-minute feature on your show. You could get a full-length documentary out of this."

Phyllis saw the interest spark to life in Felicity's eyes. She tried to keep her expression and voice neutral, though, as she said, "Do you mean my crew and I could go along with you while you're interrogating suspects?"

"More than that. You can *help* in the interrogations."

Felicity shook her head and said, "I don't understand. How would that work?"

"You'll be interviewing the suspects. Everyone likes to be on TV." That isn't strictly true, Phyllis thought, but most people won't turn down the chance to be a celebrity, even a temporary one. "But I can tell you what to ask them, and I'll be there to hear their answers."

Felicity's lip curled in a sneer.

"I have my own journalistic instincts," she said. "I don't need anybody to tell me what questions to ask."

"I'm sure that's true, but I know the case. I'm just talking about steering you in the right direction."

Phyllis could tell that Felicity was considering the idea. However, the young woman didn't want to give up any control. Phyllis would have to make Felicity believe that she was still running the show.

Josh spoke up, saying, "Felicity, before you can agree to something like this, you'd have to check with the producers first —"

"Shut up, Josh. I'm the biggest personality on that show."

"But Spencer's still the host —"

"Spencer's a has-been! Everybody knows

that. I'll be in the anchor chair before another six months has gone by. Everyone says so."

Josh sighed and said, "Okay. It's your decision."

"Damned right it is." Felicity's eyes narrowed in thought. "I can see it now . . . An *Inside Beat Special Edition with Felicity Prosper: Murder in Texas.*"

"That's kind of a generic title —"

"How do you think you get big ratings? You have to give people something they can grasp easily! What's easier than *murder* and *Texas*?"

"That's true," Josh admitted.

Felicity swung back toward Phyllis and said, "You have to give me your word you won't hold out on me. I want the whole story, and I want it exclusively."

"That's what I had in mind," Phyllis said, nodding.

"How close are you to nabbing the killer?"

"Not that close, I'm afraid."

"Good! We don't want the viewer to feel cheated. You're sure Hollingsworth is innocent?"

"I'm positive of it," Phyllis declared.

"All right. How do we prove it?"

Felicity, Josh, and Nick had a computer in

their van, and Felicity was willing to let Phyllis use it in return for an explanation of what she was looking for.

"Each of the county commissioners has a particular precinct within the county where he's responsible for the upkeep of the roads. That's why you sometimes hear them called road commissioners, even though they handle other county-related business as well."

"So?" Felicity asked impatiently. "What does that have to do with murder?"

"There's what they call a precinct barn in each precinct, even though it's not actually a barn. It's the headquarters for that particular commissioner. There's an office, and some metal buildings and sheds where all the road equipment is kept and serviced. There are usually piles of sand and gravel there as well, to be used as needed. People can bring certain items there to be recycled, too." Phyllis saw the frown on Felicity's face deepening, so she pointed to the computer screen and went on. "This is the location of Clay Loomis's precinct barn."

"Loomis," Felicity repeated as her expression cleared a little. "He's the guy who was in Santa's sleigh with McCrory."

"That's right. And nobody loves a TV camera more than a politician."

That brought an actual smile to Felicity's face.

"You want to question Loomis."

"Well, I don't know if he'll be at the barn or not, but at least we can talk to some of the people who work for him."

"Wait a minute," Felicity said as her frown came back. "Loomis couldn't have shot McCrory. I think somebody would have noticed if Santa Claus had a rifle. Anyway, he was *behind* McCrory."

"Exactly. But what if Loomis was the target instead of Mr. McCrory?"

The theory appeared to burst on Felicity like a bomb. Her eyes grew wide, and her jaw sagged for a second before she snapped her mouth shut. She peered intently at Phyllis for a heartbeat longer, then said, "That opens up a whole new area of the case."

"Yes, it does. An area that the police aren't even investigating because they're convinced they already have the killer."

"Yeah, they wouldn't go out of their way to look for anything that would shoot holes in that theory," Felicity muttered.

Josh spoke up, asking, "Why would anybody want to shoot Loomis?"

Phyllis took a deep breath. Sharing the theory she and Sam had come up with was one thing. Giving all the information they had uncovered to Felicity on a silver platter was something else. She had no way of knowing for sure that the reporter would keep everything to herself for the time being. Felicity might go on the air with all their speculation and ruin everything. If they were right, such a revelation would spook the killer and prompt him or her to hide the tracks so well, the truth might never be found.

But at the same time, Phyllis needed these TV people to open doors for her. Felicity and Josh were watching her with avid interest. Nick didn't really seem to care about much of anything other than pointing his camera where Felicity wanted it pointed.

"You have to give me your word you won't broadcast this until I say it's all right."

Felicity scowled and said, "I don't like making promises like that. I won't compromise my journalistic integrity."

As far as Phyllis could see, she had already done that by going to work for a program like *Inside Beat,* but sharing that opinion wouldn't accomplish anything.

"Maybe it'll be all right," Josh said. "I mean, we don't even have a story without Mrs. Newsom's cooperation."

Felicity turned her scowl toward him and said, "Didn't they teach you in journalism school about the adversarial relationship between reporters and the people we cover?"

"Well, yeah, but a little quid pro quo doesn't hurt anything, either."

"You've got the makings of a producer, all right," Felicity said. "You're a weasel." She sighed. "But you may have a point." She turned to Phyllis. "All right, you've got my word. But if my gut tells me you're lying to me or trying to trick me somehow, the deal's off."

"I'm going to be honest with you. That's the only way this will work."

For the next few minutes, Phyllis laid out what she and Sam had discovered about Gene Coyle; Loomis's business partners, J. D. Ridgely and Phil Hedgepeth; his estranged wife, Serita; and his former mistress, Jaycee Fallon. When she was finished, Felicity looked impressed.

"You came up with all that in just a day or two? A couple of old geezers like you?"

"Felicity . . ." Josh said.

"Ah, she doesn't care," Felicity said with a dismissive wave of her hand.

"There are worse things to be called," Phyllis said, thinking of Elderly Angel of Death.

"So, your idea is that one of these people

took a shot at Loomis and hit McCrory by accident," Felicity went on. "That sounds reasonable enough. But if it's true, how did they get their hands on Nate Hollingsworth's rifle?"

The blunt question made Phyllis's heart sink. Mostly because she didn't have an answer for it.

"I don't know," she said honestly. "That's why we have to dig deeper into all of them."

She needed to sit down with Nate and Allyson as soon as she could, too, and go over the theory with them. Maybe they could furnish some connection she was unaware of so far.

"All right, let's start with Loomis," Felicity said. "You're right about politicians and cameras. Can you tell Nick how to find this — what did you call it? — precinct barn?"

Nick grunted and said, "I got a GPS."

"That's all right," Phyllis said. "I can give you directions."

Nick shrugged and settled behind the wheel of the van. Felicity took shotgun, and Phyllis and Josh sat in the back. A few minutes later, they were on their way out of Weatherford.

They followed a farm-to-market road for about ten miles, then turned right onto a smaller county road that wound among farms, ranches, and the occasional small housing development for people who preferred country living. Phyllis could understand the appeal of that, although she had lived in town for so long, she didn't think she could ever be comfortable anywhere else.

Clay Loomis was supposed to be back in his office at Cross Timbers Transport today, Phyllis recalled, but she didn't want to go there. The woman who had replaced Jaycee Fallon as office manager might remember her from her visit with Sam, when they had pretended to be soliciting donations for the Lions Club. If Loomis heard about that, he might be suspicious of her showing up with a TV crew.

"The place we're going is up ahead on the right," she leaned forward and told Nick. "I've been out here before for county cleanup days."

"What's that?" Felicity asked.

"It's when you can bring almost anything you don't want anymore and get rid of it," Phyllis explained. "Old furniture, lumber, appliances that don't work . . . By the time it's over, there are *mountains* of trash out here."

"What in the world do they do with it?"

"I think they load it in Dumpsters and haul it off to use for landfill."

Felicity shook her head and said, "There's just no end to the crazy things you rednecks do, is there?"

Phyllis didn't respond to that. She knew there was no point.

The road veered to the right, where another county road dead-ended into the one they were on. The gate in the high chain-link fence around the commissioner's headquarters was actually on this smaller road. It was open, so Nick turned in and drove across a large, gravel-covered open area toward the metal building where the office was located.

The sheds and storage buildings were to the right and behind the office. The big piles of sand and gravel Phyllis had mentioned were to the left, scattered across the big lot. At one of them, a tractor with a front-end loader attached to it was scooping up gravel and depositing it in the back end of a dump truck.

A couple of pickups with county seals on the doors were parked in front of the office, along with a dark SUV with the letters AAA painted on its door, plus some other writing she couldn't make out. Phyllis wasn't sure what AAA was doing here, but someone could've been having vehicle trouble. A man came out of the office, got into the SUV, and drove off while Nick was parking the TV crew's van.

Another man followed the first one out of the building and started toward one of the pickups. Phyllis recognized him immediately as Clay Loomis.

"That's him," she said quickly. They had caught a break, finding Loomis here, and now they needed to take advantage of it.

"Stay out of the way," Felicity snapped as she opened her door. Sure-footed in her high heels, even on the gravel parking lot, she approached Loomis, with Nick hurrying to catch up with her.

Loomis paused with his hand on the handle of the driver's door and smiled as Felicity came toward him. Most men would smile if they saw a young woman who looked like Felicity, especially one obviously bent on talking to them, Phyllis thought. She and Josh got out of the van and followed.

Phyllis carried a clipboard she had found in the van and kept her head down. Loomis might have seen her and Sam talking to McCrory on the night of the parade, so it was possible he could recognize her. She didn't think that was very likely, but she wanted to blend into the background as best as she could for now, and minimize the chances of that happening.

"Mr. Loomis," Felicity said. "Felicity Prosper from *Inside Beat.* I'm sure you've seen our program."

"As a matter of fact, I have," Loomis replied. He wore jeans, a sheepskin jacket, and expensive snakeskin boots. "What can I do for you, Ms. Prosper?"

"I'd like to ask you some questions," Felicity said, "about the night Barney McCrory was murdered right in front of your eyes."

Chapter 20

Loomis's smile disappeared and was replaced by a solemn expression.

"A terrible, terrible tragedy," he said. "I can't tell you how upset I still am about the whole incident."

"You were playing the part of Santa Claus in the annual Christmas parade on the evening of the murder, is that correct?"

"Yes, I was giving the, ah, real Saint Nick a hand that night," Loomis replied with a half chortle, and shifted emotional gears again without missing a beat. "Filling in for him, you might say, since the old fellow can't be everywhere at once. Now can he, kiddies?"

Loomis smiled into the camera as he said that. Felicity said, "We don't have a lot of children who believe in Santa among our viewers, Mr. Loomis. We specialize in the truth."

Phyllis saw Josh wince at that. She understood the feeling. What was the point in alienating viewers who might have small children in the room? Josh was thinking like a producer, going after the biggest audience possible, Phyllis realized. It could be he was smarter than she had given him credit for at first, when he was toppling off a bicycle in the middle of the street.

"Maybe you can fix it in editing," Phyllis whispered to him. He rolled his eyes and nodded, safely behind Felicity, where she couldn't see him.

Felicity was still talking to Loomis, saying, "Tell me what it felt like when you realized that a man had been violently killed just a few feet away from you."

Loomis still didn't show the least bit of hesitation about answering Felicity's questions — a combination of his politician's thirst for publicity and the natural male urge to keep a pretty girl happy, Phyllis thought. The commissioner spread his hands and said, "Well, at first I didn't even know what was happening, of course. I wasn't aware that my good friend Barney had been shot."

Phyllis made a mental note to ask Allyson and Nate if McCrory and Loomis really *had* been friends. She hadn't gotten any sense of that so far in the investigation.

"All I knew," Loomis went on, "was that

the horses pulling the carriage had stampeded, and we were careening along the street much faster than was safe. I kept shouting for people to get out of our way, and then I tried to see if I could climb up to the driver's seat to get the team under control. I knew I had to keep a cool head in order to prevent a greater disaster."

That was certainly an interesting version of what had happened. Phyllis didn't recall the incident quite that way. To the best of her memory, Loomis had been screaming his head off and clutching those teenage elves as if to shield himself with their bodies.

"Luckily, someone else stopped the horses," Loomis said. Phyllis shifted slightly, keeping Nick's burly shape between her and the politician. She didn't want Loomis's memory jogged enough that he would recognize her. "That was when I had the chance to check on my old friend and saw that he'd been injured."

"He'd been shot," Felicity said. "Murdered."

Loomis sighed and said, "Yes. It was . . . an utterly shocking discovery."

He was solemn again now, trying to look properly sympathetic.

"You're aware that the police have made an arrest in the case?"

"Yes, I heard. It's unbelievable that Barney's own son-in-law would do such a thing."

Loomis's voice had a tone of finality about it, as if he expected that to conclude the interview, but Felicity pressed on without hesitation.

"This is just the latest example of trouble in your life, isn't it, Commissioner Loomis?" she asked briskly.

Loomis's forehead creased in a surprised frown as he said, "What do you mean by that?"

"I mean that your own life has been in turmoil recently, even before you were involved in a murder."

"Wait a minute. I'm not involved in Mr. McCrory's murder. I just happened to be there. I could have been hurt, too, when that team bolted!"

As if he hadn't said anything, Felicity went on. "At the moment, you're defending yourself in three ugly legal disputes, isn't that correct? You're being sued by your own business partners, who say that you've stripped the company coffers of funds and run it into the ground. Your wife has initiated divorce proceedings against you and vowed to take everything you have. And your former mistress has threatened to file a sexual-harassment suit against you, charging that she was pressured into having an affair with you."

The words came out of Felicity's mouth a mile a minute, and she needed to talk fast to get them all out, because Loomis's face was turning a bright red, and it looked like he was going to explode at any second.

When Felicity finally had to pause to draw a breath, Loomis roared, "How dare you! Get off this property right now! You have no right to come here and spew this vile filth, these ugly rumors that have no basis in fact —"

He had to stop short because he was shaking so hard and gasping for air. Phyllis suddenly had the awful thought that he might have a stroke or a heart attack right there in front of them, judging by the way he looked. If Felicity thought the same thing, she would probably just consider it a bonus, a dramatic climax to an act of journalistic ambush.

"All these things are a matter of public record, Commissioner," Felicity said. "You can't deny that your life has been in an uproar. With all this going on, you might think that murder was a welcome diversion from your own woes. In fact, given all the hatred directed at you recently, would you say that you're lucky no one has taken a shot at *you*?"

There it is, Phyllis thought.

Felicity had gotten to the point, and, in doing so, she had worked Loomis up into such a state that he shouted, "None of those idiots would have the guts to come after me like that! Not unless it was that bitch of a wife of mine. She's twice the man that Ridgely and Hedgepeth are!"

"What about Jaycee Fallon?"

"She's a simpering little imbecile. She's got no case. She's the one who came after me —"

He stopped short as he realized he was saying things he shouldn't, especially on camera. He turned toward Nick and made a slashing motion across his throat.

"Stop that," he snapped. "Turn that camera off."

Loomis took a step forward, and Nick began to back away with the camera still on his shoulder, still shooting.

"Commissioner Loomis, are you threatening my cameraman?" Felicity demanded. Phyllis had heard *that* before. "As a public official, you should be familiar with the concept of a free press."

"Just get out of here, all of you," Loomis said in a low, menacing tone.

"I believe this property belongs to the county, which means it's public property. You can't force us to leave."

Loomis still looked like he wanted to attack Nick, but he got himself under control with a visible effort, turned toward the building, and stalked toward the door, saying over his shoulder, "I'm going to call the sheriff!"

The door slammed closed behind him, so violently that it shook in its frame.

Felicity made her own throat-cutting gesture to Nick with one elegantly manicured finger and said, "Let's go."

The four of them went back to the van and climbed in. While Nick was starting the engine, four men came around the corner of the building. Phyllis figured they were county road workers, and from the way they started toward the van, she thought that Loomis must have summoned them. He might have even decided to tell them to try to take the camera away.

"I don't think we should waste any time getting out of here," she said.

"You think I'm scared of those bruisers?" Felicity said. "I'm not scared of them. Are you, Nick?"

As taciturn as ever, Nick just grunted.

"I'm a little nervous," Josh admitted.

"You would be," Felicity scoffed. But Phyllis thought she was starting to look a little worried, too, as Nick leisurely put the van in reverse and backed around to leave. The four men were only about twenty yards away when Nick gave the van some gas and headed for the gate. The road workers stopped and glared after them.

Felicity turned halfway around in the front passenger's seat and grinned at Phyllis.

"What did you think of that?" she asked. "Pretty good job of rattling his cage, wasn't it?"

"He was rattled, all right," Phyllis said, "but I'm not sure we found out anything helpful."

"What are you talking about? He practically pointed the finger at his wife. He said if anybody tried to kill him, it'd be her. What do we know about her?"

"You mean other than the fact that she's divorcing Loomis?"

Felicity rolled her eyes and said, "Josh, I need background. Fast!"

"You bet," Josh said as he took out his phone and started punching buttons. Phyllis tended to forget that people could get on the Internet just as easily on their phones as they could on a computer. She'd been carrying the same cell phone for years, and all it would do was make calls and take pictures.

By the time they were halfway back to Weatherford, Josh said, "Okay, Mrs. Loomis is the former Serita Lopez. Born in Corpus Christi. She and Loomis met while they were students at the University of Texas in Austin. He was a business major; she was premed. Looks like she dropped out to support him and never went back."

"So she gave up being a doctor for him, and then he cheated on her with some bimbo who works for him," Felicity said. "Sounds like a motive for murder to me."

"And she has a concealed-carry license," Josh added. "So she's used to handling guns."

Phyllis said, "How did you find that out?"

"Oh, I just hacked into the state database," Josh said, as if it were the easiest thing in the world.

"Won't that get you in trouble?"

"If it does, *Inside Beat* will foot the bill for his lawyers," Felicity said. "Journalism knows no price."

Reporting on the sleazy antics of rich, pretty people who were famous for no other reason than being famous didn't really strike Phyllis as journalism, but she wasn't going to argue. Not while Felicity and the others were trying to help her clear Nate's name by finding Barney McCrory's murderer.

"I can't get into the ATF database to find out if Mr. or Mrs. Loomis has a rifle registered to them," Josh said. "After all the uproar about data leaks over the past few years, they've gotten harder to crack. And with all the surveillance they've got going on, if I try, they'll track it right back to me."

"Mr. D'Angelo might be able to find out," Phyllis said. "He has a friend who works for the ATF."

"The guy better be careful. He'll get hauled off to some NSA black site and never be heard from again."

Phyllis wasn't quite sure what that meant, but it couldn't be anything good.

Felicity said, "See what you can find on Loomis's business partners, Ridgely and Hedgepeth."

"I've looked them up already —," Phyllis began.

"Let Josh take a crack at it, okay? He's got to be good for something, and this is it."

As Felicity turned to face forward again, Josh gave Phyllis a weak smile, as if to tell her he didn't care about the things Felicity said. Phyllis thought he did, though. She had seen the way Josh looked at the reporter when Felicity wasn't paying any attention to him. He had a crush on her, probably because of both her beauty and the fact that she was on-air talent. To a lowly intern fresh out of college, Felicity was close to TV royalty.

At the moment, however, Josh was concentrating on his research, and after a few minutes he said, "Here's something." He held the phone out so Phyllis could see the screen. "The guy on the left is Phil Hedgepeth."

"Oh, dear Lord," Phyllis said as she looked at a newspaper photo of two men in hunting garb, standing next to the carcass of a bear. "They killed that poor animal?"

"Yeah, on a hunting trip to Canada. The other guy is the guide. Hedgepeth's the one who brought down the bear."

Phil Hedgepeth had a big, proud grin on his face. He held a rifle in front of him.

"Let me see," Felicity said from the front seat. She looked at the picture on Josh's phone and went on. "If Hedgepeth can shoot a grizzly bear, he could shoot a person."

"I'm not sure one thing follows the other," Josh said. "And it's a brown bear, not a grizzly —"

"A bear is a bear, okay? I don't care if it's freakin' Yogi or Boo Boo. How about Ridgely?"

Josh went back to work, but after a few minutes he shook his head and said, "Nothing connecting him with hunting or shooting or anything like that. He doesn't seem to be an outdoorsman."

"That leaves Jaycee Fallon. We already know that the other guy who ran against Loomis — what was his name? Coyle? — we already know he's a shooter."

Several more minutes passed before Josh said, "Nothing on Jaycee Fallon, but I've got a Jaycee — spelled the same way — Dobbs in a picture from about fifteen years ago."

"Let me see," Phyllis said.

Josh turned the phone. Phyllis looked at the picture of half a dozen high school cheerleaders. Jaycee Dobbs, according to the caption, was the head cheerleader at the high school in one of the communities outside Weatherford that had its own school district.

"Is that the same person?" Josh asked.

Phyllis cast her mind back to the one photo she had seen of Jaycee Fallon. The hair was the same color, although styled differently, and the faces could be the same as well, taking into account that fifteen years had passed.

"I think it is," she said.

Josh showed the photo to Felicity, who said, "So, she was a cheerleader in high school. That doesn't mean anything. *I* was a cheerleader, in high school and college both, and it didn't turn me into a killer."

"No, of course not," Josh said hastily. "That's just the only thing I've been able to find about her so far."

"Well, go back to Loomis's wife. She's our best suspect. I want to talk to her. Where does she live?"

Phyllis said, "If she's filed for divorce against Loomis, there's a good chance he had to move out of the family home and she's still living there. That's usually the way things work."

"Yeah, it is," Josh agreed. "I'll see if I can find Loomis's address."

That didn't seem to take any time at all. A few minutes later, Josh gave Nick an address, then asked Phyllis, "Do you know where that is?"

"No, I'm afraid I don't recognize that street name."

" 'S okay," Nick said. "I got a GPS."

CHAPTER 21

Clay Loomis's house was located on Lake Weatherford, northeast of town. Years of prolonged drought, plus the exploding population of the area and the resulting increase in demand for water, meant that the lake was not what it used to be. It stayed at a lower level than it was when Phyllis and Kenny would bring Mike out here as a little boy. Now it was primarily a reservoir and not a recreational destination.

But there were still areas where the lake and the hills that surrounded it were quite pretty, and the houses in those areas were large and expensive. Clay Loomis's home was one such house, an oddly cantilevered structure that stuck up out of the trees at eye-catching angles as it sat on a hill overlooking the water.

A black iron fence surrounded the property, and the gate had a speaker and keypad attached to a pole that stuck out by the driveway. Since none of them knew the code to open the gate, Nick had to punch the call button on the keypad.

A minute or so later, a woman's voice asked over the speaker, "Yes?"

Felicity leaned toward the driver's side of the van so the camera mounted on the speaker could see her past Nick. She said, "Hi, I'm Felicity Prosper from the TV show *Inside Beat* —"

That was as far as she got before a squeal of recognition came from the speaker.

"Oooh, I know who you are!" the woman exclaimed. "I watch you all the time!"

Felicity put a dazzling smile on her face as she said, "We'd like to speak to Serita Loomis."

"That's me! That's me! I'll open the gate. Come on up. Just follow the driveway and I'll meet you in front of the house."

With a low rumbling sound, the two halves of the gate began to swing back. When they were far enough apart, Nick eased the van through the opening and followed the asphalt driveway as it wound uphill through the trees.

"She didn't even ask you what you wanted to talk to her about," Phyllis said to Felicity.

"It doesn't matter. It's TV. And she's going to be on it."

The driveway leveled out and turned into a circle drive in front of the house. Serita Loomis stood just outside the front door, wearing pastel blue sweats. Her long dark hair was pulled into a ponytail that dangled far down her back. She was a petite woman, and even in the casual getup she was very attractive.

She hurried down a short flagstone walk to greet the visitors as they got out of the van.

"I can't believe it," she said. "Felicity Prosper at *my* house. I've always thought that you should be the lead anchor instead of Spencer, you know."

"From your mouth to the executive producer's ear," Felicity said with a smile.

"But what are you *doing* here? Why do you want to talk to me?"

"Actually, it's about your husband —"

Serita's gushing attitude disappeared in an instant. She said, "That lying, cheating, no-good — Wait a minute. Are you here to do an exposé about him? Are you doing a story on corrupt small-town politicians? Because Clay is the poster boy for that, let me tell you!"

"Maybe we could go inside and talk," Felicity suggested.

"Yeah, sure. I wish I'd known you were

coming. I could have fixed the place up. I could have fixed *myself* up!"

"Oh, I'm sure that's not necessary," Felicity said. "You look gorgeous."

"Oh, I do *not*! But it's so nice of you to say. Come on in, Ms. Prosper — you and your assistants."

"Call me Felicity."

"Can I? That's so . . . I mean, I just can't *believe* it! You're actually here!"

As they followed Serita into the house, Phyllis thought about what Josh had found out about her. This woman had been in the premed program? She had planned to become a doctor? And now she was prattling on with excitement because a reporter from a tabloid TV show had come to talk to her? Being all . . . What was the term Sam might have used? Being all fan-girl-y over a minor TV personality?

Clearly, years of being married to Clay Loomis had changed Serita.

The house was as eccentric on the inside as it was on the outside. The Loomises had probably hired some trendy decorator who was more concerned about feng shui than about comfort. But the sofa that Phyllis and Josh sat on wasn't too bad. Felicity and Serita perched on angular chairs that looked like they'd be easy to fall off of. Nick stayed on his feet, with the camera in its usual position on his shoulder.

One wall of the room where they sat was mostly glass. In summer, the view down over the lake would probably be spectacular, but right now, with the trees bare because of the season, it was a little bleak.

Phyllis looked around the room for a Christmas tree or other decorations but didn't see any. Either Serita hadn't gotten around to putting them up yet, or else she wasn't much on celebrating the holiday. It seemed like fewer and fewer people really cared about Christmas nowadays.

"All right," Serita said as she leaned forward eagerly. "What do you want to know about Clay?"

"The two of you are getting a divorce, is that correct?" Felicity asked.

"That's right." Serita didn't appear to wonder how Felicity had found out about that. "He cheated on me."

"With a woman who works at his company, isn't that right?"

"Jaycee." Contempt dripped from Serita's voice as she said the name. Her lip curled in a sneer. "A little blond piece of trailer trash." Serita shook her head. "But she doesn't work at the company anymore. She quit when she found out what a scumbag

Clay really is. And she probably realized that with all the trouble he has going on, he's not going to be able to afford to be the sort of sugar daddy she was looking for."

Phyllis hadn't heard anybody use the term *sugar daddy* in a long time. She was especially surprised to hear it from someone as young as Serita. Of course, Serita couldn't be as young as she appeared, considering when she and Clay Loomis had been in college. There was a good chance she'd had some work done over the years to preserve her youth.

"Tell me more about that trouble," Felicity said in a voice that invited Serita to confide in her.

"Well, there's the lawsuit, of course. The one that J.D. and Phil have filed against him. They're his partners in Cross Timbers Transport. I guess something must have happened to make them suspicious of Clay, because they brought in an independent accountant to audit the company's books, and he found that the company doesn't have nearly as much money as it ought to. Clay couldn't really account for that. He tried to sell them some story about how the economy has been bad —"

"The economy *has* been bad," Felicity put in.

"Well, yeah, sure, but not bad enough to account for all the money that was gone. If you ask me" — Serita lowered her voice to a conspiratorial tone — "I think he's got it stashed somewhere in an overseas bank. In the Cayman Islands or somewhere. He just doesn't want any of the rest of us to get our hands on any of it."

"That must make you really angry, when you think about all the things your husband has done."

"Angry?" Serita repeated. "*Angry?* When I found out he was cheating on me, I wanted to kill him!"

Felicity smiled and said, "I'm sure that's just a figure of speech."

"I don't know," Serita said slowly. "I guess, yeah, I wouldn't really try to hurt him, but with all the people he's crossed, Clay's lucky nobody's taken a shot at him. You know" — Serita leaned forward and poked holes in the air with an index finger — "when I heard about what happened the other night at the parade, how that poor man got shot, I mean, one of the first things I thought was that I wondered if whoever shot him was aiming at Clay instead!"

"Really?" Felicity murmured.

"Yeah." Serita laughed. "I was a little surprised the cops didn't come around, asking me where I was that night. Not that I could have done something like that. That poor man was shot with a rifle, wasn't he?"

"I believe he was," Felicity said.

"Well, I've never shot a rifle in my life. I have a little pistol that I carry in my purse, but that's all. I admit, there were times when I thought about what it would feel like to shoot Clay, after everything he's done, but I'd have to get really close to do that."

"Because of your aim, you mean?"

"No," Serita said. "If I were going to do it, I'd want to be close enough to see the look in his eyes when I pulled the trigger."

There didn't seem to be much else that Serita could tell them, so when she offered them something to drink, Phyllis caught Felicity's eye and gave a tiny shake of her head. Felicity made their excuses, saying they had to get back to process some footage, whatever that meant. It worked on Serita.

"When will this air?" she asked breathlessly. "I'll want to tell all my friends about it so they can watch."

"I'll have to get in touch with you so I can let you know," Felicity said. She took out her phone. "Give me your number."

She put Serita's number into her phone, then got up and led the way to the door. Serita followed them outside, still gushing, and was standing there with a huge smile on her face when they drove off.

"Good Lord, what a shallow woman," Felicity said as they reached the bottom of the hill. The gate was open again so they could get out. "But I have to admit, she has good taste."

Phyllis didn't know if she meant because of the house or because Serita was a fan. Either way, it wasn't important.

Josh said, "Well, we know she can't be the murderer, anyway."

"How do we know that?" Phyllis and Felicity asked at the same time. Phyllis wasn't sure she liked the idea that her mind worked the same as the reporter's.

Josh frowned and said, "She brought it up herself. I mean, the idea that the killer was really aiming at her husband instead of Mr. McCrory. She wouldn't just drop that theory on us like that if she had done it, would she?"

"She might if she were clever enough," Felicity said. "She might be trying to make us think she's some airheaded trophy wife instead of a diabolical killer. Although she can't really be considered a trophy wife —

can she? — since it's the first marriage for both of them? Isn't that right, Josh?"

"Uh, yeah, they got married while they were in college. I didn't see any record of either of them being married to anybody else."

Phyllis said, "I'm not sure she's devious enough to try to divert suspicion that way. I think she was telling us the truth."

"My instinct says she was, too," Felicity agreed. "I was just playing devil's advocate. So where does that leave us now?"

"We should probably talk to Gene Coyle and Phil Hedgepeth. We know both of them are marksmen."

Phyllis's phone rang before she could say anything else. She looked at the display and said, "It's Sam."

When she answered, he said, "Well, the bail hearin' is over. I wasn't sure the judge was gonna even grant bail, but in the end he did. Half a million bucks."

Phyllis gasped.

"Was Nate able to arrange that?" she asked.

"Yeah, Jimmy knows a bail bondsman who was willin' to post it."

"Where are they now?"

"Back at your house for the time bein'. Ally wanted to come by to get her things, and Carolyn convinced ’em to stay for lunch. Where are you?”

Phyllis glanced at her companions and said, “You might not believe me if I told you. But warn Carolyn that there are going to be three more guests for lunch.”

Felicity looked at her and cocked an eyebrow.

“We’ll be there in a little while,” Phyllis went on. “I want to have a talk with Nate and Allyson.”

“Shouldn’t be any trouble keepin’ them here for that. Both of ’em are pretty down in the dumps, as you’d expect. If there’s anything you can tell ’em that might give them some hope . . .”

“I don’t know yet,” Phyllis said. “There’s something — some connection I’m not quite seeing. But we’ll talk about that in a little while, when I get back.”

“I don’t suppose you want to give a hint who these three mysterious guests you’re bringin’ to lunch might be.”

“We’ll let it be a surprise,” Phyllis said.

Judging by the expressions on the faces of everyone in the living room, it certainly *was* a surprise when Phyllis walked in with Felicity, Josh, and Nick.

Allyson had been sitting on the sofa with

Nate, holding his hand, but she leaped to her feet at the sight of the TV people.

"You!" she said as she glared at Felicity. "What are *you* doing here?" She switched her gaze to Phyllis and asked in disbelief, "Mrs. Newsom, you brought them here?"

"Miss Prosper and I have come to an agreement," Phyllis said, keeping her voice calm and level. "She and her friends are trying to help me find the real killer and clear Nate's name."

"It's going to take more than a TV show to do that," Nate said dispiritedly. "The cops think they've got the goods on me. And, to tell you the truth, if I didn't know better, I might think they were right."

"Don't say that, Nate," Allyson said.

"With all the evidence they have, a person'd have to be crazy to think I'm innocent."

"I suppose I'm crazy, then," Phyllis said, "because I don't believe that you killed your father-in-law. I don't think poor Mr. McCrory was even the target."

Carolyn came in from the dining room and said, "Crime solving will have to wait. I have lunch on the table."

They all filed into the dining room, Nate and Allyson with obvious reluctance. After the past twenty-four hours, it was understandable that neither of them had much of an appetite. Carolyn was determined that everyone should eat, though, and the food certainly looked good. She had made spaghetti and meatballs and served it with hot garlic bread.

Josh seemed to enjoy the meal more than any of the other guests. After washing down a bite of garlic bread with a long swallow of iced tea, he said, "This reminds me of being at my grandparents' house."

"We seem to provoke that reaction," Phyllis said dryly. "Where did you grow up, Josh?"

"In Fort Worth, but my grandparents lived in Brownwood. We went down there a lot when I was a kid. They've both passed away now, but I sure remember all those times."

"Everybody needs a couple of good sets of grandparents growin' up," Sam said. "That gives people a sense of bein' connected to history. All four of my grandparents, for example, were born in the 1870s."

"Wait a minute," Felicity said. "That's nearly a hundred and fifty years ago. Frontier days. How is that even possible?"

"I was born durin' World War II. That probably seems pretty prehistoric to you, young lady."

Felicity just made a scoffing sound.

"I taught history," Phyllis said. "Most people don't really grasp just how close we are to the events of the past. While Sam and Carolyn and Eve and I were young, there were a number of Civil War veterans still living as well. I remember some of the old-timers who came into town for First Monday when I was a child. It's entirely possible that some of them could have fought at Bull Run or Gettysburg."

Josh looked interested, but Felicity's eyes were starting to glaze over with boredom. All of Nick's attention was focused on the plate of food in front of him.

"Why don't we get back to the subject of murder?" Felicity suggested.

"Over lunch?" Carolyn sounded horrified.

Felicity nodded toward Nate and said, "Hey, the sooner this guy gets rid of that cloud hanging over him, the better, right?"

Allyson said, "I still can't believe you're trying to help us. Why would you want to?"

"Because of the story, of course. A guy murders his father-in-law — it's a good story." Felicity held up a hand to forestall Allyson's angry protest and went on. "A guy is accused of murdering his father-in-law but he really didn't — that's an even better story. Especially when you throw politics and corruption and adultery into the mix. Nothing appeals to the public more than sin in high places. Not that a county commissioner in Texas is all that high, you understand, but, hey, it's a place to start. And we've got the notorious crime-busting granny, too."

She gave Phyllis a sweet smile.

Phyllis sighed and said, "Let's just finish lunch. Then, and I know you two are tired of this" — she looked at Nate and Allyson — "we're going into the living room and starting from scratch. Something's missing, and I need to figure out what it is."

CHAPTER 22

The living room was full with Phyllis, Sam, Nate, Allyson, Felicity, and Josh all sitting on the sofa and in various armchairs. Nick, surprisingly, had volunteered to help Carolyn and Eve with cleaning up after lunch. Phyllis thought all the talk of solving murders bored the cameraman.

"Should Mr. D'Angelo be here for this?" Allyson asked with a suspicious glance toward Felicity and Josh. "Can we trust these people?"

"We're not here to cause trouble for you, sweetie," Felicity said. "Mrs. Newsom convinced me to focus on the bigger picture. Pestering you with 'How does it feel to be married to a murderer?' questions gets me a few minutes on the air. Exposing a killer and freeing an innocent man gets me the job of hosting my own special edition of the show."

"So you're just trying to help because it's

in your own self-interest."

"If it keeps your husband out of prison and finds out who really killed your father, what does that matter?"

Allyson sighed and nodded. She said, "You're right, of course." She looked at Phyllis. "What did you want to ask us?"

Phyllis leaned forward in her chair and said, "Nate, tell me about that rifle. Did you ever have it in the travel trailer parked next to your house?"

Nate shook his head.

"No, I wouldn't have any reason to put it out there. We didn't take the rifle with us when we used the trailer for vacations. I kept the rifle, unloaded, in the closet in the guest bedroom. The shells for it were in a drawer in our bedroom."

"You used it for hunting?"

"A few times," Nate said with a shrug. "Barney and I went deer hunting now and then." He swallowed hard, evidently affected by the memories of those times. "And I took it with me out to the ranch to help him chase off some coyotes a while back."

"You didn't ever leave it at the ranch?"

"Not that I recall. I'm pretty sure I didn't."

In a matter of life and death, *pretty sure* might not be good enough, but Phyllis understood what he meant. The rifle hadn't been a focus of his thoughts. He'd had no idea that it would one day become a piece of evidence against him in a murder case.

"Allyson said you took it to a gunsmith to have something done on it recently."

"Well, not that recently. It was a month ago. I could give you the guy's name. I'm sure he'd have a record of it, and that would have the date on it."

"We may need that later, but for now let's concentrate on how you got the gun to him. Did you take it directly from your house to his shop?"

"No, I put it in my SUV and dropped it off at his place after work one day."

"And when you picked it up from him?"

"I took it straight home and put it in the closet, as usual," Nate said.

"Do you know a man named J. D. Ridgely?"

The abrupt switch in subject made Nate frown. He thought for a moment and then shook his head.

"I don't think I've ever heard of him."

"How about Phil Hedgepeth?"

Again Nate thought about it, then said, "Doesn't ring any bells. I don't think I know him."

Allyson asked, "Who are these people, Mrs. Newsom?"

"We'll get to that," Phyllis said. "What about Gene Coyle?"

Nate said, "No, I . . . Wait a minute. That name *is* vaguely familiar for some reason. But I'm pretty sure I've never met the guy, whoever he is."

Phyllis thought that answer made sense. Nate would have seen Coyle's name on campaign signs during election season earlier that fall. The memory was fresh enough that he recognized the name but not the context.

"You know who Clay Loomis is, of course."

"Yeah. Couldn't very well miss hearing about him the past few days," Nate said with a little edge of bitterness in his voice.

"What about his wife, Serita?"

"Never met her." Nate looked at Allyson, who shook her head to indicate that she didn't know Serita, either.

"How about a woman named Jaycee Fallon?"

"Nope."

Allyson said again, "Who are these people? I don't understand this at all, Mrs. Newsom."

"They're people who had a reason to shoot Clay Loomis," Phyllis said.

"Loomis?" Nate repeated, his eyes widening. "I don't understand. It wasn't Loomis who . . ." His eyes got even bigger as what Phyllis was getting at dawned on him. "Oh! You think the killer was really aiming at Loomis instead of Barney, like you talked about before."

"Given what we know, that's the only thing that makes any sense," Phyllis said. "No one else had any reason to kill Mr. McCrory, at least that we've been able to figure out so far, and those people I asked you about all have possible motives for wanting Clay Loomis dead. Some of them are excellent marksmen, too."

"But the police are acting like they have proof my rifle fired the fatal shot," Nate said. "How is that possible?"

Felicity said, "Someone could have broken into your house and stolen it, right? Then put it back in the travel trailer and tipped off the cops that's where it was? They're trying to frame you!"

Nate gave her a dubious frown and said, "I suppose that's possible. We talked about a burglar getting in there and stealing just the gun, so that we didn't notice the house had been broken into, but that's just really far-fetched."

"Unless he broke in specifically to steal the rifle, knowing that he was going to use it to shoot Mr. Loomis," Phyllis said. "Then he would have been careful not to disturb anything else so that you *wouldn't* notice. So you'd think the rifle was still in the closet."

"Which is exactly what I did think," Nate said as he rubbed his chin and frowned in thought.

"But that still doesn't make any sense," Allyson said. "How would any of those people even know that Nate owns a rifle?"

Phyllis sighed and said, "That's why I wanted to talk to the two of you. I thought there might be a connection I'm not seeing, but it's just not there. If you're not acquainted with any of the suspects, none of them would have known about the rifle, and so they couldn't have used it to try to frame you."

Josh said, "Wait a minute. Why not see if we can expand the circle of suspects? Nate, do you know anybody else who might have known about the rifle *and* had a reason to shoot Clay Loomis?"

Felicity looked at him in surprise and said, "That's a pretty good question, intern." She turned to the others and went on. "From what I saw of this Loomis guy, he might have dozens of enemies who'd want him dead. Hey, we only spent fifteen minutes with him, and *I* felt like shooting him!"

Nate just shook his head and looked like he was baffled. He said, "I'm not sure I could tell you who knew I owned a rifle. I haven't been hunting all that much, but I've gone with at least half a dozen guys. Plus I've had the gun out at the ranch, so the hands who work there could have known about it."

Sam asked, "What about those hands? Any of them have a grudge against Barney? Any of 'em been fired recently?"

"No, and I'd know if they'd had, since I handle the payroll. Look, I'm not out there all the time, so I don't know everything that goes on, but Barney was pretty good about telling me if there was any trouble, and there hasn't been. My impression has always been that the men who worked for him were very loyal to him. Sure, he could be loud and get after somebody if they fouled up, but they all respected him."

Allyson nodded and said, "I agree. I'd go so far as to say that most of the hands loved Dad."

Of course, Allyson is prejudiced in favor of her father, Phyllis thought. She would feel that way whether there was any basis in reality for it or not.

Something else occurred to Phyllis, and she said, "You know, all of our thinking about this has hinged on the theory that your rifle was the murder weapon, Nate. But we're not absolutely certain of that. I think we need to find out."

"How do we do that?" Felicity asked.

"Mr. D'Angelo might be able to get the information. The district attorney has to reveal his evidence to defense counsel before the grand-jury hearing." Phyllis paused. "Or perhaps you might be able to find out, Ms. Prosper."

"Me?"

Phyllis smiled slightly and said, "District Attorney Sullivan might respond to a question if you asked it."

"You mean he might like seeing himself on TV?"

"I think he's the sort of man who might appreciate that, yes."

In fact, District Attorney Timothy Sullivan *is* an arrogant, self-satisfied, pompous windbag who once ordered me thrown in jail, Phyllis thought. But she didn't say that. If a stunning female reporter shoved a microphone in his face and asked him a question, he would answer it, all right. And he would try to make himself look as good as possible while he was doing it, too.

Felicity got to her feet and said, "Sounds like a good idea. Want to come with me?"

"No. If Sullivan sees me with you, he won't cooperate. We have some history."

"You mean he doesn't like it that you've made him look like a fool in the past, when he's prosecuted the wrong person," Felicity said with a smile.

"That sums it up pretty well," Phyllis admitted.

"Well, I know how to handle guys like that. Josh, go find Nick."

Josh scrambled to his feet and said, "Yes, ma'am."

"By the time I'm done with him," Felicity purred, "we'll know everything that District Attorney Sullivan does."

Felicity, Josh, and Nick headed over to the courthouse and the district attorney's office. Before they left, however, Phyllis brought out the baklava macarons that had been chilling overnight and passed them around. Everyone exclaimed over how good they were, and Phyllis was quite pleased with them herself.

Allyson gathered the things she had brought with her so she and Nate could go home. While she was doing that, Nate said, "I appreciate everything you've been trying to do for me, Mrs. Newsom, and you, too, Coach. It's starting to look like the deck is just too stacked against me, though."

"I don't believe that," Phyllis said.

"Naw, the case against you is just a house of cards, if you want to throw card playin' in there," Sam added. "We've just got to find the right one and pull it out, and the whole thing'll come tumblin' down."

"I hope you're right," Nate said with a faint smile. Clearly he didn't believe that was going to happen, though.

Once the two of them were gone as well, Phyllis headed upstairs to put the finishing touches on her first draft of the column for *A Taste of Texas.* With everything else that had been going on, it would have been easy to forget about that, so she wanted to seize this opportunity. When she was done, she e-mailed the file to Eve so the former English teacher could proofread it.

Then she gave in to curiosity and checked the true-crime websites that posted things about her and the cases in which she was involved. The furor over Barney McCrory's murder had faded somewhat, she discovered. There were still a few recent comments on the blogs, but Nate's arrest seemed to have diminished the interest. A few people who commented even expressed disappointment that Phyllis hadn't solved this murder.

They are giving up too soon, she thought, but at the same time, she understood the feeling.

As Nate had said, the deck was stacked.

But the antidote to frustration is action, she told herself. Instead of just sitting around waiting to hear from Felicity, maybe there was something else she could do. She went downstairs and found Sam at his workbench in the garage, sanding a piece of wood. She couldn't tell if he meant to build something with it or if he was just passing the time, like she had been.

"Let's go take a look at Loomis's trucking company again," she said.

"What for?" he asked.

"Just a hunch." Really, she needed to be doing something instead of sitting here, spinning her wheels. "He leases trucks to various companies, right?"

"Yeah, that's the way I understand it," Sam said, nodding slowly.

"Maybe we can find out what some of those companies are. That might give us more leads to someone who'd have a grudge against him, and if we could connect that person back to Nate . . ."

A grin spread across Sam's face as he said, "That might be the connection you said was missin'."

"Exactly."

Her restlessness, her need to be out and moving around, had actually led her to come up with an idea that might hold some promise. They already had an abundance of suspects, just not the right ones.

So, the only answer was to keep looking.

Phyllis told Carolyn where they were going; then she and Sam left in his pickup, heading north out of town toward the headquarters of Clay Loomis's company.

The day was sunnier and warmer than the last time they had visited the site, but the place still had a certain bleakness to it. The acres of gravel and rows of trucks just didn't hold much warmth. As they neared the gate in the fence, Sam asked, "Are we goin' in?"

"Yes, go ahead," Phyllis told him. "I only see one car parked at the office, and it's one that was here the other day. It must belong to that lady who took over for Jaycee Fallon."

"Looks like Loomis doesn't actually spend much time here," Sam commented as he parked the pickup in front of the office.

"He's probably too busy with county business . . . or hiding out from other people who want to serve him with lawsuits."

When they went inside, the same gray-haired woman looked up from the desk behind the counter. She must have remembered them, because she said, "Oh, you just missed Mr. Loomis! You're not having very good luck catching him here." She shook her head. "Not that it would have done you much good. I asked him about making a contribution to the Lions Club, but he said he couldn't afford it right now."

"Well, we appreciate your checking with him," Phyllis said. "I was wondering . . . Do you think any of the companies he leases trucks to might be willing to contribute? If you had a list of them . . ."

The woman frowned and said, "I don't know if Mr. Loomis would want me sharing that information." She shrugged and went on. "Then again, the company logo is on all the trucks, along with the names of the companies that lease them, so it's not like it's any great secret."

"That information would certainly be helpful," Phyllis said.

"The problem is, a list like that doesn't really exist. I'd have to go through the files and put it together, and I'm not sure I have time."

"If you handle the billing, maybe you remember some of them," Phyllis suggested. "It doesn't have to be a complete list. Just a few more places for us to try."

The woman thought about it and then nodded. She said, "I could do that, I suppose. We lease trucks to several of the regional supermarket chains." She named them. "There are some oil-field supply companies and energy companies, like Cherokee and Anderson Brothers and Winchell and Devstar and Hawkins Supply. They get all of their trucks from us. Oh, and one of the hardware-store chains and any number of construction companies. Aren't you going to write these down?"

"Of course," Phyllis said. She fumbled in her pockets. "I just don't seem to have any paper or a pen."

The gray-haired woman shook her head and said, "I'll write them down for you."

"Thank you so much."

The woman spent several minutes making a list of companies that did business with Cross Timbers Transport. She said, "I wouldn't be doing this if it weren't for a good cause."

"I know the children will be very grateful on Christmas morning," Phyllis said. She made a mental promise to get several of those angels from the Angel Tree and make sure they had good Christmases. Even doing that, she might still feel a little guilty for using the Lions Club's project in this manner.

But saving an innocent man from prison and finding a killer are good causes, too, she reminded herself.

The woman handed the sheet of paper over the counter and said, "There you are."

"Thanks again," Phyllis said as she took it.

"We're much obliged," Sam added with a nod. They turned toward the door.

It opened before they could get there, and a woman stormed into the office. She demanded, "Where is he? Where is that lying, no-good —"

She stopped short at the sight of Phyllis and Sam standing there. Phyllis recognized her right away. She had seen two pictures of this woman, albeit taken fifteen years apart.

The blonde standing there with an angry expression on her face was Jaycee Fallon.

CHAPTER 23

"Sorry," Jaycee muttered without much sincerity. She looked around Phyllis and Sam at the woman behind the counter and went on. "He's not here, is he?"

"No, he left a little while ago," the woman said. "Was he expecting you?"

Jaycee laughed and said, "Are you kidding? If Clay knew I was coming, he'd run the other way as fast as he could. That's why I tried to catch him here. He owes me, the son of a —"

"Please," the woman said. "I know how upset you are with him, Jaycee, but there's nothing I can do about it."

Jaycee nodded and sighed.

"I know," she said. "I'm sorry, Martha. I don't mean to take it out on you. I'm just frustrated because I know how slick Clay is. He's going to weasel out of all his responsibilities somehow. And I . . . I . . . don't know how I'm going to get through this."

She put her hands over her face as it unexpectedly crumpled into tears.

The gray-haired woman — Martha, Jaycee had called her — hurried out from behind the counter and put an arm around the blonde's shoulders.

"Oh, dear," she said as she steered Jaycee toward the little leather sofa against one wall. "What in the world is wrong?"

They seemed to have forgotten that Phyllis and Sam were still there, which was just fine with Phyllis. She hated to see anyone as upset as Jaycee obviously was, but sometimes when people were caught up in such an emotional state, they revealed more information than they intended to.

"I — I've just been to the doctor," Jaycee said as she sat down on the sofa with Martha. "I was pretty sure already, but now it's certain . . ."

"You're pregnant?" Martha whispered.

Jaycee swallowed hard and nodded.

"I told Clay a couple of weeks ago that I thought I was, and he said . . . he said it wasn't his. I told him it had to be, but he didn't believe me. And he was really rude about it! That's why I got mad and threatened to sue him for sexual harassment." Jaycee clenched her right hand into a fist and thumped it against her knee. "I am *not* going to let him get away with not taking responsibility for this. I'll keep him in court from now on, if that's what it takes to make him stand up and do what's right."

Martha shook her head and said solemnly, "It won't do you any good, dear. Between you and me, he's broke. I'm not sure if he'll even be able to pay my salary this month." She seemed to realize the two of them weren't alone and shot a glance at Phyllis and Sam. "Oh, my. Please pretend you didn't hear that. I had no right to speak out of turn."

"Don't worry," Phyllis said. "It's none of our business. Right, Sam?"

"That's right," Sam said. "In one ear and out the other."

"Thank you," Martha said.

Jaycee frowned at them and asked, "Who are you people?"

Martha said, "They're collecting donations for the Lions Club. You know, for the Christmas Angel Tree."

"Oh, sure." Jaycee sighed. "My kid may wind up being one of those angels in a few years, if his father doesn't provide for him. And from the sound of it, he won't. Or can't."

"It's none of my business, but I'd be tempted to shoot a man like that," Phyllis said. It was a leading comment, and she wanted to see how the blonde would react to it.

"You and me both!" Jaycee responded with a hollow laugh. "That's about what Clay deserves, all right. If I'd ever shot a gun in my life, I'd be tempted to get one and put a hole in him. Like I said, though, I'll deal with him in court. It just won't be as *satisfying* as shooting him would be."

"I hope things work out for you," Phyllis said. She put a hand on Sam's arm and urged him toward the door. We got what we came here for, she thought. Actually, they had gotten even more. Jaycee barging in like this had been a stroke of luck.

As they were pulling away in the pickup, Sam said, "Well, we already knew that gal had a grudge against Loomis. I reckon now she's got even more of a reason to be mad at him."

"And she said she already suspected she was pregnant a couple of weeks ago, well before the parade," Phyllis mused.

"You think she was lyin' about never havin' fired a gun, just to keep anybody from gettin' suspicious of her?"

Phyllis gave that some thought, then said, "I don't think so. She had no idea who we really are, so she wouldn't have had a reason to think we might suspect her of anything. Not only that, but if she was pregnant, then killing Loomis wouldn't do her any good. You can't sue a dead man for child support."

"So, we cross her off the list?"

"Tentatively," Phyllis said. She looked down at the piece of paper in her hand. "And we need to talk to Nate again and see if he has a connection to any of the companies on this list. If his rifle really is the murder weapon, then the killer had to know that he owned it and where to find it."

"Headin' back to the house, then?"

"Yes. I'll see what I can find out about these companies on the Internet."

After driving for a few moments, Sam said, "You know, from everything we've heard about the dire straits ol' Loomis is in, it seems almost like *he'd* be the one desperate enough to kill somebody."

"Yes, it does," Phyllis said as she frowned in thought. "But we know Loomis couldn't have killed Barney McCrory. Besides, he doesn't profit from McCrory's death in any way, and he was in some danger himself when McCrory was shot."

"Yeah, I know. It was just a stray thought."

And not a bad one, Phyllis decided. Under different circumstances, Clay Loomis certainly would fit the profile of a potential suspect. As things stood, though, Phyllis couldn't see how the theory would work.

It kept lurking in the back of her brain anyway as Sam drove back into town.

Carolyn and Eve hadn't heard anything from Felicity by the time Phyllis and Sam returned. Phyllis headed for the computer to start checking out the names Martha had given her at the Cross Timbers Transport office.

It seemed too far-fetched to think that somebody from one of the major grocery-store or hardware chains would have tried to murder Clay Loomis and accidentally shot Barney McCrory instead, so she concentrated on the smaller companies Martha had written down. Most of them were construction companies or energy companies based in the area.

Devstar, for example, was owned by a man named Devin Scott, and its headquarters was in Fort Worth. Anderson Energy was owned by three brothers of that name from Mineral Wells. Hawkins Supply operated out of Granbury. Phyllis spent more than an hour on the computer and didn't discover anything the least bit suspicious about them or any of the other companies she checked out. All of them seemed to operate in an honest and aboveboard manner, with no trace of controversy about their dealings.

And nothing that would seem to tie in with murder, either.

Eve came into the living room and said, "I've gone through that file you sent me, Phyllis. I didn't see anything wrong with it."

"No spelling or grammar mistakes?" Phyllis was surprised.

"Oh, I moved a comma or two," Eve said. "Nothing really important. You just can't expect a former English teacher to go through something someone has written and not make a correction or two. It's instinct, you know."

Phyllis understood. She was the same way when someone made a historical reference that was wrong. She kept her mouth shut most of the time, though. She wasn't being paid to set people straight about history anymore.

"Anyway, I sent the file back to you," Eve went on. "It's very good, by the way. The recipe makes scrumptious cookies, and you wrote about it in a very clear, easy-to-understand manner."

"I can't tell you how relieved I am to hear you say that. This is the first thing I've actually written for publication, and I wasn't sure if I was up to it."

"Oh, you are," Eve assured her. "You certainly are." She looked out the front window and added, "That TV reporter is back."

Phyllis looked, too, and saw Felicity getting out of the van. Josh followed her as she came up the walk toward the house. Nick stayed in the van. He is probably going to try to catch a nap, Phyllis thought.

She had the front door open before Felicity could ring the bell. It was hard to tell from the reporter's face what she had found out from District Attorney Sullivan, if anything. It was possible that Sullivan had refused to talk to her, although Phyllis still thought that was unlikely.

"Come in," she said. "Were you able to talk to the district attorney?"

"Oh, I talked to him, all right," Felicity replied. "I just wish what I'd found out was better news."

After that statement, what Felicity had to report was pretty much a foregone conclusion. As she and Josh sat down in the living room, along with Phyllis and Sam, Felicity told them, "The test bullet from Nate's rifle matches the one they took out of Barney McCrory's body. There's no chance that it wasn't the murder weapon."

"Sullivan came right out and admitted that?" Phyllis asked.

"Not at first. I had to flatter him for a while. That man's really full of himself, isn't he? I'm not sure I've ever seen anybody that vain."

Josh glanced away as Felicity said that, Phyllis noted. She suspected it was because Josh thought Felicity ran a pretty close race with Sullivan in the vanity department. Though that didn't seem to stop Josh from having a crush on her. For a young man, Felicity's drop-dead-gorgeous looks would make up for a lot of shortcomings in her personality.

"Anyway, once I convinced him I thought he was the greatest district attorney on the face of the earth, he was more than happy to let me in on the details of his latest legal triumph," Felicity went on. "He's got all the evidence he needs to convict Nate Hollingsworth, he said, including the murder weapon. I asked him if he meant Nate's rifle, and he said yes, that the ballistics evidence was conclusive. He made me promise not to broadcast that until he gives me the go-ahead, of course. Said that for now everything he told me was off the record." She snorted contemptuously. "Sure, I won't broadcast anything. I won't broadcast anything until we can blow his case right out of the water!"

"I hope you're right," Phyllis said. "Sam and I went back out to Loomis's trucking company to look around some more, but we didn't find out anything useful. In fact, I think we may have eliminated Jaycee Fallon as a suspect."

She went over what they had learned from Martha, and then told Felicity and Josh about how Jaycee had barged into the office, looking for Loomis.

"She's pregnant by him?" Felicity said. "And he claimed he wasn't the baby daddy. That made her so mad she dumped him, but now she wants him to pay up. Yeah, that just about rules her out as a suspect. Loomis wouldn't be any good to her if he were dead!"

"If he's as broke as the woman running his office claims, he won't be any good to her alive, either," Phyllis said. "In fact, with people coming after him from all directions, it sounds like his troubles are just going to multiply if he doesn't come up with some cash flow."

Felicity frowned and said, "Being in a corner like that is enough to make anybody a little desperate. Desperate enough to kill somebody, maybe."

"That's what I thought. But it's physically impossible for Loomis to have killed Barney McCrory."

"He could have paid somebody to do it," Josh said. The other three looked at him. "I mean, if he had a reason to."

"That's the other problem," Phyllis said. "McCrory's death doesn't benefit Loomis in any way that I can see. The only connection between them is that they were both on that carriage for the Christmas parade."

Felicity blew out an exasperated-sounding breath and said, "We just go around and around with this, and all the evidence still points to Nate. Maybe we're wrong about him."

"We're not," Sam declared. "That boy is no murderer. Somebody got his rifle, used it to kill Barney, and put it back in that camper to frame him."

"That's a neat little theory, but it's not worth a thing if there's no evidence to back it up. It's just wishful thinking."

The same possibility had nagged at Phyllis, but every instinct she possessed told her that Nate was innocent. She had to decide if she trusted and believed in those instincts.

Maybe I'm just too stubborn for my own good, she thought. But the idea of giving up didn't sit well with her. It wouldn't hurt to keep looking into this case. Christmas was coming, and, as always, celebrating the holiday properly would take some time, but it was still more than two weeks away. There would be plenty of chances to put up the Christmas tree and the other decorations.

"Let's keep digging," she said. "According to Mr. D'Angelo, the grand-jury hearing won't be until after the first of the year. Surely we can turn up something to clear Nate before then."

"I can't wait that long!" Felicity said. "My producers sent me here to get a story — a story about a guy who shot his father-in-law during a Christmas parade. I can only stall them for so long with vague talk about something even better." She sighed. "I may wind up having to go with what I've got, and that's a whole pile of evidence pointing right at Nate Hollingsworth."

"You can't do that," Sam said. "That'll just make things worse for him and Ally. A lot of folks are probably convinced already that he's guilty, and if you broadcast what you know about the rifle, then everybody will think he killed Barney."

"Hey, maybe that'll be a good thing," Felicity said with a shrug. "D'Angelo can get a change of venue that way, because the jury pool will be contaminated. It won't be possible for Nate to get a fair trial here. That might be the only thing we can do for him."

Phyllis leaned forward and said, "Is there any chance you can wait a little longer? Just a few days. You've helped a lot so far, Ms. Prosper. Give us a chance to investigate a little more."

"Do you really think you're going to find anything?" Felicity asked skeptically.

"Of course I do," Phyllis said. "The answer is out there. I know it is. There's something we haven't found yet, one piece that will finish filling in the picture so it makes sense."

"That missing connection you were talking about?"

"That's right. The one piece that connects everything and makes it work."

"Well, if you can find it, more power to you." Felicity stood up. Josh got hurriedly to his feet as well, following her lead as usual. "I can put off the producers for another day or two and make them think I'm about to break an explosive story. But not for any longer than that. Bring me something really good between now and then."

"I'll do my best," Phyllis promised.

"And remember, whatever it is, it's got to

be explosive. Make sure it blows up real good."

CHAPTER 24

Felicity and Josh left with Nick, heading back to the motel where they were staying while they were in town. By now it was fairly late in the afternoon, so Phyllis didn't want to set off on any new investigations — even if she could think of some angle she hadn't explored yet, which she couldn't.

Sometimes things occurred to her when she had her mind on another subject entirely, so she retrieved her e-mail and looked at the corrected file Eve had sent back to her for the magazine article. Eve was right, of course; the commas she had moved were now in their proper places. Phyllis read over the whole piece carefully, changed another few words, and then attached the finished file to an e-mail addressed to the magazine's editor.

She took a deep breath as she sat there with her hand on the mouse and the cursor hovering over SEND. This was taking a big step. She had submitted many, many recipes she had written to various contests, including some to this very magazine. Writing a column was different. People would be judging her not just on the recipe, but on the quality of the writing as well. It was a scary feeling. As a person grew older, it became a little easier not to worry about the opinions of other people, but that desire for approval never went away completely, she supposed.

But she had never been one to say that she couldn't do something without giving it a try. If she had been, she never would have solved any murders and some innocent people would be sitting in prison instead, including some of her friends.

She clicked SEND.

Like it had wings, the column was off to her editor.

Phyllis sat back and sighed, but it was, at least for the moment, a contented sigh. She had done the best she could, and now she would wait to see what happened.

A knock on the front door made her sit up straighter. Most people used the doorbell, but Mike sometimes knocked. She turned and glanced through the window, saw a cruiser from the sheriff's department parked outside, and knew it was him.

"Come on in," she said as she opened the door. "Nothing's wrong, is it?"

"Can't a guy come by to see his mom without something being wrong?" Mike asked as he stepped into the house.

"Of course, and I'm always glad to see you."

From the hallway, Carolyn said, "Mike, are you staying for supper?"

"No, but I wish I were," he told her with a shake of his head. "Thanks, anyway." He turned back to Phyllis. "My shift's starting soon, but I wanted to stop by and let you know about something. Sarah and Bobby and I won't be here for Christmas."

"You won't?" Phyllis tried to keep the disappointment out of her voice, but she wasn't sure if she succeeded very well.

"No, Bud and Katherine invited us out there, and Sarah wants to go."

"Well, of course she does."

Sarah's father, Bud, had been battling cancer for several years. More than once the doctors had warned him that his time was just about up, but he had hung on stubbornly. Sarah flew out to California to see him several times a year, and Phyllis couldn't blame Sarah's parents for wanting her to bring the whole family with her.

"How is Bud doing?" Phyllis went on.

"About as well as can be expected, I guess. But with something like that . . . Well, you never know."

"No, you don't." She patted Mike's arm. "We'll miss the three of you, of course, but you're doing the right thing."

Mike smiled and said, "I'm glad you feel that way. I was worried that you'd be upset."

"Nonsense. You're a part of their family, just like Sarah is part of ours. When are you leaving?"

"Don't know. Haven't made the reservations yet."

"Well, when you find out, let me know. We'll have a big dinner and holiday celebration here before you go."

Mike's smile widened into a grin. He said, "I was hoping you'd say that." He leaned down and kissed her on the forehead. "Gotta go. You're the best, Mom."

"The best mom you have, that's for sure," she told him.

He chuckled and waved as he went out and started along the walk toward his car.

"Did I hear right?" Carolyn asked from behind Phyllis. "Mike's not going to be here for Christmas?"

"No," Phyllis said, turning around. "I don't blame him, though."

"I suppose I could be here Christmas day

instead of going to Sandra's."

"That's not necessary. Spend the day with your daughter like you usually do."

"All right. But if you change your mind . . ."

"I won't. It's fine, really."

Life always holds changes, she thought. No year was exactly like the one before it. Someone was always gone, sometimes for good, leaving a hole that would never be filled. For Allyson, this would be the first Christmas without her father. And by next Christmas, Nate wouldn't be with her, either, if he was convicted of murder and sent to prison.

Once again, Phyllis was convinced she was right to be stubborn. She wasn't going to let that happen if there was anything in her power she could do to prevent it.

Supper was a subdued affair. The chicken and spinach salad Carolyn had made was excellent, and Phyllis enjoyed it, but her mind was on the McCrory case, and on the news that Mike had brought as well. The past few days had been busy ones, and weariness was catching up to her.

She tried to distract herself by telling Eve, "Thanks again for helping me with the column. I sent it to the editor."

"I'm sure he'll love it, dear," Eve said. "And it won't be long before we'll have a famous author in the house."

"Oh, I doubt that!"

"You never know. Famous writers have to come from somewhere, after all."

Phyllis couldn't argue with that, but she thought Eve was being too optimistic. A few columns in a food magazine weren't going to make anyone famous.

Sam brought her back to reality by asking, "What's our next step in the investigation?"

"We need to get together with Nate again and go over that list of companies we got out of the secretary. Maybe one of them will ring a bell for him."

"Still lookin' for that missing piece, eh?"

"It's all we've got left," Phyllis said with a shrug.

Her sleep that night was restless. She had never been one to be haunted by nightmares, but when she woke up the next morning she thought she'd had some, even though she couldn't really remember them. But the disturbing sensation lingered.

Carolyn had coffee waiting and muffins in the oven when Phyllis came into the kitchen. Phyllis took a deep breath and said, "That's a wonderful smell."

"I hope you like the muffins," Carolyn said. "They're gluten-free. I've been reading about how gluten can cause arthritis flare-ups, and I thought maybe at our age we could stand to do with a little less pain."

Phyllis thought about it, nodded, and said, "I'm willing to give it a try."

By the time the muffins had come out of the oven and cooled, Sam and Eve were in the kitchen, too, sitting at the table, drinking coffee. Carolyn set out muffins on saucers for everyone. Sam took a bite of his and said, "Mmm. Mighty good. A little different, but still good."

"They're gluten-free," Carolyn said.

"Ah. That explains it." Sam grinned. "I've always been fully glutened. But, hey, I'm willin' to try new things, and this is good."

"Carolyn says it's supposed to be good for arthritis to not eat gluten," Phyllis put in.

"Well, I'm all for that." Sam took another bite and seemed to enjoy it.

After breakfast, Phyllis called the number she had for Nate and Allyson's house. Allyson answered, hope sounding momentarily in her voice when she realized it was Phyllis calling.

"Is there something new in the case?" she asked.

Phyllis hated to disappoint her, but she

said, "No, I'm afraid not. I have some more questions for Nate, though. Is he there?"

"No, he was going to the office for a while and then out to my dad's ranch this morning. He said he wanted to carry on like normal as much as possible, and things on the ranch need to be checked on. Is there anything I can help you with?"

Phyllis had handy the list Martha had written. She looked at it and asked, "Do any of these names mean anything to you?"

She read through the company names, pausing slightly after each one to give Allyson time to respond, but she got all the way to the end before the young woman said, "Sorry, I don't think I've heard of any of them. Am I supposed to recognize them?"

"No, not necessarily. But that's what I want to ask Nate."

"You can call him. You have his cell phone number, don't you?"

"I do," Phyllis said. "Thanks."

"I'm the one who's grateful to you for not giving up on us."

"I'm not going to do that," Phyllis declared.

She broke the connection with Allyson and tried Nate's number. The call went straight to voicemail, which meant Nate was either in an area where there was no service or had turned off his phone. Maybe he just didn't want to be disturbed for some reason.

But Allyson had said he was going to his office in the Cranmoor Building, and that was close by, so Phyllis decided she might go by there and talk to him. Most of the time, she preferred talking to people face-to-face rather than over the phone, anyway.

She went to look for Sam, thinking he would go with her. When she found him on the back porch, sitting in one of the rocking chairs while Buck sniffed around in the yard, he was talking on his phone.

He told whoever he was talking to, "Hold on a second," and moved the phone away from his mouth. "You need me for something?" he asked Phyllis.

She looked at the phone and raised her eyebrows quizzically.

"My daughter," he said.

"Oh. Well, you go right ahead and talk to her. I'm just going to run an errand. I'll see you later."

Sam nodded, and Phyllis went back in the house. She didn't want to disturb Sam while he was talking to his daughter, Vanessa. She was the only child he and his late wife, Victoria, had had, but she and Sam weren't particularly close. There were no problems between them as far as Phyllis knew, but

Vanessa had married and moved out of state to some place up in the Northeast, and she and Sam just didn't see each other or even talk very often. Phyllis certainly didn't want to intrude on one of their rare conversations.

There was no reason she couldn't run over to Nate's office by herself.

After telling Carolyn where she was going, she put on a jacket and went out to her car. The day was overcast again, and it just looked chilly outside. That proved to be the case, but the air was crisp, not unpleasantly cold.

The parking spaces around the square were mostly full. With the approach of Christmas, more people were out shopping. She hated to think what the traffic would be like for the next few weeks on the south side of town, where Main Street crossed the interstate. That was the main shopping area now, with dozens of stores big and small on both sides of the freeway, and the congestion was so bad that whenever Phyllis ventured down there, she felt like she was in Fort Worth or even Dallas. And it would only get worse between now and Christmas.

Maybe for once she would give some thought to doing the shopping she had left online. That still seemed a bit unnatural to her, but it might be better than trying to navigate through those crowds.

With that on her mind, she almost missed seeing a good parking place. She spotted it in time to maneuver the Lincoln into it, though, and then got out to walk toward the Cranmoor Building, which was less than a block away.

A few people were going in and out of the building as she entered the lobby. She climbed the stairs with their ornate banister, and turned toward Nate's office when she reached the second-floor landing. The door was closed, and a man was coming along the hall toward her.

He jerked a thumb over his shoulder at the door behind him and said, "If you're looking for Nate, he's not there."

"Oh?"

"Yeah, I came by to talk to him, but the door's locked."

Phyllis was disappointed. She had hoped to catch him here so she could ask him about those companies Clay Loomis did business with. The list was folded up and in her jacket pocket.

The man who had stopped her smiled and said, "I'm Frank Holbrook, by the way." He held out his hand.

The name rang some sort of bell for Phyllis, but she couldn't place it. She shook hands with Holbrook and introduced herself.

"You must be a friend of the family," he said. He was in his forties, a pleasant-looking man with thinning brown hair. He wore a brown leather jacket over a flannel shirt and khaki trousers.

"That's right," Phyllis said. It was easier than trying to explain her connection to Nate and what she was doing here. She gave in to her natural curiosity and asked, "What about you?"

"Oh, I'm just a business associate, although I'd like to think Nate is a friend, too. I've spent a lot of time talking to him over the past few months."

Something about that jogged Phyllis's memory. She said, "You're the oil-and-gas man."

Holbrook grinned and said, "Yeah, I guess you could call me that. I'm a landsman. I was hoping to do some business with Nate, but . . ." He spread his hands and shrugged. "So far it hasn't worked out. And after this terrible business with Barney McCrory . . ." Holbrook shook his head. "It's hard to believe Nate would do something like what they're accusing him of."

"He didn't," Phyllis said flatly. "I'm sure of it."

Holbrook frowned slightly and asked, "What did you say your name was?"

"Newsom. Phyllis Newsom."

"The detective lady!" Holbrook grinned again. "Sure, I've read about you."

"Well, you can't believe everything that you read. But I believe in Nate's innocence."

"And you're trying to clear his name?"

"That's right."

"Well, more power to you," Holbrook said emphatically. "If he's innocent, somebody needs to prove it."

"I'm going to do my best."

"I'm glad to hear it." Holbrook leaned his head toward the staircase. "Since Nate's not here, why don't I walk you back out?"

"You're sure?" Phyllis stepped over to the office door and tried the knob. It was locked, all right, and no one responded to her knock on the wood beside the frosted-glass panel. She sighed.

"Maybe he's out at the McCrory ranch," Holbrook suggested.

"Possibly," Phyllis said, without mentioning that Allyson had said he might be there if he wasn't at the office. She didn't know if he would want the landsman pestering him today. Holbrook obviously held out hope that he could still make a deal for a gas lease on the ranch.

She headed for the staircase and Holbrook fell in alongside her, still chatting pleasantly. When they reached the sidewalk outside the building, Holbrook said good-bye and turned to his right. Phyllis went the other way toward her Lincoln.

Something made her glance back. She saw Holbrook get into an SUV, back out of the space, and drive away. Something about the vehicle struck her as familiar. It had the letters AAA painted on the driver's door, and under each letter was a name written in fancy script: *ARTHUR, ALAN,* and *AMOS.* ANDERSON ENERGY was written under the names.

Phyllis stumbled a little, but not because she had tripped.

She had just caught her balance when a vehicle pulled up in the street beside her and a voice asked, "Mrs. Newsom, are you okay?"

Phyllis looked over to see the van belonging to the TV crew. Felicity Prosper had rolled down her window to ask the question. The reporter went on. "It looked like you almost fell."

"I'm fine," Phyllis said. "Were you looking for me?"

"Yeah, we went by the house, and Mrs. Wilbarger said we might find you up here. Were you talking to Nate?"

"No, he's not in his office. I think he's out at the McCrory ranch." Phyllis took a deep breath. "And that's where we're going."

Felicity frowned a little and said, "What?"

"I need to ask Nate a question, and you might as well go along, if that's all right."

"Sure, climb on in." Felicity looked behind her. "Josh, don't just sit there. Open the door."

The van's side door slid back, and Phyllis got in and sat next to Josh. From behind the wheel, Nick grunted and said, "Where'd you say we were goin'?"

"The McCrory ranch," Felicity told him. "I figured we'd shoot some footage out there sooner or later, so the location is programmed into the GPS."

"Umm," Nick said. He pushed buttons on the little instrument mounted on the dashboard.

Felicity turned in her seat to look back at Phyllis and asked, "What is it you're going to ask —" She stopped short and her eyes widened as she took in the expression of grim determination on Phyllis's face. "Oh, my God," she said. "You've solved the case, haven't you?"

"That's what we're going to find out," Phyllis said.

Chapter 25

A multitude of thoughts cascaded through Phyllis's head as Nick drove out of town, following the GPS's directions to Barney McCrory's ranch. As she had hoped, once the missing piece was in place, everything else started to click together. She needed confirmation from Nate about a few things, but if his answers matched up with what she was thinking, then she knew who had killed Barney McCrory and why.

Proving it to the satisfaction of the police and the district attorney might be another story altogether, but if she could present the whole theory to Chief Whitmire and Detective Largo, she thought they would be intrigued enough to investigate.

Felicity's voice from the front seat broke into her thoughts.

"Come on!" the reporter said. "You've got to tell me what you figured out."

"Yeah," Josh urged. "I'm really curious, too."

Phyllis considered for a moment, then nodded and said, "All right. But remember this is just a theory. It's mostly supposition, connecting dots that may not be really be connected."

"With your track record, I doubt that," Felicity said. "But go on."

"The key is that I was wrong all along about one thing: Barney McCrory's death wasn't an accident. He was the intended victim right from the start, so the shooter didn't miss."

"Who had a reason to kill McCrory except Nate?" Felicity asked.

"Clay Loomis and one other man: Frank Holbrook."

Felicity and Josh stared at her in consternation. It was Felicity who asked, "Who?"

"He's a landsman who works for a gas company owned by the Anderson brothers." Phyllis turned to Josh. "Can you look them up on your phone?"

"Sure." The young intern took out his phone and started pushing buttons.

While he was doing that, Phyllis went on. "Holbrook had been trying for months to get Barney McCrory to agree to give the Anderson brothers a gas lease on his ranch."

"We know that," Felicity said, impatience creeping into her voice. "That's what caused the trouble between McCrory and Nate that the police are using as the motive for murder. You're not saying Holbrook wanted that lease so bad he shot McCrory over it, are you?"

"I'm not sure he would have done that right off the bat," Phyllis said, "but once Loomis got involved, he must have sweetened the deal for Holbrook."

"I've got the Anderson brothers," Josh said.

"Arthur, Alan, and Amos," Phyllis said, remembering what she had seen written on the door of Frank Holbrook's SUV.

"Yeah. Good grief."

"Three *A*'s," Phyllis said. "That's what they use as the company logo, too. I saw it on an SUV out at the precinct barn when we went to talk to Loomis. I thought it was from Triple A, you know, the ones you call when you have car trouble. But I'll bet it was Frank Holbrook talking to Loomis about the next step in their plan."

Felicity said, "So Loomis and Holbrook are working together to do what, exactly?"

"Get that gas lease. The Anderson brothers lease all their trucks from Loomis." Phyllis held up the paper she had gotten from the woman who worked at Cross Timbers Transport. "I know that for a fact. If they were to put a bunch of gas wells on the McCrory ranch, they'd need a lot of trucks for the operation, and Loomis is in desperate need of the money such a deal would bring in."

"You know," Josh said slowly, "that makes sense."

"Holbrook wanted to sign up the lease, too, and when Loomis offered him a cut of the money he'd make, that was the tipping point. Holbrook agreed to kill Barney McCrory for him."

"So Holbrook is the missing piece you talked about," Felicity said.

"I think so, yes."

"That's a fine theory, but it's spun practically out of thin air! You're basing it on seeing an Anderson brothers truck at Loomis's precinct barn. It might have been somebody else, on some other business entirely, instead of Holbrook."

"No, I'm sure it was him," Phyllis said. "Now that I've met the man, I'm certain he's the one I saw leave the office, get in that pickup, and drive off just as we were getting there."

"Loomis and Holbrook will deny it. It'll be your word against theirs."

"Other people out there at the precinct barn must have seen Holbrook, too."

"What of it? Loomis has a business arrangement with Holbrook's employers. They can just say that Holbrook was out there talking to him about something else. About those truck leases, more than likely."

"Holbrook is a landsman. He doesn't have anything to do with leasing trucks for the Andersons."

"That you know of," Felicity said. "Look, I know I'm playing devil's advocate here. I don't want to shoot holes in your theory — really I don't. But if it's not going to hold together, we can't put our faith in its chances of saving Nate."

Josh said, "What about the rifle? You haven't even addressed that part of it, Mrs. Newsom. How would Holbrook know about the rifle, and why frame Nate? Even if you're right about Loomis and Holbrook plotting to get Mr. McCrory out of the way, it seems like they'd want Nate around to sign that gas lease they were after."

"The rifle is one of the things I want to ask Nate about," Phyllis admitted. "As for why they would frame him, Nate can't sign the lease. Legally, Allyson inherits the ranch, so she would have to agree to it. Knowing how strongly her father was opposed to the idea, she might decide not to go along with it, to honor his memory if nothing else. But if she lost Nate, too, by his being convicted of her father's murder and sent to prison, she'd be more likely to be desperate enough to agree to anything that would bring in money to pay for lawyers and appeals."

"Maybe," Felicity agreed with a dubious frown. "But somebody would have to be awfully diabolical to come up with that line of reasoning, don't you think?"

"Not so diabolical that I'd put it past Clay Loomis."

"So if Loomis is the mastermind, how come he almost got killed, too?"

"You're talking about the runaway horses?" Phyllis asked. "Mastermind or not, he couldn't have predicted they'd do that. He was supposed to have the perfect alibi, sitting right there in the carriage with Barney McCrory when the fatal shot was fired. What happened after that was just a stroke of bad luck that left Loomis genuinely terrified for his life. But as it worked out, that just helped to shield him from suspicion."

"It sounds like you've got most of it covered," Felicity admitted with a shrug. "If you can close one or two loopholes, that is."

"Is that explosive enough for you?" Phyllis asked.

"If we can prove it, yeah."

Phyllis hoped it wouldn't be much longer before they could do just that. They had been following a farm-to-market road with a tall white boundary fence running along the left side. Up ahead were a couple of stone pillars flanking a gate.

As they came closer, Phyllis saw the words MCCRORY RANCH on an arched sign above the gate. On the other side of the gate, a gravel road twisted up into the rolling, tree-dotted hills. Both sides of the wooden double gate were open. A cattle guard across the entrance would keep the ranch's live-stock from straying.

"This is it," Felicity said.

Nick turned and drove through the gate onto the gravel road. Phyllis saw a house and some barns and corrals on the third hill back, about a mile off the main road. Because Nick couldn't drive very fast on the narrow, twisting road, it took several minutes to get there.

A large, level parking area lay between the house and the nearest barn. The house was a sprawling rock-and-frame structure that looked like it had been there a hundred years or more. Phyllis thought it was very impressive. The barns were much newer, probably built to replace the original ones from when the ranch was established.

A car that probably belonged to Nate was parked near the house, but Phyllis didn't see anyone around. She and Felicity and Josh got out of the van, and as they closed the doors, Nate came through one of the open doors of the barn. He stopped short, looking at them in surprise.

"Mrs. Newsom," he said. "What's going on? Is there some new development in the case?"

Phyllis and her two companions hurried forward to meet him. A glance back told Phyllis that Nick was still in the van, doing something with his video camera. She wasn't technologically adept enough to have any idea what the problem might be.

"Nate, I need to ask you some questions," Phyllis said. "We've come up with an idea, but I need some more information to know if it's possible."

"Sure," he said. His face was haggard, showing the strain he'd been under. "Why don't you come on in the barn? We can get out of the wind to talk."

There was a fairly cold wind blowing on the hilltop, so Phyllis nodded and said, "All right."

Nate turned and led the three of them into the barn, where the metal walls blocked the wind. It felt warmer inside, whether it really was or not.

"Now, what's this about needing to ask me some questions?"

"They're about Frank Holbrook."

Nate's forehead wrinkled as he frowned. He said, "The gas-lease guy?"

"That's right. He came to your office fairly often for a while, didn't he?"

"Yeah," Nate replied with a shrug. "He was there once or twice a week, it seems like."

"Including the day you had your rifle with you, so you could drop it off at the gunsmith's shop."

Phyllis phrased it as a statement, not a question, but Nate's eyes widened slightly as he answered, "Yeah. Yeah, now that I think about it, you're right. We even talked about it. He said he did a lot of . . . target shooting." Nate's voice had gotten hollow. "Oh, hell!"

"Did you tell him where you kept it at home?" Phyllis asked quietly.

Nate lifted both hands and pressed them to his temples as he closed his eyes and moaned softly. He said, "I think I did. I seem to remember telling him I never used it much, so I kept it put away. He's just such a friendly, talkative guy, I never even thought about it again."

"He's a salesman, in a way," Phyllis said. "They know how to get information out of people and then turn it to their advantage."

Nate stared at her. He asked, "Are you saying you think Frank Holbrook is the one who shot Barney?"

"He knew you had a rifle, he knew where you kept it, and he had a reason for wanting Barney out of the way."

"Over a blasted *gas lease*?"

"That's only part of it," Phyllis said. "The rest involves Clay Loomis."

Since she had laid out everything for the others earlier, it was all straight in her mind now, so it took her only a couple of minutes to piece together the theory for Nate. As she was finishing, he started to nod.

"It could have happened that way, I suppose. But how do we prove it?"

"I think we have plenty to get the police interested," Phyllis said. "I know both Chief Whitmire and Detective Largo have too much integrity to just ignore this. If they start looking into it and put some pressure on Holbrook and Loomis, there's a good chance they'll turn on each other."

A voice from behind them said, "That

weasel Loomis would, for sure."

Phyllis turned and stiffened as she saw Frank Holbrook standing in the shadows of the barn, pointing a revolver at them.

"Oh!" Felicity said. "Oh, crap!"

"Frank, what are you doing?" Nate said as Holbrook came closer to them.

"Something I never wanted to do, buddy," the landsman said. "I really liked you, you know. Loomis just made me too good an offer to pass up. I've got gambling debts to pay — those damn Cowboys — and the money he offered me was enough to keep me from getting my legs broken. It's a real shame about your father-in-law, though. If that old buzzard had just had the good sense to sign off on that lease, none of this would have had to happen."

Josh's jaw hung open in fear. With a visible effort he forced it closed and then asked, "You . . . really did kill Mr. McCrory, like Mrs. Newsom said?"

"Not much point in denying it now, is there, kid?" Holbrook motioned with the gun. "All of you bunch up a little more there, okay?"

"To make it easier for you to shoot us?" Phyllis asked. She was as scared as any of the rest of them, but she knew she had to keep that fear under control. "Does committing one murder make it that much easier to kill again?"

"I didn't come out here to kill anybody but Nate," Holbrook snapped. "And he was going to commit suicide, if you know what I mean. Out of remorse over killing his father-in-law. That would have wrapped everything up nice and neat." Holbrook sighed. "I didn't expect to find the rest of you here, too. Now I suppose he's got to go on a killing spree and get rid of you three first before shooting himself. It'll really be a terrible tragedy, especially this close to Christmas. I can't risk you stirring everything up, though. I don't trust Loomis not to crack."

"But — but we don't have any real evidence!" Felicity said. "It would be your word against ours. You can still afford to let us go."

Holbrook shook his head and said, "Nah, I don't think so," as he started to lift the gun.

With no warning, Josh lowered his head and charged like a bull. He bellowed like a bull, too, as he pounded straight at Holbrook. The landsman yelped a startled curse and pulled the trigger. The revolver went off with a boom that hurt Phyllis's ears. Josh stumbled, fell to his knees, and then pitched forward. The others stood there, frozen in shock.

Phyllis saw movement in the shadows behind Holbrook. Nick, with the fingers of his hands laced together, stepped up to the killer and swung his clubbed fists against the back of Holbrook's neck. Holbrook fell forward and jerked the revolver's trigger again. The gun exploded a second time, but this bullet went harmlessly into the dirt.

Nate moved fast. He rushed past the fallen Josh and kicked the gun out of Holbrook's hand. Then he reached down, grabbed the stunned landsman's jacket, and hauled him to his feet.

"You killed Barney!" Nate yelled as he swung a punch that landed solidly on Holbrook's jaw. Holbrook's head slewed to the side, and when he went down, it was obvious to everyone else in the barn that he was out cold. Nate stepped back, jumping up and down a little as he shook his hand and repeated, "Shoot, shoot, shoot!"

"Break it?" Nick asked.

"I think so," Nate said, grimacing. He looked down at Holbrook's sprawled form and added, "But it was worth it."

Phyllis was about to see how badly Josh was hurt when Felicity ran past her. The reporter's short skirt wasn't meant for kneeling on the hard-packed dirt floor of a barn, but she did so anyway as she grabbed Josh's shoulders and struggled to roll him onto his back.

"Josh!" she cried. "Josh, damn it! He shot you! Why'd you do that, you crazy fool?"

Phyllis knelt on Josh's other side and said, "I think he was trying to protect you."

"Why would he —" Felicity's eyes got big. "You mean . . . Oh!" She still gripped Josh's shoulders. She shook him and said, "Josh!"

He opened his eyes behind the thick glasses and looked up at her. "Felicity . . ." he said. "You're all right?"

"Of course I'm all right, thanks to you!" Felicity bent down and pressed her mouth to his in an urgent, passionate kiss. After a moment Josh's hands began to wave around feebly. With a little gasp, Felicity broke the kiss and straightened. She asked him, "How bad is it? Are you going to make it?"

Phyllis sort of hated to do it, but she said, "I, ah, don't actually see any blood on him."

"What?" Felicity said with a frown. She jerked Josh's Windbreaker open. His sweatshirt didn't show any bloodstains or bullet holes. "You're not shot?"

Still lying on his back, Josh swallowed, pushed up his glasses, and said, "I think I kind of tripped and fell just as Holbrook shot at me. He must've missed."

"Then you're not dying?" Felicity's face darkened. "I *kissed* you! I wanted you to have a good memory to take with you!"

"It . . . it really was good," Josh said.

"Oh!"

Felicity looked like she was about to start kicking and punching him when Phyllis said, "Whether he was hurt or not, he did risk his life to save you, Felicity. We all saw that."

Cradling his injured hand against his chest, Nate said, "Just like we all saw Holbrook confess to Barney's murder and then try to kill us. Will that be enough to convict him?"

"With this, it ought to be," Nick said as he retreated a few steps and picked up the video camera he had set down before cold-cocking Holbrook from behind. "I got his whole confession. I saw him sneaking around the barn and figured he was up to no good, so I sneaked in after him."

That was probably the longest speech Phyllis had ever heard the taciturn cameraman make, and she was glad to hear it.

"It'll do more than just convict Holbrook," she said. "It'll convict Clay Loomis, too." She smiled at Felicity and asked again,

"Explosive enough for you?"
"Boom," Felicity said.

CHAPTER 26

The footage of Clay Loomis being arrested for conspiracy to commit murder is bound to be rerun again and again, Phyllis thought as she, Sam, Carolyn, and Eve watched it that evening for the first time. As a pale, handcuffed Loomis, jaw hanging open in shock, was put into the rear seat of a police car by Detective Isabel Largo, the camera panned back to a beautiful but solemn Felicity as she said, "This is Felicity Prosper reporting exclusively for *Inside Beat.* Be sure to watch for our upcoming special edition that will detail all the facts about this sensational case — and the crime-busting, cupcake-baking Texas granny who broke it wide open! At *Inside Beat,* our business is the truth!"

"Good Lord!" Carolyn said, as Sam used the remote to mute the TV.

"My sentiments exactly," Phyllis said with a sigh.

"You have to admit," Eve said, "that young woman knows how to catch an audience's attention. Of course, the skirt doesn't hurt, either."

Sam said, "I'm still annoyed that you didn't take me out there with you. You could've gotten yourself hurt, Phyllis."

"And it's not the first time, either," Carolyn said. She looked at Sam and added, "Both of you have tangled with killers before."

"As it turned out, there wasn't time to come and get you, Sam," Phyllis said. "If we hadn't gotten out to the ranch when we did, Holbrook might have killed Nate and made it look like suicide so he could get away with it."

"Yeah, I guess," Sam grumbled. "Next time you go pokin' into a murder, though, I'm not lettin' you out of my sight."

"With any luck, there won't be a next time."

Carolyn snorted and asked, "Do you really believe that? Because I don't."

Phyllis didn't know how to answer that. She supposed time would tell.

Sam said, "Just don't go chasin' murderers until I get back, all right?"

Phyllis turned on the sofa beside him and frowned at him.

"Get back?" she repeated. "Where are you going?"

"Well, I feel bad about sayin' this," Sam replied, "but when I was talkin' to Vanessa this afternoon, she asked me to come up to Pennsylvania to spend Christmas with her and her husband and kids. I really haven't seen my grandkids much over the past few years, so I, uh, I thought I might just do that."

Phyllis felt her heart sink a little. Mike had already told her that he and Sarah and Bobby wouldn't be here for Christmas, and now Sam was talking about being gone, too.

She caught herself immediately and told herself not to feel like that. Sam had every right to see his family. This was a good thing, in fact. Sam and his daughter weren't estranged or anything like that, but this was a chance for them to get closer again. She took his right hand in both of hers and squeezed it.

"Of course you should go," she said. "In fact, you have to. I insist."

"I was thinkin' . . ." He drew in a breath. "I was thinkin' you could come with me."

Phyllis was touched and pleased that he had made the invitation, and for a second she was tempted to accept. But then she shook her head and said, "No, that might not be a good idea. You've told me about how hard Vanessa took it when her mother passed away. If I go with you, she might think I was trying to replace Vicky or something like that. You need to mend those fences and go by yourself. This time."

"Does that mean . . . ?"

"We'll see," Phyllis said, smiling.

"Dang right we will," Sam said.

"In the meantime, we were already going to have an early Christmas celebration, since Mike and his family won't be here on the twenty-fifth, so we'll pick a time when you'll still be here, too, Sam. We'll just have Christmas on our own schedule this year."

Carolyn said, "That means we'd better go ahead and get the tree and the decorations up. And start baking!"

Phyllis laughed, snuggled a little closer to Sam, and said, "That sounds good to me."

Late that night, Phyllis was in the kitchen in her pajamas and bathrobe and fuzzy slippers, looking for something to eat. As far as she knew, everyone in the house was asleep. She was getting one of the gluten-free muffins left over from breakfast from the container where Carolyn had stored them when she heard footsteps in the hall.

Eve, also attired in pajamas, bathrobe, and

slippers, came into the kitchen. She said, "I thought I heard you moving around, Phyllis, and I couldn't wait to give you this." She held out a small thumb drive. "Consider it an early Christmas present, I guess . . . If you like it. If you don't, I suppose you can call this fair warning."

Phyllis took the thumb drive and frowned in confusion.

"I don't understand," she said. "What's on here?"

"It's a novel," Eve said. "The novel that I've been writing."

Phyllis stared at her and said, "A novel? I knew you'd been in your room a lot, but . . . you've been writing a novel?"

"I have, and I just finished it tonight."

"Why, that's wonderful!" Phyllis hugged her friend. "I'm so proud of you. That's what you meant when you said there was going to be a famous author in the house. It's you!"

"Well, I don't know about that, but it *is* going to be published. A while back I sent the first few chapters to an agent, and she sold it."

"Eve, that's incredible news." Phyllis was smiling so broadly it made her face hurt. "We should wake up Carolyn and Sam and tell them all about it."

Eve shook her head quickly and said, "Oh, no. In fact, I don't want you to say anything to them until you've read it. You're going to be the first."

"Well, I'm honored, of course, and I'll be glad to read it. I'm sure I'll love it. What's it about?"

Eve hesitated, looking as though she was gathering her courage. She said, "It's about a woman who lives in a small town in Texas. She's a retired teacher, you see, and she lives in a house with some of her friends, and she . . . well, she solves crimes and catches murderers. Oh, and she bakes a lot."

For a long moment, Phyllis couldn't find her voice. She could only stare in shock. She took a step back, found one of the chairs at the kitchen table, and sank blindly into it.

"You're serious?" she finally said.

"Yes, but if you hate the idea, I don't have to do it. I can call off the whole deal."

Phyllis shook her head and said, "No, absolutely not. I wouldn't hear of it. I'm just . . . surprised, that's all. Who would want to read something like that?"

Eve smiled weakly and said in a hesitant voice, "I suppose I really shouldn't say anything about the movie deal . . ."

Phyllis started to laugh. She stood up,

hugged her friend again, and said, "I can't wait to read it!"

Recipes

CANDY CANE CUPCAKES

Ingredients

1 1/2 cups all-purpose flour
1 cup granulated sugar
1 1/2 teaspoons baking powder
1/2 teaspoon salt
1/2 cup (1 stick) unsalted butter, room temperature
1/2 cup plain Greek yogurt
1 large egg, room temperature
2 large egg yolks, room temperature
1 1/2 teaspoons vanilla extract

Directions

Preheat the oven to 350 degrees F. Line a standard muffin/cupcake tin for 12 muffins with paper or foil liners.

In the bowl of a stand mixer fitted with the paddle attachment, whisk together the flour, sugar, baking powder, and salt.

Add the butter, yogurt, egg, egg yolks, and vanilla. Beat at medium speed until smooth, about 30 seconds. Scrape down the sides of the bowl with a rubber spatula and mix by hand until all the flour is incorporated.

Divide the batter evenly among the cups. Bake until the tops are pale gold and a toothpick inserted into the center comes out clean, 20 to 24 minutes. Remove the cupcakes from the tin and transfer to a wire rack; allow to cool to room temperature.

Makes 12 cupcakes.

Peppermint Buttercream Frosting

Ingredients

2 sticks unsalted butter, softened
2 pounds confectioners' sugar, sifted
1 1/2 teaspoons peppermint extract
6–8 tablespoons milk or heavy cream
Crushed candy cane pieces (as much as desired)

Directions

Cream the butter in a large mixing bowl. Add in the sugar, one cup at a time, and continue until all the sugar is creamed together with the butter. Add the peppermint extract and 3 tablespoons of the milk or cream and mix. Keep adding a tablespoon of the milk or cream while mixing, until the frosting is smooth. Frost the cupcakes and garnish with crushed candy cane pieces.

Makes frosting for 12 cupcakes.

MACARONS

You will notice this recipe uses mostly weight, grams and ounces. It's a cookie that doesn't convert well to just cups and spoons. A good kitchen scale is necessary for this recipe.

Basic Macaron Cookie Recipe

Ingredients

7.4 ounces (210 grams) powdered sugar
4.4 ounces (125 grams) almond flour
4 large egg whites, at room temperature
1/4 cup granulated sugar
Macaron filling of your choice (see p. 363)

Directions

Make the Batter

Line 3 large baking sheets with parchment paper and set aside.

In a large bowl, sift the powdered sugar and almond flour; set aside. In the bowl of a stand mixer fitted with the whisk attachment, whip the egg whites on medium speed until foamy. Add about a third of the granulated sugar, and continue to whip for another 30 to 45 seconds. Repeat twice more with the remaining granulated sugar. Once all of the sugar is mixed in, continue whipping the whites until they turn glossy and stiff. When you lift the whisk from the bowl, the whites should hold a straight peak that doesn't curl at the tip.

Using a large rubber spatula, fold in half of the powdered sugar / almond flour mixture. Once most of it has been incorporated, fold in the remaining mixture until just combined. *Do not overmix.*

Pipe the Batter.
Using a piping bag fitted with a large round tip, pipe the batter onto the prepared baking sheets in rounds about 1 1/2 inches in diameter and 1/4- to 1/2 -inch thick, spaced about 1 inch apart, until you've made 30 rounds. As you pipe, hold the bag perpendicular to the baking sheet to avoid making peaks. Tap the sheet against the counter several times to flatten the mounds and pop any large air bubbles. Let the rounds rest until the meringues no longer feel sticky, about an hour at room temperature. If your oven has a warm setting, put the baking sheets inside and leave the door cracked open to more quickly dry out the tops of the macarons. This step is very important; if the rounds are baked while the tops are still sticky, they will not rise properly.

Increase the oven temperature to 300 degrees F. Place one baking sheet on the top rack and bake for 7 minutes. Rotate the sheet and continue cooking about 6 more minutes, or until the cookies are slightly golden around edges. Repeat with remaining baking sheets.

Remove the baking sheets from the oven and place on racks to cool completely. Remove the cookies from the parchment and pair them by size.

Fill the Cookies

Make ganache filling (see p. 363) or other filling of your choice. Using a piping bag with the same tip used to pipe the cookies, pipe 1 to 1 1/2 teaspoons of the filling onto half of the cookies; use just enough filling that it spreads to the edge when topped with another cookie. Top the filled halves with their partners. The macarons are best the day they're made, but they can be stored in an airtight container at room temperature for up to a day, or in the freezer for up to two weeks.

Makes 15 macarons.

BAKLAVA MACARONS

Recipe for Basic Macaron Shells

(See Recipe on Previous Pages)

For the Ganache/Filling

Ingredients

3.5 ounces (100 grams) cream
8.8 ounces (250 grams) white chocolate
1.75 ounces (50 grams) honey
1 teaspoon ground cinnamon
1/4 teaspoon ground nutmeg
2 tablespoons finely ground pecans (optional)

Directions

In a small saucepan, heat the cream on a low setting. Add the white chocolate and mix until smooth. Add the honey and spices, mix, and refrigerate overnight.

Pipe some ganache on half of the cookies, and add a sprinkling of the ground pecans, if desired. Top with the remaining cookies. Place in the fridge to mature for 24 hours before serving.

Fills 15 macarons.

CRUSTLESS SPINACH AND BACON QUICHE

Ingredients

5 or 6 slices of bacon, cut into small pieces
1 small white onion, chopped
1 cup frozen chopped spinach, thawed and drained
5 eggs, beaten
1 cup cheddar cheese, shredded
1 cup mozzarella cheese, shredded
1/4 teaspoon salt
1/8 teaspoon ground black pepper

Directions

Preheat the oven to 350 degrees F. Lightly grease a 9-inch pie pan.

In a large skillet over medium-high heat, cook the bacon until crisp. Drain the bacon on paper towels. Discard all but 1 tablespoon fat from the pan. Add the onion and sauté, stirring occasionally, until soft. Stir in the spinach and bacon and continue cooking until the excess moisture has evaporated.

In a large bowl, combine the eggs, cheeses, salt, and pepper. Add the spinach mixture and stir to blend. Scoop into the prepared pie pan.

Bake until the eggs have set, about 30 minutes. Let cool for 10 minutes before serving.

Makes 6 servings.

TOMATO AND MOZZARELLA SALAD

Ingredients

1 pound cherry tomatoes
1/2 pound mozzarella cheese
1/2 cup chopped basil leaves
1 garlic clove, finely minced
3 tablespoons olive oil
4 teaspoons balsamic vinegar
Salt to taste

Directions

Cut the cherry tomatoes in half, and the mozzarella into cubes. Add the basil and garlic. Drizzle with olive oil and vinegar. Stir lightly. Sprinkle with a little salt. Chill at least one hour before serving. Store in refrigerator.

Makes 4–6 servings.

SAUSAGE EGG MUFFINS

Ingredients

Vegetable oil spray
1 pound ground sausage
12 eggs
1/4 teaspoon salt
1/8 teaspoon ground black pepper
1 cup cheddar cheese, shredded
1/2 cup mozzarella cheese, shredded

Directions

Preheat the oven to 350 degrees F. Lightly spray a 12-cup muffin pan with the vegetable oil of your choice.

In a large pan, brown the crumbled sausage on medium heat setting. Drain the grease. Set aside.

In a large bowl, whisk the eggs with the salt and pepper. Add the cheeses and mix. Spoon the sausage evenly into the bottom of each muffin cup. Pour the egg mixture over the top, filling almost to the top of each cup.

Bake for 20 to 25 minutes, until the eggs are set. Remove, and serve while still warm.

Makes 12 servings.

RED POTATO SALAD

Ingredients

5 pounds medium red potatoes, halved
3 eggs, hardboiled and chopped
1/2 medium white onion, chopped finely
1 cup Miracle Whip
1/2 cup sour cream
2 teaspoons mustard
1/4 cup sweet-pickle relish
2 tablespoons dried parsley flakes
1/8 teaspoon ground black pepper
1 teaspoon salt
2 tablespoons sugar
1 teaspoon apple cider vinegar

Directions

Place the potatoes in a large kettle; cover with water. Bring to a boil. Reduce the heat, cover, and cook for 15 to 20 minutes, or until tender. Drain, and allow to cool. Cut the potatoes into 3/4-inch cubes.

In a large bowl, combine the potatoes, eggs, and onion. In a small bowl, combine the remaining ingredients. Pour over the potato mixture and stir gently to coat evenly. Cover and refrigerate for 6 hours or overnight.

Makes 12–15 servings.

POTATO SOUP

Ingredients

1 pound bacon, chopped
1 onion, chopped
3 cloves garlic, minced
8 Russet potatoes, peeled and cubed
4 cups chicken stock, or enough to cover the potatoes
3 tablespoons butter
1/4 cup all-purpose flour
1 cup heavy cream
Salt and ground white pepper to taste
1 cup cheddar cheese, shredded
1 cup green onions, chopped

Directions

In a Dutch oven, cook the bacon over medium heat until crispy. Remove the bacon from the pot, and set aside. Drain off all but 1/4 cup of the bacon fat.

In the bacon fat remaining in the pot, sauté the onion until it begins to turn translucent. Add the garlic, and continue cooking for 1 to 2 minutes. Add the potatoes and toss to coat. Sauté for 3 to 4 minutes. Return half of the bacon to the pan, and add enough chicken stock to just cover the potatoes.

Cover, and simmer until the potatoes are tender.

In a separate pan, melt the butter over medium heat. Whisk in the flour. Cook, stirring constantly, for 1 to 2 minutes. Whisk in the cream. Bring the mixture to a boil and cook, stirring constantly, until thickened. Stir the cream mixture into the potato mixture. Using a potato masher, mash the ingredients 5 times. Taste, and add salt and pepper if needed. Most store-bought stock has a lot of salt, so you really need to taste before adding salt.

Spoon the soup into bowls and top each with the remaining bacon, the cheddar cheese, and the green onions.

Serves 8.

HOT HAM AND CHEESE SLIDERS

Ingredients

1/4 cup melted butter
1 tablespoon Dijon mustard
1 teaspoon Worcestershire sauce
1 clove garlic, minced
12 sweet dinner rolls
1/2 pound thinly sliced cooked deli ham
1/2 pound thinly sliced smoked provolone cheese

Directions

Preheat the oven to 350 degrees F. Grease a 9-by-13-inch baking dish.

In a bowl, mix together the butter, Dijon mustard, Worcestershire sauce, and garlic.

Separate the tops from bottoms of the rolls, and place the bottom pieces, insides facing up, in the prepared baking dish. Layer the ham onto the rolls. Arrange the cheese over the ham. Place the tops of the rolls onto the sandwiches. Pour the mustard mixture evenly over the rolls.

Bake until the rolls are lightly browned and the cheese has melted, about 20 minutes. Slice into individual rolls, through the ham and cheese layers, to serve.

Makes 12 sliders.

BAKED MEATBALLS

Ingredients

2 pounds lean ground beef
1 cup Italian-style bread crumbs
1/2 cup milk
1 teaspoon salt
1 teaspoon Worcestershire sauce
1 teaspoon pepper
1 small onion, finely chopped (about 1/4 cup)
2 cloves garlic, minced
2 eggs

Directions

Preheat oven to 400 degrees F. Spray two 9-by-13-inch pans with cooking spray.

In a large bowl, mix all the ingredients lightly; don't overwork. Shape into 40 to 48 1 1/2-inch meatballs. Place 1 inch apart on the pan. Bake, uncovered, for 18 to 22 minutes, or until no longer pink in the center.

Serve with your favorite sauce on pasta.

Serves 8 with pasta.

GRILLED CHICKEN AND SPINACH SALAD

Ingredients

4 (6-ounce) skinless, boneless grilled chicken breast halves, sliced
1 bag baby spinach, washed and dried
1/3 cup sweetened dried cranberries
1/4 cup chopped pecans, toasted
3 green onions, thinly sliced
4 tablespoons olive oil
2 teaspoons fresh lime juice
1 teaspoon sugar

Directions

In a large bowl, toss the chicken, spinach, cranberries, pecans, and green onions.

In a small bowl, combine the olive oil, lime juice, and sugar; stir well. Add the oil mixture to the chicken mixture; toss to coat.

Serves 4.

ABOUT THE AUTHOR

Livia J. Washburn has been a professional writer for more than twenty years. She received the Private Eye Writers of America Award and the American Mystery Award for her first mystery, *Wild Night,* written under the name L. J. Washburn, and she was nominated for a Spur Award by the Western Writers of America for a novel written with her husband, James Reasoner. Her short story "Panhandle Freight" was nominated for a Peacemaker Award by the Western Fictioneers. She lives with her husband in a small Texas town, where she is constantly experimenting with new recipes. Her two grown daughters are both teachers in her hometown, and she is very proud of them.

The employees of Thorndike Press hope you have enjoyed this Large Print book. All our Thorndike, Wheeler, and Kennebec Large Print titles are designed for easy reading, and all our books are made to last. Other Thorndike Press Large Print books are available at your library, through selected bookstores, or directly from us.

For information about titles, please call:
(800) 223-1244

or visit our Web site at:
http://gale.cengage.com/thorndike

To share your comments, please write:
Publisher
Thorndike Press
10 Water St., Suite 310
Waterville, ME 04901